Write ... ers: The Wo ... rchid

A novel

By

S. Cunliffe

S. Cunliffe

S. Cunliffe Press

ISBN: 9781738550203

"Money is power, freedom, a cushion, the root of all evil, the sum of blessings."
Carl Sandberg

Prologue

We all do the best we can in this life, and when my business was struggling and debts threatened to overwhelm me, I clung to a lifeline that would secure my future. That is my excuse, anyway. Perhaps I should have been more discriminating, but we do what we can in the heat of the moment. Having my debts cleared and money in the bank again meant so much to me that I failed to understand how letting strangers into your world can impact your whole life and not just your business.

But I am getting ahead of myself. My name is Jinni and I am a 43-year-old Thai woman who lives in a small southern city in the USA. I own a nail salon, the Purple Orchid in the upmarket Walks shopping district. By the spring of 2023, I had also committed to extend my business by leasing and converting a former factory in the regeneration area of the city into a nail salon and coffee shop. My business had been very successful, and in 2022 it was voted on social media as the best nail salon in the whole metropolitan area. However, in winter that year, due to my love affair with Song, a Chinese woman who had worked illegally in my salon and had gained notoriety in a court case in Atlanta, I had alienated some customers and my business had suffered. I had worked tirelessly to attract customers back and by October 2023, the salon was operating at near capacity again. However, the impact on my finances had been disastrous.

I had business loans which were overdue, and I was even struggling to pay my manicurists' wages. It was a very difficult time for me.

This is the story of what happened when I took action to secure the future of my business.

November, 2023

An investor is found for the Purple Orchid

Chapter 1

Jinni meets an investor

By November 2023, things were so dire I had to let my long-term accountant go as I could no longer afford to pay her fees. I had taken on a new firm of accountants who were willing to do the same work for half the price. My contact at the firm was Carole Parks – a certified public accountant and senior manager.

I met with Carole in late October 2023 at her office. The office was in a 1960s building near to the regeneration area on a street that had seen better days. The building was tired and rundown, and the elevator taking me up to the 6th floor smelled of vomit and needed a clean. I told myself I was supporting the firm as they were an all-woman operation, but in truth it was because they were cheap. When I walked into the reception area I could smell a faint whiff of disinfectant, so at least it was cleaner than the elevator, but the furniture and carpet seemed worn and tired. I was told by a bored looking receptionist to wait, and I sat playing on my phone for a good fifteen minutes. I was just about to leave when Carole appeared and asked me to join her in her office.

Carole was, I guess, in her early fifties. She was a tall, plain woman who seemed weary of life. Her face was deeply wrinkled, perhaps because of living all her life in a sunny climate. She had her greying blonde hair in a messy bun and had perched her glasses on the end of her nose. She was my financial adviser but would never use any of my services. Her nails were short and bit to the quick. She needed a professional manicure and also, in my honest opinion, a facial. I briefly wondered if I should offer her my services for a reduction in the fee. While I mused about this, Carole sat behind the desk and asked me to sit opposite her in her shoebox of an office. I was not offered any refreshments and for a few moments, she sat glued to the computer screen without looking at me. I guessed she must be looking through my file, although she did not enlighten me on this fact.

It seemed like an eternity before she spoke and when she did speak, she certainly did not waste time on pleasantries.

“How is business, Jinni?” she enquired.

“Getting back to 2022 levels – busy,” I replied, smiling falsely.

Carole did not immediately answer as she seemed to be intent on something on the screen. “Still giving it away? Continuing to use offers to attract customers?”

“In business we must be competitive. My offers have resulted in new customers.”

“Yes, *turnover* has increased but your net profit has not, Jinni.” At this point, she turned from the screen to look me straight in the face. “The truth is you are making a loss. You must face up to the fact that you are not even breaking even. Looking at your loan on the new premises, it is overdue – you have missed the last two payments.”

I was beginning to feel defensive. Did the woman not have any subtlety?

"It has been hard, but I feel I am on track to sort out all my financial difficulties by the end of the year."

"I have an email here from Brotherton's contractors who are saying they have not been paid for the refurbishment they did at the new premises. You paid a deposit of ten thousand dollars, but as of now you owe them forty thousand dollars for the work they did, and the payment is overdue by thirty days. They are giving you another thirty days, after which they will take you to court for the money. You will have to borrow this money to pay them. I have made some preliminary enquiries with several banks and so far, none have given the go ahead to a loan."

"Someone will loan me the money. I have a viable business, and I am expanding."

At this point, Carole took her glasses off and stared me straight in the eye. "I must be honest with you Jinni, at this rate you will be lucky if you are not out of business by the end of the year."

She paused and polished her glasses on her sleeve, a move I found intensely irritating. "I'm sorry to be so harsh, but there is no sugar coating the situation. You really are struggling financially."

Another pause, this time glancing back at the computer screen. "I feel you would benefit from an investor – someone who would pay off your creditors and put money into the business so you can go forward with the new premises and continue with your existing business, the Purple Orchid.

An investor? That was something I had never given any thought to. I had always operated solo, and that was how I liked it.

"I know this is difficult for you, Jinni." She was now removing an imaginary piece of lint from her sweater. "Give it some thought, I don't want to rush you. An investor would take away your financial worries and save your livelihood. I think you will see it is the best solution for you and for your business."

That was the end of that meeting – at least as far as I was concerned. I don't remember what else she said. Platitudes, I believe, about how other businesses had used investors and were now booming.

I walked to the train station feeling sick and anxious. An investor – what a thought!

That evening, I rang my friends for advice. Everyone told me to go ahead and bring an investor into the business, mainly so I could go ahead with my plans to expand.

In the salon I asked a couple of my loyal customers. Janine was married to a partner in a firm of certified public accountants. She promised to ask her husband what he thought. He was very positive and suggested that it would be a good move at present. He also said, and this I took to heart, that I could buy out the investor when my new business was up and running and was successful. This statement said to me that this arrangement is only temporary, and to go ahead and be positive. It was his advice that I relied on – *the investor is only going to be temporary*.

I can move back to being on my own again when I buy them out sometime next year.

So, I told Carole to go ahead and find an investor. She promised to put feelers out and to get back to me when one was found. Very quickly it seemed, she got back to me to say that a potential investor had come forward to show their interest in the Purple Orchid. This person was interested in agreeing terms with me. They initially wanted 65% interest in return for investing $100,000. After much discussion, we reduced this to a 30% interest and $60,000 investment. The agreement was to be signed the following Monday when we would meet.

"He is a British man named Bill Underwood," Carole informed me.

Chapter 2

Southern Hills – Janine and Gene's House

A first meeting with Bill Underwood

A couple of weeks before Bill Underwood agreed to invest in Jinni's business, Janine and her husband hosted a dinner party at their home. Bill Underwood and his wife, Patrice, were guests at the dinner party.

When Gene had made partner at Alex Gold Certified Public Accountants, the first thing he did was buy a beautiful large home in the Southern Hills fit for entertaining and which matched his status in the world. His wife, Janine, was an artist, and very creative. She had decorated the home, so it was undeniably beautiful, with incredible features. The main living area featured soaring ceilings, wood floors, and floor-to-ceiling windows that flooded the home with natural light and highlighted panoramic vistas over the city.

Expansive multi-level decks invited the visitor to enjoy sunsets and city views. Once it went dark, the views of the city lights were breathtaking.

The home featured four distinct living areas making it ideal for both entertaining and everyday living. The chef's kitchen boasted mitred quartz countertops, a large island, gas cooking, built-in refrigerator, Wi-Fi-enabled dishwasher, and pantry. The adjoining prep kitchen was worthy of inclusion in a style magazine and elevated the kitchen's convenience and design, making it ideal for both hosting and daily life.

Today, Janine was putting the finishing touches to a dinner party for 12 people. This was intended to be a welcome meal for a new resident and member of the country club, Bill Underwood and his wife Patrice. Gene had chatted to Bill and found out he was the newly appointed chief operating officer for the Southern States at a right-wing conservative media company – Stermer, that had its headquarters in Los Angeles but was expanding. Stermer produced podcasts and news shows by specific commentators including Jack Ryan and Bill Dexter, that were available to license to local radio stations. The company had been successful in recruiting some Southern radio stations and wanted to expand their presence outside of Los Angeles. In addition, Stermer had a small boutique publishing house. It specialized in right-wing and Christian fiction and non-fiction. It had been successful in the publishing area and had signed some popular non-fiction authors who wrote about politics and current affairs. Authors received a higher level of service than would be typical from a larger publishing house. Stermer also welcomed submissions from literary agents.

Gene knew that there was a lot of competition in the conservative media sector, but he felt that Stermer had a good chance to be successful. He had glanced briefly at their website and saw a list of commentators and authors and was quite impressed. There were several famous right-wing commentators that had been discussed in the mainstream media.

Bill was a certified public accountant, who, it seemed, had enjoyed a career working in financial roles at media companies. From a brief review of his background bio on the Stermer website, Gene was happy to welcome him into the community.

When the guests began to arrive, the house was full of beautiful, scented flowers and the caterers were putting the final touches to a Southern banquet in the chef's kitchen.

Bill and Patrice Underwood had arrived slightly early. Gene was pleased about this, as it gave him time to have a quick chat with Bill before the other guests started to arrive.

Janine looked stunning in a white, off the shoulder gown, and she made sure she introduced the Underwoods to the other guests as they arrived.

It was only after the meal that Janine was able to sit and chat with Bill and Patrice. Listening to Bill talk during the meal Janine could hear that he was British, and she always enjoyed talking about the time she and Gene had lived in London. She noticed that Patrice was American and seemed much younger than Bill. She was wearing a very low-cut red designer gown that also had a high cut displaying her legs. Her watch was Rolex, and she wore diamond earrings and a huge diamond ring on her wedding finger.

Patrice chatted a little bit about the city and then asked Janine about Gene's career.

Janine indicated that Gene was a CPA and a partner in the firm Alex Gold and had had a good career with them.

"In my opinion, accounting can be a testing choice of career for a Black man," mused Patrice, "that is why I was asking." She smiled at Janine and without waiting for her to reply, carried on. "My mother is Black, so I know a little about the challenges faced when trying to make it. My father is a white man who my mother met while she was working as a dancer in a Las Vegas show. In those days, it was difficult to get beyond the chorus line if you were Black. My father was an actor who used to vacation in Vegas. He was moderately successful and persuaded Mom to come to LA. Once they married and I was on the way, she gave up her career to be a stay-at-home mom. She wanted me to follow her into the theatre, but the makeup department is where I felt most comfortable."

"You are a makeup artist?" Janine asked.

Bill, who had been talking to Gene, interrupted here. "Patrice is excellent, and has worked on some big movies providing makeup for the stars. Recently, she expanded by having her own small beauty shop in Hollywood. Moving out here I feel a bit guilty that we had to sell her business which was, I have to say, a huge success."

"Would you like to work in this area again?" asked Janine.

Patrice indicated that she would, either as a stylist or an adviser.

Janine mentioned that a local business, the Purple Orchid, was looking for an investor. She was a regular customer and a friend of the owner. The

Purple Orchid had started as a nail salon in the Walks shopping district, and the owner had purchased premises in the regeneration area of the city, hoping to expand. The salon already sold well-being products, but she could see the new premises offering a beauty salon with makeup and beauty treatments.

Patrice and Bill looked at each other and seemed very interested. “Do you know how we can follow this up?” Bill asked.

Janine offered to send details.

It turned out that Janine was as good as her word. She did send details, and Bill decided he would invest – but he had no intention of being a sleeping partner. His intention was that his beloved wife, Patrice, should be able to continue her beauty treatments from the Purple Orchid as the wife of the part owner and investor.

Chapter 3

A kind man visits the Walks shopping center

On the Saturday after Jinni agreed to sign an agreement with an investor, and before the agreement was signed, the Walks shopping area was busy with people browsing in the upmarket shops and stopping for lunch either at La Luce, an upscale Italian restaurant, or The Pearl, a new dining experience which had opened to great acclaim the previous month. The Tory Burch store seemed busy, but next door, the Purple Orchid nail salon had a sign in the window, which a year ago would have been unheard of – 'Walk-ins Welcome'.

Two women had stopped to look in the window of Josie Fine Jewelry.

"Oh wow," one was saying, "just so beautiful, they are definitely on my Christmas list." She was referring to a pair of diamond encrusted drop earrings.

"I prefer the bracelet." Her companion bent down to look at the bottom of the display. As she stood up, unnoticed by her, a small parcel on the top of her bag fell to the ground. As the ladies moved away, they heard a man's voice behind them.

"Hey!" he exclaimed, and as they turned, he held out the package. "Is this yours?"

The ladies regarded the tall man who may once have been slim, but was now running to middle-aged spread. The tweed jacket was buttoned, but the button was straining. The blue shirt was slightly the wrong color to wear with the jacket, and the chinos were just a bit too tight. He had a face which only a mother could love. His nose was slightly too big, and his chin receded. He did still have a full head of hair which he had combed into a style that resembled a helmet. The sun glinted off his glasses as he held the small parcel aloft.

“Oh wow, thank you,” the woman said, smiling from ear to ear. “I had no idea that had fallen off my bag, it’s a gift for my daughter.”

“It’s my pleasure.” The man spoke formally, and his accent was British with a very faint American twang.

Handing the parcel back, he continued to stride purposefully along the Walks.

The two women stood for a moment watching him.

“Wow, that was Cleo’s birthday present,” said one. “I can’t believe it had fallen off, I almost lost it.”

“Where did he come from?” asked her friend. “Was he standing next to us at the window? I can’t say I noticed anybody.”

The last they saw of him was when he turned left and went into the Purple Orchid nail salon.

Chapter 4

Jinni

A first meeting with Bill

I first met Bill Underwood when he came by the Purple Orchid – unannounced. I have no idea if this was a normal thing to do or not, after all, it turned out he was thinking about putting money into the business. I expect that as a potential investor, he would want to check out the salon. However, the visit did not get off to a good start.

I was in reception with a group of people. There were about 25 paperback books piled onto the reception desk, and we were discussing them. *Summer at the Malami Hotel* was a book which had been written by my friend, Noi. It was her second novel and had been self-published the day before. I was so proud of her. This was Noi's second book about a woman who ran a boutique hotel on the Hawaiian island of Kaui, and it followed the adventures she had with her guests who were often quirky and had back stories of their own. It was a work of fiction, but Noi went every year on vacation to Hawaii and stayed at the same, small hotel. She had chatted to guests who had provided inspiration for some of the back stories. Lila, my receptionist, was handing the books out and we were deep in conversation.

I guess we initially did not notice the man who had entered the salon and was standing by the door next to a display of orchids. I don't know how long he stood there before I went over and acknowledged him.

“Good morning, sir.”

He seemed distinctly unimpressed. He was a tall, white man who towered over me. He had a florid complexion and big hair. His face was contorted into a slight sneer. I was used to this type putting me down, but I was determined not to be intimidated.

“And how can I help you, sir?”

It was only after what seemed like an eternity he spoke. “I would like to meet with, Jinni, I believe the name is, the owner of this establishment.”

Establishment! Oh my!

“I am Jinni.”

“And I am Bill Underwood, who has spoken to your accountant and hopes to invest in your business.”

After that, I quickly ushered him into my small office at the rear of the salon. I offered him a seat and asked Lila to make him a drink of coffee.

“You seem surprised to see me?” He was now smiling and sitting back in the chair. “I would always go to visit a business I was going to invest in. The financial accounts, of course, tell a story, but the real story is to see the business in operation. Today, a Saturday, should be a very busy day for a nail salon. Am I not correct?”

I was on the defensive. “We are busy,” I spluttered. “As you can see, most of the chairs in the salon are occupied, and we are booked for most of the day. We will get walk-ins later."

"Yes, I understand business has been picking up, which is good."

He sipped his coffee, studying me and my small office.

"Would you like to see the appointment book?" I didn't really know what to say. I was sure this was irregular, but what did I know?

He shook his head. "I just wanted to see the salon. I love all the flowers – Ylang-ylang and the scents from the other tropical flowers. Beautiful. It reminds me of the time I visited China. Where are you from?"

"I am Thai, but I have lived in America for a long time now."

He nodded and continued to study me.

He had me on the wrong footing and I started to get verbal diarrhea, going on about the shop and Noi's books!

When he finally left, I realized that he had said very little. On the way out, he shook hands with Lila on reception and purchased one of Noi's books.

I told myself everything was going to be okay, but later that day I got a call from Carole saying that the investor wanted to make a visit to my new premises before finally signing the agreement. He did not need me to be there when he toured the new building, and she would ring again when he had completed the tour.

A week later, we arranged a meeting at Carole's office and we both signed the agreement.

Bill shook my hand and said he would be along to discuss the investment and to introduce me to his wife, Patrice, the following week. His wife! Oh my! What had I let myself in for?

In the meantime, my loans were paid off and there was money again in the bank. I waited to hear from Bill and to be introduced to his wife. I did not have to wait long.

December, 2023

Meetings with the new investors

Chapter 5

Jinni

Meeting with Bill and his wife Patrice at the new premises

For a brief period, my anxiety was alleviated. My loans were paid off, and there was money in the business bank account again. In addition, the Purple Orchid seemed to be making a return to profitability. There was a marked increase in bookings in the period leading up to the December holidays.

Bill sent me a WhatsApp, asking to meet with me at the new premises in the regeneration area, on Monday afternoon, December 20th. I left the Purple Orchid under the direction of one of my manicurists, Julie, and took an Uber over to the regeneration area of the city.

This area still looked like a mess, but great effort was being made to refurbish the old buildings. The Institute for the Blind and Visually Impaired occupied an old factory and was the flagship building in the area. This building had been completed for over a year and was in full use as a school. I loved the mural on the side of the building that had been painted by Janine.

A couple more buildings were now in occupation, including a fresh food store and a do-it-yourself store. My new premises was in the middle of the block, wedged between two, as yet empty properties. It was a former commercial premises – I believe it was used for manufacturing clothing, which had been sold in a small retail shop at the front of the property. I saw that the building to the right of mine was being refurbished, and work was being carried out painting the outside white. A banner above the door announced that this would be Jenny's BookStop. I liked the idea of my nail salon being next door to a bookstore. I felt that the bookstore gave the area a classy feel.

My own building had been painted purple and white and was very striking, in my opinion. The door was open when I arrived, so I went straight inside to the reception area. I could hear voices coming from upstairs. Originally, I was only intending to refurbish the reception area and the room behind it. I did not plan to refurbish upstairs until I was more established.

I called out, "Hi, it's me, Jinni!" but no-one answered, so I climbed the stairs.

Bill was standing in the middle of the upstairs room with a woman who I assumed was his wife, talking to Ron, my contractor.

They smiled and waved as I came to the top of the stairs.

What were my first impressions of Bill's wife, Patrice Underwood? She was certainly a striking woman who gave the impression of being rich. She was wearing a floor- length cashmere coat over a white cashmere sweater and black pants. Her boots had vertiginous heels of about (it seemed to me) 5 inches. She was either light- skinned Black or of mixed race, it was hard to tell. It was 2 p.m. in the afternoon on a Monday, and she was wearing full makeup and expensive jewelry. She appeared young at first sight, but it was difficult to put an age on her – I guessed early thirties.

Bill was quick to introduce us. “Jinni, this is my wife, Patrice,” he said, ushering me over to her.

“Hi Jinni,” she smiled.

“Well,” said Bill, clapping his hands together, “this area still needs a lot of work. I can see how downstairs can be transformed into a coffee shop and a nail bar, and work is well underway. But up here, it is a blank canvas, yes?”

I explained how I was planning to leave the upstairs until I was more established and maybe convert it within a year or so.

Patrice looked at me. “Why not now? I can see great potential for this space.” She seemed almost excited.

Bill then decided to fill me in. “Patrice is a beauty therapist and had her own beauty salon in Hollywood. She specialized in anti-aging treatments and had a number of famous clients. Billie Keagan was a big fan.” He stopped for a moment, gazing at her. “I know you don’t like me name-dropping darling, but I can’t help it when I talk about your business.”

A sick, sinking feeling started to overtake me. Oh no, I thought, Bill is not a hands-off investor – he wants a business for his wife to play around in. Yes, I know dear, you must think that I am completely stupid to have never considered this before. I guess I had worried that he would come along and try to be involved in the management, but I had never suspected he might want a business for his wife. Not for one moment. It floored me, to put it mildly.

Patrice clapped her hands together like a seal and began to walk around the room excitedly. “We could have some small consulting rooms back there, and a reception desk here with products for sale, oh, and a waiting area...”

We had hardly exchanged names, and there she was planning her beauty parlor upstairs at my nail salon!

But what could I do? Bill had invested in my business and was now part-owner. Without him I would go bankrupt.

“Are you sure this is what you want?” I stammered. “Have you done any market research to see if another beauty salon is needed in this area?”

“Oh, darling.” Patrice came over and towered over me. I am sure she was about 6 foot 5 in those shoes. I craned my neck to look up at her and could see she was smiling broadly. “Just think. A fabulous nail salon downstairs and an equally fabulous beauty salon upstairs. People will come from miles around to visit. We will be the talk of the city.”

“It’s just a lot for me to take in,” I stuttered. I was on the back foot again, and I was aware I seemed awkward and not very articulate.

“Sure, I can see that,” said Bill, “but Patrice was very well known in Hollywood, and has the most fabulous ideas.” He spread his arms wide. “I can see a brilliant partnership here.”

I know I should have asked for the name of Patrice's salon in Hollywood, but I was totally out of my depth. I still had 70% ownership, so I could have said no, but they totally overwhelmed me. Within a few moments, Bill was talking about extending the arrangements with the contractors so that they could convert the upstairs.

I explained that this would require more money to be invested. As it stood, we could run the existing business and refurbish the nail salon, but no funds had been set aside to refurbish the upstairs.

Bill then indicated that he was happy to invest more money. We agreed that he would speak to the contractors to work out the cost of refurbishing the upstairs into a beauty salon, and that he would invest this money into the business. This, however, would then give Patrice a 20% share in the ownership.

As we were walking down the stairs to leave, Patrice waved her arms, motioning to the rear wall. "This wall would be perfect for a mural. I love the mural Janine has painted on the wall of the Blind Institute – an interior mural would be just perfect for the salon. Don't you agree?"

Bill clapped his hands together. "What a brilliant idea. Yes, we should ask Janine."

I had to agree it was a good idea, but I was out of control again.

So that was that. Based on that short conversation and visit, I allowed Bill and Patrice to convert the upstairs of the building into a beauty salon. Carole Parks, the accountant, was consulted again and came up with an agreement that worked out the share of profits from the nail salon, the beauty salon and the ownership. After all the negotiations, I was left with 50% ownership, while Bill had 30% and Patrice 20%.

Additionally, they got Janine to paint a mural of a beautiful woman's face onto the interior rear wall where the stairs were. The woman had her hand to her face, and her nails were elaborately decorated. I have to say it was absolutely stunning.

Still, I couldn't shake the feeling of being overwhelmed and totally out of my depth. I had no idea what beauty treatments Patrice offered, but at least I still had my nail salon which I would run personally downstairs, and I told myself that we could co-exist side by side. And I was solvent again, so what was there to complain about?

January and February, 2024

Getting ready for the opening of the new premises

Noi the author receives a proposition

Chapter 6

Patrice

Patrice Underwood had risen early and gone for a short jog along the bike trails in the neighborhood where she and Bill lived. Their home was large and beautiful, with terraces overlooking the swimming pool. It did not have city views like Janine and Gene's home, instead, it looked northwards towards the hills and lakes outside the city. They had moved there two months previously, when Bill had taken up a new position in the city.

The reason the house did not have city views is that it was a new construction. The lots with stunning views had been built on first. However, the lack of view was made up in the incredible architecture of the house. It was truly beautiful. It had an open living concept with a grand thirty-foot, two-story entry, floating staircase and twelve-to-sixteen-foot illuminated ceilings throughout. The lead crystal chandeliers were unique and had been sourced in Europe. There were three linear gas fireplaces for the cooler season. Specialty rooms, such as a glass wine room and game room could be found upstairs, and there were wet bars on both levels. There was also a media room complete with projector, sound system and kitchenette. Bill was able to obtain advance copies of the latest movies through his position at the media company.

Natural light flowed into the house from floor-to-ceiling windows in the living areas and study. The kitchen had top of the line Thermador appliances, featuring dual ovens, dual dishwashers, a coffee machine and an induction cooktop. A covered outdoor patio overlooked a sparkling pool with waterfalls and an infinity-edge hot tub.

As she jogged, Patrice thought about the move from Los Angeles. It had been quite sudden with Bill announcing that he was resigning from his position at Avalon Media and moving to Stermer. A consequence of this move was that she had to give up her business and work as a beautician in Los Angeles. She smiled as she remembered how Bill had exaggerated about her business at the recent dinner party, and to Jinni. She had been leasing a small shopfront in an area near to Hollywood that was not far from the Burbank studios – that was true, but the clientele she attracted were not usually involved in the movies. The actors she had worked on when she was employed by the studios certainly had not made the move to her salon. She had one famous client, Billie Keagan, an aging child star who was trying to turn back the years. Billie was very well known for her roles twenty or so years ago, but not so much nowadays.

She felt warm inside as she thought about Bill. He was always talking up her achievements, and he spoiled her, that she knew was true. It hardly seemed like eighteen months since they first met, and it had not been under the best of circumstances. She had suffered sexual harassment from a director while she was working on his makeup before a media appearance. Bill had intervened and made sure that her side of the story was heard, and she had also received compensation. He not only helped her – he befriended her. When she found out he was the chief operating officer of a media company and lived in Calabasas, she could hardly believe it. He was about fifteen years older than her and, if she was very honest, not a handsome man, but he made up for it in other ways. He was kind, considerate and caring, and acted like a perfect gentleman. Unlike men who wanted sex almost as soon as they met her, he was a very different proposition. In fact, she had been a bit worried after a few dates that he might not find her attractive, as their dates were so chaste. That is when she had taken matters into her own hands and invited him back to her studio apartment in Burbank. Waking the following morning in his arms, she felt that this time she was going to be lucky. That this was the perfect man for her. They were married very quickly after that, and Patrice moved into his beautiful home in Calabasas.

She had been sorry to give up her salon in Los Angeles, but Bill had assured her that he would sort her out with a new business. True to his word, he had come up with a new business and she was thrilled about her new venture in the regeneration area of the city. Today she was going over there to find out how the work was coming along to transform the upstairs of the old building into her new beauty salon. She had designed the layout herself and was very proud of what she had envisioned.

She also had a meeting with Jinni to discuss the grand opening of the new premises. This was planned for 1 p.m. at the Purple Orchid, during Jinni's lunch break.

Returning home from her jog, Patrice showered and dressed and headed out to the regeneration area of the city. The work was coming along well at the new premises, and soon she found herself at the Purple Orchid in the Walks shopping district, a few minutes early for her meeting with Jinni. Walking into the salon, she was struck by how beautiful and upscale it was, full of the scent of exotic flowers. Jinni was just finishing up with her customer, who was paying for her manicure at the reception desk. Patrice was surprised by how inexpensive the manicure seemed to be, compared to Los Angeles prices.

Jinni told Patrice that she was taking her to La Dolce Vita for lunch and they left the salon with Jinni's senior manicurist, Julie, in charge.

At the restaurant, they were shown to a table overlooking the Walks pedestrian area and they sat sipping sparkling water while they each studied their menu. Neither woman spoke for a few minutes, and then Patrice set her menu down.

"I'm very pleased with the way the work is progressing at the new premises, in the upstairs salon. I feel we are on target for a March 2nd opening day."

Jinni nodded. "I agree, and we should go ahead with sending invites out for the grand opening. I have about a hundred people who I am planning to invite. I will have drinks and snacks available and provide tours of both floors."

Patrice nodded thoughtfully and let a moment or two go by. "Can you share the invite and names please?

I also have a few people I want to be sure are on the list."

"Of course, I will email you the list today."

"I had a look through your price list while I was waiting, and I wondered if you had thought about 3D nail art. It's very big in LA now."

3D nail art is a technique where three-dimensional designs are created on the nail. This is not like traditional nail art where designs are painted flat onto the nail surface. 3D designs pop out. This can be achieved in a variety of ways.

"I am aware of 3D nail art," Jinni said flatly, "but no, we haven't offered it as a service at the Purple Orchid."

"When I was in LA, I had space-age blob nails done. Fantastic! I had a rubber base coat with jewels and pearls attached which gave it a futuristic look."

Jinni didn't know what to think but smiled politely.

"You could increase your prices if you did something different. I couldn't believe your prices. So cheap compared to LA. Invest and then reap the benefits, that's what I say."

And so it went on over lunch – endless comparisons of the Purple Orchid to LA, and discussions of the people who frequented Patrice's salon.

Finally, it was 2 p.m. and calling for the bill, Jinni told Patrice she really would have to get back to the salon. They kissed politely as they said goodbye, and each woman went in their own direction. One to a mansion in the Southern Hills, and the other back to filing nails and applying polish.

Chapter 7

Jinni

Events leading up to the opening of the new salon

"In LA you can charge double what you do here for a manicure, in LA *everyone* has 3D art on their nails, in LA women really care about their appearance," and blah, blah, blah.

What an intensely irritating woman Patrice Underwood was. *Who cares about LA*? This is not LA, lady, and I know what the prices are in this city.

Of course, after I sent her the email showing her the design of the invite and the people invited, she was right back at me. The design was too pedestrian and conservative. It should be more contemporary. Had I thought about a modern, minimalistic design? She could recommend a brilliant designer from LA who would put together something more striking.

She also wanted to add to the list of people I had invited. She recommended the following people – the mayor, Edgar Dumont and his assistant, the head of the local TV station, Robin Bridges, and the CEO of her husband's media company, Jennifer Morgan. "We need local dignitaries to make a splash," she said. Also, had I informed the local radio station about the opening? We could get a spot on the commuter show.

She was probably right about a lot of this, but it felt exhausting and as if I was being walked all over. I was sick of the constant references to LA as if we were a little backwater here.

Then she started to go on about nail art again. She sent me a picture of a set of nails with gummy bears stuck on them! For goodness' sake! In my opinion, this was not art. However, I did promise to talk to my senior manicurist, Julie, about it. Julie seemed to think it was a good idea to do something different, and we could put the 3D designs on the Purple Orchid Instagram. Julie knew someone, Robbie, who could do 3D art on nails. She currently worked for another salon but might be tempted to leave if we made her an attractive offer.

I was not keen on this at all but agreed to meet Robbie. She came to the Purple Orchid one Tuesday evening just as we were closing. I liked her immediately. She was in her early twenties, I guess, and was very pretty with long dark hair and blue eyes. She was slim and natural-looking. It was her smile though, that got me. It lit up her whole face and was so infectious.

I have to admit that since my relationship with Song I had been celibate. Song was now back in her native China after running away from university here in the USA and having a very bad experience in Atlanta. Employing her even though she did not have working papers was the start of my financial downfall. I kept in touch with Song via Zoom. We spoke once a week. Song was now at college and studying business to keep her father happy. At least he had not insisted that she go to Australia to study. Deep down I knew that Song and I would never be together, and I was beginning to accept that fact.

I was not really looking for another relationship when I met Robbie, but there was something between us. Deep down where I had been numb, I felt a warm feeling again looking at her.

After chatting for a while, she agreed to come and work at the new premises as our specialist in 3D nail art. I knew that I was going against my better judgement agreeing to have 3D nail art in the salon, but I was much happier about including it now I had met Robbie. I couldn't wait to work with her.

The following morning, I put on KAVC98 radio station when I got to the salon, as I like the commuter show with Jerry Levens. He was playing some classic hits and talking about crime in the city. This related to the new regeneration area, and how it was gradually being cleaned up. He talked to the chief of police about what was being done, so of course I was interested in this with the new premises being in the area.

Then, to my astonishment, he announced, "Today we have a very special guest in the studio who is currently investing in the regeneration area." He paused for a moment for dramatic effect. "Ms. Patrice Underwood, who is opening a beauty salon in the area on March 2nd. Hi Patrice."

"Hi Jerry and hi, everyone."

I recognized the voice and could feel my mouth gaping open.

"I just wanted to say that we are having a grand opening of the Purple Orchid – Second Wave on March 2nd, and everyone is welcome to come down from 3 p.m. onwards. Come and tour the premises and see what we have to offer. There will be a coffee shop in the reception area, where you can sit and chat with friends while you wait for your beauty or nail appointment. The nail salon is under the same management as the Purple Orchid in the Walks district. The nail salon is downstairs, and the beauty salon is upstairs. I will be running the beauty salon personally – not two months ago, I was working in LA in the movie industry helping people to look incredible."

"That is fantastic, Patrice – have you worked on any celebrities we might know?"

"Too many to mention here." This was accompanied by a laugh. "But let's say my prices are competitive and you don't have to be a movie star to come for a treatment."

I was beginning to feel nauseous. The woman was taking over and this radio show was unbelievable. I had not even been consulted! But at the same time, part of me felt sure it was good publicity for the new premises.

I decided to text Patrice and tell her that although I thought the radio appearance was good publicity, I would like to be consulted in future. I also mentioned about the name for the new premises, the Purple Orchid – Second Wave. This was the first time I had even heard this name!

A message immediately came back. “The appearance was arranged by Bill through his company. It was all very last minute as it turned out, but I did suggest it to you a couple of weeks back. And I was surprised you had not consulted the radio station.

Bill and I came up with the name and thought it sounded cool. What do you think? Do you like it? We can change it if you don’t like it.”

I wasn’t going to change the name now she had mentioned it on the radio. It wasn’t a bad name and, of course, by appearing on the radio Patrice had got good publicity for the new salon. But it was the way she did things! Well not just her! Patrice *and* Bill! What had I agreed to, letting investors into my business? Whatever next?

Chapter 8

Noi the author

Noi had been so proud when she self-published her first novel, *The Malami Hotel*. She self-published it through Delta Online. It was free to upload there, and authors received royalties. Seeing it there available to purchase either as an e-book or paperback was exciting, until a few weeks later she checked the sales figures, and they were remarkably flat. There were 25 paperbacks sold – to herself and her friends in the city. She could account for all of them. Plus, there were 20 copies of the e-book sold online. Her friends had told her how much they had enjoyed the book, and a couple had written reviews which had been published online. Hardly a New York Times bestseller when her friends were the only readers!

But what was I expecting? Noi asked herself. Can I really expect thousands of sales when I am a completely unknown author and immigrant to the USA?

Noi was a member of the Thai community in the city, and a very good friend of Jinni. In fact, Jinni often referred to Noi as her best friend. Noi and her husband, Niran, ran a small Thai restaurant in the northern suburbs. Their restaurant was called Ao Nang after the town in the coastal province of Krabi in Thailand. Niran did all the ordering and accounting for the restaurant, and Noi was the cook. It was well-known in the Thai community that Noi was a brilliant cook, and the restaurant was usually busy.

Niran was born in America, and Noi was an immigrant from Thailand. They had met when Niran went on a vacation to visit his uncle in Bangkok in 2008. Noi could write and speak some basic English before she moved to the USA, but once she arrived, she had enrolled in evening classes to improve her skills.

To have written one novel was, Noi felt, an amazing achievement and although it had not sold many copies, it was available for people to buy all over the world. Her Thai friends had been so encouraging, and had told her repeatedly how proud they were and how much they had enjoyed the book.

Niran was another story, though. "You are wasting time, Noi, help the children with their homework," and "stop wasting time on that pointless hobby," were his favorite comments. He felt that the book was a waste of time. Noi felt she spent plenty of time with their two children, Anong and Ariya, and was not neglecting them by her writing. They were very lucky in that Niran's parents were also very involved with the children and babysat so that Noi and Niran could work in the restaurant.

The restaurant was moderately successful, and Niran had felt proud being able to pay for the whole family to go to Hawaii on vacation and stay at a small, family-run hotel. He then found out that Noi had written a novel based on the hotel – featuring different guests who went on holiday there. How ridiculous, he thought. Has she lost her mind?

He liked to gossip with their elderly next-door neighbor, Stan. When the restaurant was closed on

Sundays, Niran would have a beer with him. They sat on the porch laughing and joking. Stan took a swig of his beer and laughed, "Is it *The Love Boat*, Hawaiian style?" when Niran complained about Noi and her writing. *The Love Boat* was an American sitcom which had run for 10 seasons starting in 1976. The show featured the ship's passengers and their romantic shenanigans. Niran had no idea what Stan was talking about, but to be polite, he laughed along.

"Poor Noi, she is so naïve," he told Stan. His wife needed to get her head out of the clouds. Who was going to read the rubbish she wrote?

Noi was not put off by her husband's comments, and although she had to acknowledge that numbers had been disappointing, she still went ahead writing the second book in the series, *Summer at the Malami Hotel*.

Jinni had promised to display the second novel in the reception of the Purple Orchid, and although Noi was grateful, she knew she had to promote the book herself to get more sales and it was proving to be far from easy. She didn't really understand American advertising, and she realized that she needed to get her head around what was involved to promote a book.

One day when she was collecting the children from school, Noi decided to ask their teacher for some advice. Unfortunately, Ms. Rogers was rushing around, collecting her phone and laptop when Noi, going red in the face and stumbling over her words, tried to pluck up her courage.

"I'm sorry but today I have a staff meeting," Ms. Rogers said. "Can we set another time to chat?"

Noi could hear Niran's voice in her head. "Your writing is rubbish. Who will take you seriously?"

Taking hold of Anong and Anya's hands, Noi bolted out of the school. She had to find another way.

The friendly women's group that she had joined on Facebook seemed like the perfect place to get help from Americans and to advertise her book. When her post appeared on the site, she was pleased with how it looked and felt confident it would result in sales. She had talked about her two novels and asked for advice on the best way to carry out advertising.

A couple of days after posting, she received a comment on the post from '@lulub':

"I have purchased your book, and it is a magnificent work of fiction. Your characters are believable and engrossing. I have laughed. I have cried. How are you promoting your novel? DM me to discuss further."

A magnificent work of fiction! Noi was delighted with the feedback and clicking on @lulub she sent a message:

"Hi lulu. Thanks for the comment. I would love to talk further. Please send me a private message."

A few minutes later, Noi received a DM from @lulub:

"Let me know how many sales you have made so far and how you are promoting your novel and then we can discuss how I may be able to help."

After Noi had explained how sales were going so far, @lulub came back to say that Noi's writing deserved more recognition and that they really wanted to help.

Noi asked if she could know more about @lulub and her background. It turned out that @lulub – Lulu – was an author herself, and had written her own novel, called *Breaking Waves*. She said that she wanted to help a new author, and could put feelers out in the literary world.

How kind, thought Noi. But the cynic in her said to wait and see first as it sounded too good to be true!

A week later, Noi received a message from a person called Robin Pine, asking if he could DM her. She had never heard of this person, but was curious who it might be. Her thoughts went immediately to Lulu and how she had been looking for advice. She accepted the message and Robin wrote:

"I have just read your novel on the recommendation of Lulu Bartlett. It was magnificent. I see it as a movie filmed on location in Hawaii with beautiful scenery and amazing vignettes about the different characters. Perhaps even a series with a different character each week."

Noi felt excited. Wow! This person was talking about filming her book!

"That would be amazing! Are you a movie producer?"

The reply came back very quickly:

"No, I am not a producer. Usually, a producer will not speak directly to an author. You need a middleman, an agent who can talk to production companies for you. That is where I believe I can help you."

It all seemed very exciting, but, although Noi didn't want to put herself down, it did seem a little quick based on the level of sales of her novel.

That day the restaurant was very busy, and Noi was working hard in the kitchen. She did not have time to keep looking at her cell phone, but she was very flattered when she saw that another message from Robin Pine had come through:

"I know this might seem very quick after the release of your novel, but I have worked in this business for a long time. I can now recognize books that will be best-sellers or translate into movies, and I think your novel is going to be a huge success. I would like to be there when you achieve this success."

Noi wanted to believe everything he said. She wanted to believe in herself, and she wanted to prove Niran wrong. In that moment, she decided to cast any doubts aside. She couldn't wait to tell her friends and to ask Robin Pine what the next step would be.

March, 2024

The opening of the new premises

A new love affair for Jinni

Kevin reads Noi's book

Noi talks to Robin Pine

Chapter 9

Jinni

The Grand Opening of the Purple Orchid – Second Wave

March 2nd seemed to come around very quickly. By this time, Patrice had interfered in every aspect of the grand opening. She changed the invitations to a more 'upmarket, muted' style – her words not mine – and had invited people who she felt would be appropriate. I had lived in this city for years and her for about two months, yet *she* had a list of appropriate people? Unfortunately for her, not all of her special guests could make it. The mayor had turned her down, saying he was double booked that day. Also, it seemed Jennifer Morgan from her husband's media company had a prior engagement. Reanne Colter, a presenter from the local radio station, however, agreed to come along and tape a small interview with Patrice and I.

The day before, I went along to the new premises to look around before the grand opening. I had to admit everything looked stunning. Patrice had good taste and was very knowledgeable about interior design. The décor was purple and white to reflect the Purple Orchid and the floors were bamboo. Patrice had explained that she wanted bamboo as it is sustainable and renewable, and they looked very warm and inviting against the color of the walls. The reception area was light and welcoming. Four small sofas, scattered with plump cushions, waited for customers to sit and enjoy coffee, and an open cupboard displayed luxurious well-being products.

The reception area was an open, communal space, and took up the whole of the left side of the building. An archway from the reception area led customers to the right side of the building to the nail salon, where there were four top-of-the-line chairs for manicures and two for pedicures.

The rear wall of the reception held a floating staircase, and displayed an intricate mural painted by Janine. It displayed a beautiful woman's face with her hand held up to her cheek, her nails sleek and decorated with nail art. It was a thing of beauty to look at, especially when one was walking up the stairs to Patrice's beauty salon, where no expense had been spared. There were four small rooms for private treatments and a waiting area in the middle with comfortable sofas and a display of products.

I was so proud of the new premises. I couldn't wait for the grand opening and have customers in there and see their faces. It was so exciting.

We were so busy on March 2nd and the opening went by like a blur in my consciousness. I remember friends coming and making appointments, and also many newcomers who were interested in both my nail salon and Patrice's beauty treatments. Robbie had come in to demonstrate the 3D nail art and people were really impressed – several appointments were made.

Reanne Colter came in about halfway through the day. She brought with her a small team to record the interview, and I was looking forward to it. She was very keen to interview Patrice about the beauty salon, and also in discussing the 3D nail art with

Robbie. In the end, she had a very short interview with me about the nail salon. Later, when I listened to the interview on the radio, it seemed my part had almost been cut out altogether – I only featured for about five seconds! Patrice and Robbie had been the main feature.

By the end of the day, I was exhausted and couldn't wait to sit down. Patrice, however, still seemed energized.

"I am sure we will be in all the local papers tomorrow," she said, walking around smiling and flapping her arms. "I am booked up for the next three weeks! This is better than I could have hoped for."

At that moment, Bill arrived to pick her up. He seemed delighted with how things had gone.

We had employed a firm of caterers, and they had provided canapes and drinks during the day. I had also employed Randi –the sister of my part-time receptionist, Lila – to clean both premises, and as the caterers were finishing tidying, she arrived to start work.

As I was chatting to Randi about the cleaning, Robbie came out of the nail salon. I introduced them to each other, and then I plucked up the courage to ask Robbie out for a drink to celebrate.

About an hour later, Robbie and I left to grab a drink at the White Horse cocktail bar, which was in walking distance from the regeneration area.

We sat at the bar and ordered beers. We seemed to hit it off very easily. We were soon laughing and joking and all the worries of the day just evaporated.

I couldn't believe how fast time went and before I knew it, it was 10 p.m. and we had been talking for hours. Saying goodnight, I had such a good feeling about Robbie and for the first time in months, I felt relaxed and happy inside. I hoped that I was finally on the way to recovery after my disastrous relationship with Song, and the financial meltdown that followed.

Sitting on the train, I pushed aside any negative feelings about having allowed investors into my business. Today had been a good day, I told myself, and the start of many more to come.

Chapter 10

Jinni

The new business

Noi has news about her book

So, after the grand opening I had two premises to manage. I divided my time between them as best I could, relying on Julie to run the Purple Orchid at the Walks and Robbie the nail salon at the Purple Orchid – Second Wave in my absence. Business was good at the new salon, and from what I could see, Patrice's beauty salon was booked up every day.

A week after the grand opening, Noi came over to my apartment to see me. It seemed that she had a literary agent interested in her book. She told me his name was Robin Pine, and that he saw her book being developed into a movie. She was very excited, and showed me his messages. How wonderful for her, I thought. She deserves recognition.

The following week I was doing a manicure on Ellie, who is a regular customer of mine. Ellie and her husband Kevin both teach at the State University, and were very kind to me when there were all the issues with Song. Recently, Ellie and Kevin had become parents to a beautiful daughter, Lily. Ellie was British and had been interested to hear about Bill Underwood and his wife, Patrice. She mentioned that she might like to book a facial with Patrice at the new premises.

We then moved on to talking about Noi. Ellie had purchased her book when it was available in the reception of the Purple Orchid, and I was keen to know if she had enjoyed it.

“Mmm, well, it is very difficult finding time to read with a newborn, and as you know, I am still working part-time too. My life consists of rushing from pillar to post. When I finally get five minutes at the end of the day, I fall asleep.”

So, from that I guessed she had not read the book. I decided to bring up Robin Pine.

“An agent has been in touch with Noi via text message and he is interested to find a film company who will make her book into a movie or TV show.”

Ellie smiled. “Wow, that is really something.” She then paused and thought for a few moments. “Is it a literary agent that represents you to contact commissioning editors at the big book publishers? I am not sure how it works.”

“Oh yes, I am sure that is what it is,” I said. I really didn’t have a clue about publishing, so I had not asked Noi many questions! “Except in this case,” I continued, “he was talking about making a movie.”

“Did you say Noi contacted the agent or was it the other way round?” Ellie queried.

“The other way round – the agent contacted her through a Facebook group she joined.”

“I would check out his credentials if I were her – just to be sure,” urged Ellie. “You have to be so careful online nowadays.”

That seemed like good advice, and I meant to tell Noi but I was very busy that day, and then my brother, Somchai, came to see me after work the following day. He was living with his American wife, Barb, in the Southern Hills again. He should have been happy but there was always friction between them. I do not know if it was because they were from different cultures, or because she was the one with all the money, or because she was not a nice person – or actually, all three.

We spent the evening in the back room. Somchai was supposed to be sober now after ending up in hospital with alcohol poisoning last year. I did not offer him any Thai rum. Instead, I offered him Iced Tea. We sat there sipping it while he told me about his latest marital woes. Barb was not interested in sex, and he felt unloved and ignored. I knew how this would go. Before we knew it, he would have another woman. This was the same complaint he had before he got into the relationship with Randi, who now cleans for me at the salon.

Noi was also very busy during the week, cooking at the restaurant. It was not until the following weekend that we managed to get together, and I was able to ask her about Robin Pine. I wondered if she had heard from him again.

“As a matter of fact, I have heard from him,” Noi said, excitedly. “He feels that my book has great potential, but I need to establish a presence on the internet before he pitches it to producers.”

“What do you think about that?” I asked.

"I have paid him seven hundred dollars where he will devise a strategy for me, and then we can start a PR campaign."

A PR campaign! Things were moving fast!

"Have you been able to check him out?" I felt awkward asking that question. She had paid him money so obviously, she trusted him.

Noi seemed slightly irritated. "What do you mean? *Check him out*? He is an agent who puts authors in touch with film studios. He told me I wouldn't be able to do that myself as they only speak to agents."

"I mean, is he able to tell you about other authors whose books have been made into films where he acted as the middle-man?"

Noi's agitation increased. "I haven't asked – but I will if you feel that it is important. I was just flattered that he contacted me and was willing to represent me and my book. I am a new author just finding my feet. I am not writing in my native language and to have this type of recognition is beyond my wildest dreams."

"I think you should ask him about other people he has helped," I said. I didn't know anything about publishing and movies, but I wanted to be sure Noi was okay. I wondered if Ellie was too cynical. Perhaps she was. I just wanted Noi to be happy and successful. My best friend Noi, a best-selling author. What would people think?

Chapter 11

Patrice's Salon

Patrice was fully booked during her first month in the new salon. During this time, she was the only beautician but she had plans to take on a second in the summer if the salon continued to be so popular.

During her final months in Los Angeles, she had been on a training course to learn how to use a new anti-aging treatment. This treatment used electric currents to stimulate the customers' facial muscles to contract and tighten. The idea behind this was that the muscles would tone up and tighten, thus giving the customer a more vibrant appearance. Wrinkles should be smoothed out, and the customer should look more youthful. Patrice had featured this technique heavily in the promotional material for her new salon and had received a number of bookings. She also offered facial massage, semi-permanent makeup and makeup lessons.

The days went by quickly, as Patrice worked on a steady supply of customers who seemed delighted with her work.

The salon was open until 7 p.m. in the evenings, and 9 p.m. on Thursdays. As Patrice was closing, Randi came in to clean the salon. Patrice treated hygiene with the utmost importance, and paid for a full clean every day.

It was on Wednesday at the end of March that Bill had come to the salon to pick up Patrice and take her out for dinner. Randi was sweeping in the waiting area when he arrived, and he acknowledged her briefly. He put his cashmere coat over a chair and went to the restroom. Shortly after, he and Patrice left the salon, leaving Randi to clean and lock up as she normally did.

Returning to the main waiting area after cleaning the salon, Randi noticed something stuck down the side of one of the chairs. Going over, she saw it was an iPhone. She picked it up, wondering whose it was. She had not noticed it when she was sweeping earlier. It pinged in her hand as a message came in. She decided it was most probably Bill Underwood's phone, and that she would give it to Patrice as soon as possible.

She messaged Patrice to say she had found a cell phone in the salon, and would give it to her the next day.

Patrice received the message while sitting in La Dolce Vita waiting for their dinner order. She asked Bill if he had his phone, and as she spoke, he realized he did not. He seemed to go into a panic and said he would go back immediately to retrieve it.

"There is no need for that – our food will be here in a minute. I can get it for you from Randi in the morning." Patrice hoped she sounded soothing, as he appeared very stressed.

"My phone is my lifeline," Bill growled. His face was going red and his tone darkened. "I can't let some bimbo of a cleaner have my phone. There is highly confidential material on that phone she might get access to."

"Your phone is password protected, and I doubt Randi would understand anything about your business even if she could get access to it. Don't worry." Looking beyond him, she leaned over and whispered, "Our food is on its way, you should eat, darling."

"Don't tell me what to do!" Patrice had never seen Bill like this in all the time she had known him. "I can't have company secrets spread everywhere. I must have my phone!"

At that moment the food arrived, but it seemed Bill had no appetite for it. After taking a couple of reluctant bites, he insisted they leave and contact Randi before she left the salon.

It was an unbelievable transformation. Patrice could not believe what she was seeing or hearing.

They drove back to the new salon, and Randi was waiting outside in the doorway with the phone.

"Thank you very much." Bill pocketed the phone, seemingly remembering his manners.

They drove home in silence, although Bill now seemed more relaxed.

After they had undressed and got into bed, Bill went to sleep almost immediately. Patrice stayed wide awake. It was weird in her view that someone would be so protective of their phone. She knew it might have work contacts on, but still… Patrice had a background of cheating men, and his behavior really worried her.

Getting out of bed, she went to the office and saw Bill's phone on the desk next to the laptop. It was charging and as she got near, she heard it pinging with new messages. She could not see who the messages were from as he had locked the screen, but she was intrigued. There were so many pings!

Bill had told her that they had no secrets – they shared everything. She now realized that she didn't know his password to get into his phone. A little voice told her that she shouldn't be snooping around trying to get into his phone if she trusted him. But his behavior was so odd when he realized he had left his phone behind.

It was something Patrice could not get out of her mind for days afterwards, even though Bill went back to the Bill she knew – loving and considerate.

Chapter 12

Kevin discovers a new book

Lily was the 6-month-old daughter of Ellie and Kevin. She was a bundle of pure joy and delight. After years of believing they could not have their own child, she was conceived out of the blue and had brought them nothing but pleasure.

Kevin was a professor at the State university, and Ellie, his British wife, also taught there part-time. They were lucky in that Kevin's mother, Jenny, was on hand to babysit so that Ellie could continue to teach.

Evenings were often chaotic, and by the time they had put Lily down and eaten a meal, it was time for bed. Tonight had been no exception. Ellie had decided to soak for a while in the tub while Kevin had got into bed. He was in the middle of reading *Wolf Hall* by Hilary Mantel – a masterful recreation of Henry VIII and his court. Looking through the books at his side of the bed, he was at first alarmed that he could not find it. He rolled over to see if it had been put at Ellie's side by mistake. He was surprised when he found a book with, in his view, a very garish cover there called *Summer at the Malami Hotel.* The author's name seemed to be Thai and vaguely familiar, but he couldn't place it. He flipped open the book and began reading. After he had read a few paragraphs, he snorted and almost laughed out loud. Goodness, what a lot of tosh. He had got to Chapter

Four when Ellie appeared, smelling fragrant from her soak in the tub.

“What on earth is this rubbish?” he teased, showing her the book.

“Do you not like it?” Ellie climbed into bed and smiled at him.

“Like it? Written by a seven-year-old for seven-year-olds. The sentence structure is infantile and the plot – wooden and going nowhere. Should appeal to people with half a brain.”

“Oh Kevin, for goodness’ sake, stop being such a snob.” Ellie was used to Kevin and his opinions.

“Seriously, who would this appeal to? I know it’s not a children’s book, but it is hardly adult reading.”

“Kevin, it was written by Noi, a very good friend of Jinni. I bought it when I went in for a manicure last week as Jinni had a few of them on reception.”

“You bought it.” Kevin was incredulous. “Well dear, you got ripped.”

“Don’t be so cruel. I think it is okay. Remember, Noi is not writing in her native language. She is Thai. She self-published the book after editing it herself. You can buy an e-book or a paperback.”

Kevin laughed out loud.

“Ellie you are way too soft, you know that don’t you?” He smiled indulgently. “We will never have any money while you continue to patronize lost causes.”

There was silence for a few moments. Ellie never really knew if he was joking or not. However, she caught sight of his copy of *Wolf Hall* buried under a couple of books at her side of the bed.

“Here’s your book, dear.” She handed it over to him. “Enjoy. I think Hilary Mantel is more your thing.”

Taking *Summer at the Malami Hotel* from Kevin, they both settled down to read until a loud cry interrupted them a few moments later. Lily was awake and needed feeding.

Chapter 13

Noi

Robin Pine had been in touch again, and he seemed optimistic. He asked for a WhatsApp call with Noi, and they had arranged for this call to take place on Thursday evening.

At exactly 7 p.m. Robin rang Noi on an audio call. So far, he had not made a video call with her.

"Hi Noi. It is good to talk."

Noi agreed.

"I really do want to get you some recognition for your book. I feel that it has such potential for a TV script. However, it seems that in its present format, TV studios are not interested to talk further. What we need is to do a rewrite of the book into a format that will be attractive."

"What do you mean a *rewrite*?" Noi was quite alarmed. She was proud of her book, and couldn't understand what he meant.

"A rewrite for American audiences. I am American and I use certain phrases that you do not. These are everyday phrases and words to appeal to an American audience. Your book is written in a very formal style which does not use these phrases, and I think we have a chance at a much wider audience if we incorporate them into the book."

Noi could see what he was saying. She was aware that Americans used certain phrases and words that maybe she did not when speaking English. She wondered if he meant profanity.

"Do you mean swear words?"

Robin laughed here. "Of course not, just general expressions. Such as the receptionist at the hotel saying 'have a nice day' to new customers. That is all. There are no plans to alter the story line, which I am so impressed with."

Noi thought that might be harmless.

"Will I get to see it after it has been rewritten?"

"Of course, and you will have the final say."

There was a brief silence here.

"What do you think? Shall I go ahead?" Robin queried.

"Yes, I think you should," Noi replied.

"I think it is the right thing to do. I will keep marketing the book while the rewrite takes place. I will send you an email setting out what this involves in detail, and a note of the charges."

The charges! Noi had not thought to ask about charges.

"Could you give me an idea of how much it would cost?"

"It is hard to say until work starts, but in the region of a thousand dollars I would expect. Fifty percent is payable up front, and the rest on delivery of the final product."

Robin hesitated before he spoke again. "I maybe shouldn't tell you this as I am not a hundred percent sure at the moment, but I spoke to Danny La Valle about some other projects, and I mentioned you and your book, and…" Robin paused here for emphasis "…he was very interested. As you know, he loves family stories with a moral. Just look at *Shamrock Isle*, his biggest success to date – set in Ireland and telling the story of a loveable family."

Noi had heard of Danny La Valle. She had watched *Shamrock Isle* on cable and loved it. She felt butterflies in her stomach, she was so excited. Danny La Valle producing her novel! Goodness, it was almost too good to be true.

After they ended the WhatsApp call, Noi checked her emails and a message had come through. It was very brief – thanking her for her time today and enclosing a proposal. She clicked on the proposal and read through it slowly.

Costs for setting up PR and marketing strategy: $700.

Cost for rewrite to be in region of $1,000. Author to have final say on rewrite.

Deposit payable immediately: $850.

Noi frowned. $850. This was a lot of money to her. However, she knew she could lay her hands on it. She and Niran had a joint savings account which they both could access for vacations, and there was enough money in that account to cover the deposit. It would be a temporary loan.

Noting the bank details, Noi went online and transferred $850 to her personal account. She then, as instructed, wired the money to the account Robin Pine had informed her about. It was amazing how quick and easy it was to do. Niran would never know. By the time next year's vacation rolled around, she would have earned the money back (and more) in royalties on her novel.

Danny La Valle! Noi was impressed. She looked him up on IMDb. He was 52 years old, she learned, and the former partner of Dino Latent in Global Films Inc. They had had a couple of surprise hits with 'feelgood' films about ten years ago. *Sunburst* was the highest, grossing $80 million at the box office. *Love in the Sun* had grossed $62 million. They then had a massive hit with *Rosy Dawn* in 2016. It seemed then that Danny had left Global Films to set up his own company, Avalon Media, and after quite a gap in producing, had come back with *Shamrock Isle*.

Wow, he might produce my book, thought Noi. She was so excited that she did a little dance in the kitchen. She knew not to involve Niran, as he had been so critical. He'll be laughing on the other side of his face when I am a Hollywood screenwriter, she thought. She went online and found Danny La Valle's Instagram account. She pressed Follow – she would be checking up on him now.

She couldn't wait to tell Jinni. She saw Jinni as her best friend and support, but decided that as it was getting late, she would not call her this evening and instead, she would speak to her on the weekend.

Things were looking up – the future was so bright she could hardly bear it.

April, 2024

The new salon

Bill acts strangely and trouble brews at Stermer Media

Noi and another author, Glenda, receive representation for their books

Chapter 14

Patrice worries about Bill's business dealings

The salon was doing very good business, and Patrice was thrilled with the way things were going. Bettina, the mayor's wife, had come along and been delighted with the facial massage she had received and told her friends. This had resulted in a flurry of bookings. After only four weeks of trading, Patrice had already taken on another beautician, Clarrie, to help her in the salon.

On Thursday evenings the salon stayed open until 9 p.m. and Patrice stayed late. At the last minute, her 8 p.m. appointment cancelled saying she had the flu and did not think it fair to come in for a facial. Patrice was not happy with the cancellation, but decided to go home early for a change. She wanted to surprise Bill. She had been working so hard she had not seen much of him, and there had been that curious incident with his cell phone.

She knew Bill usually got home about 7 p.m. so she stopped off on her way home and bought steaks, the ingredients for a salad and a bottle of Merlot. Tonight she would make him a special meal.

Driving into the motor court, she saw his BMW parked outside the house. There were lights on inside. He's home, I can't wait to surprise him, she thought.

Going into the house, she left her groceries in the kitchen and called out his name. "Bill?" She walked through to the open concept living room, but there was no sign of him.

Perhaps he is in his study, she thought as she made her way to the rear of the house. As she came up to the study, she could see the door was closed and a light glowing beneath it. She could hear Bill's voice.

Curiosity got the better of her and she stood outside the door.

She could hear him talking.

"You know I support you a hundred percent," he seemed to be saying. "All I think about is you."

Patrice felt sick. She knew you shouldn't eavesdrop, as the old saying was you never heard any good. But who the heck was he talking to?

Bill had been married before to a British woman, but there were no children, and that marriage had been over for a number of years before he had met Patrice. He had aging parents in the UK, who he spoke to on Zoom and who Patrice had never met. Other than that, she couldn't think who he would be talking to.

"Your dreams will come true now you have met me."

Oh goodness! Patrice couldn't bear it. She opened the door. Bill stared at her, and then said into the phone, "Excuse me I have to go – something urgent just came up."

There was an icy silence. You could have cut the atmosphere with a knife.

"Patrice, what a nice surprise. You are home early."

"Who were you speaking to, Bill?" She looked him directly in the eye.

There was a brief silence before Bill spoke. "Patrice, I am a businessman. I have to make work calls at home if something urgent comes up. I really don't feel I should have to explain this to you."

"Was it a woman? Is there someone else, Bill?"

"What? Are you crazy? What the heck are you talking about?"

"You talked about making someone's dreams come true."

"For goodness' sake. I was talking to a writer whose work we are going to produce. She is a born-again Christian and ardent Trump supporter who has had a very difficult life. Survived an abusive marriage and raised three children as a single parent. To have us produce her novel is like all her fantasies coming true. Have some compassion, Patrice."

Patrice immediately felt guilty that she had suspected him. He was a good man, and had been a good husband to her.

"I guess I can't get used to having your love," she spluttered. "I have had so many difficult, broken relationships and finding you was like all my dreams coming true."

She started to cry and at this stage, Bill moved out from behind the desk to comfort her.

For a while they stayed in the study – Bill hugging Patrice and stroking her back. At first, her body was racked with sobs and then gradually, this began to subside in his arms. He said, “Hush, hush, I love you, you know that. You have nothing to fear now.”

When she had finished sobbing, he began to kiss her and taking her by the hand, he led her upstairs to the bedroom where he undressed her and lay her on the bed. He was a very considerate lover, far more considerate than any of her other lovers. He made her feel like the most beautiful and desired woman on earth.

It was very much later when they got dressed again and went into the kitchen to make the steak and salad. By then, Patrice felt loved and comforted. What a fool she was to suspect Bill of being unfaithful. He was the most wonderful husband in the world.

Chapter 15

Jinni

I was pleased that bookings were good for the nail salon in the new premises. The coffee bar area was not very popular yet – sometimes customers stopped for a coffee either before or after an appointment, but it was often empty. I wanted it to be the heart of the salon, and I wanted people to call in for a coffee while they were out shopping. It was something we would have to work on, but I was sure it would become popular once other premises were complete in the regeneration area.

Patrice and Bill had met with me a couple of weeks after the opening to discuss how things were going. They suggested paying for two billboards on the busy interstate highway outside of the town advertising the premises. I had always imagined that billboards were for lawyers and much bigger businesses. However, Bill was prepared to pay for this as part of his investment, so we went ahead. I was delighted with the amount of trade we got from these billboards and by the beginning of April, the Purple Orchid in the Walks was also very busy again.

I could only be grateful to the Underwoods for what they had done for me and my business.

I was aware that Patrice was offering some new beauty treatments which were proving to be very popular. The idea of using electronic impulses on the face to tighten muscles and make people look younger was still new in our city. I knew that it had been done for a few years in bigger cities and we were probably behind the times. I was not a big fan of this type of treatment, but I understood that Patrice had trained in Los Angeles, so she knew how to operate the equipment.

One day at the beginning of April, I was at the coffee bar in the new premises chatting to Randi who was learning how to be a barista. We heard someone coming down the stairs and turned to see Kara, a loyal customer of the Purple Orchid. Kara was a real estate agent who was also a single mother with two young girls. She smiled and waved, and came over to have a quick chat.

"It's good to see the new premises, Jinni," she said as she looked around. "It's really beautiful here and Patrice is such a talented beautician. I think that is the best facial I have ever had."

"Wow, thank you, that is praise." I smiled at her. She did look good, I have to say.

"I didn't realize when I first met Patrice that you would become partners here," Kara said.

"You knew her outside the salon?" I was initially confused and then realized that of course, Kara was a realtor and Patrice and Bill had just moved to the area.

"Yes, I helped them find a home here. They leased a real beauty in the Southern Hills." Kara lowered her voice and leaned in. "I must admit to being quite envious."

I could just imagine the Underwoods having a grand house, so it was hardly a surprise to me.

Kara agreed to make an appointment for a manicure at the Purple Orchid the next week, and then she left.

I left soon afterwards and got an Uber home. It was only when I was sitting in the Uber that I started to think about the word 'leased'. I had leased an apartment when I first left my husband, but now I owned my apartment myself. It seemed strange that a man like Bill Underwood would not have bought a house. Perhaps he only intended to stay in this area for a short time. But that seemed strange when he had invested in the salon, and Patrice was working hard here to build up her business.

"You are putting two and two together and making five," I said to myself and put the conversation out of my mind. I was looking forward to arriving home, putting my feet up, and heating up a Thai red curry I had waiting for me.

Chapter 16

Stermer Media offices, early April

The offices of Stermer Media were outside of the downtown area in a business park containing a dentist, two lawyers and a chiropractor. They were modest offices, as Stermer was a relatively new company that had only been in business for five years. Keith Vickers was the chief executive officer, and he was a staunchly Christian man with right-leaning views. He worked out of the company headquarters in Los Angeles. He had recruited a chief operating officer to help him run the company. Bill Underwood had a background in finance and media companies, and Keith was convinced he was an excellent choice to help him develop the company. Bill had worked in Los Angeles, until recently, when Keith asked him to relocate to the Southern States to develop the business there. Bill oversaw the office at Stermer, and ran all the operations.

The receptionist, Becky, also doubled as the company bookkeeper – even though she had no professional accounting qualifications. Stermer Media paid her a good salary and she was happy with her job. She was sitting in the outer office working through the accounts, when the door opened and a woman entered.

“Hi and how can I help you?” Becky smiled broadly and in what she hoped was a welcoming way.

"I'm here to see Bill Underwood." The woman seemed very nervous. She was dressed in a jacket that was too big for her, and sweatpants and casual shoes. She wore no makeup and her hair was not styled.

"Do you have an appointment, ma'am."

"I don't, I'm afraid. I came on spec. I will only take up a few minutes of his time."

"And who may I say wants to see him?"

"Barbara Matthews – the mother of Leanne Matthews. He knows Leanne."

"And what is this regarding?"

The woman twisted her hair around her finger and looked around. "He will know what it is about. It is a private matter."

"Just one moment."

Becky got up from the reception and went through to the main offices. She knocked on Bill's door, and told him who was in reception.

Bill nodded. "Tell her I am very busy and have an appointment with the bank in half hour. But send her through, and I will speak to her quickly."

Becky relayed the message and sent the woman through. It was a very brief meeting, and when the woman emerged, she was visibly upset. She sat for a moment in reception.

"Ma'am, are you okay?" Becky fussed.

"Not really. I drove for three hours to get here, and now he can't help me. I really hoped for more than this."

"Bill is very busy ma'am, and he has an appointment at the bank. Is there anything I could do for you?"

"I just want my daughter's royalties. I can't believe Stermer are not paying her royalties when she is one of their best-selling authors. I just wanted to help."

Becky became curious. "We always pay royalties on books published with us. It seems strange that she hasn't received her payments. Has she given us the right information for her bank?"

The woman became annoyed now. "Of course she has! She was paid for a while, but now the royalties have stopped even though the reports show she is selling books. I don't want to see her suffer like this. It is her money and it should be paid!"

Becky agreed and made notes, and promised to discuss with Bill who she was sure would contact Head Office and follow up.

The woman left as it seemed she was going to gain nothing by staying. Her parting shot was, "If Stermer don't pay her soon, Leanne is going to the press to tell them what a fraud this company is!"

She was very agitated, and Becky was relieved when she left. Becky then went online and looked up Leanne Matthews. It seemed she had written a non-fiction book on how women can thrive using a right-leaning agenda called *The End of Woke*. It had not been on the New York Times Best Seller list, but had been very popular.

Becky knew that the Stermer Publishing House was a small press that relied on providing authors with a personal service. It seemed very strange that this woman was not receiving a personal service. Or her royalties.

Becky wanted to help, but felt all she could do was pass a message on to Bill. She was sure this was an oversight, and Bill would sort it out when he returned from his meeting at the bank. He seemed competent and this sort of thing was above her pay grade. So, bearing that in mind, she got back to her job of recording transactions in the company accounts.

Chapter 17

Glenda, the author

Glenda had a 2 p.m. manicure with Julie at the Purple Orchid. She had been a loyal customer of the Purple Orchid since it had opened, and had continued to make appointments when there were rumors going around about the employment of illegal immigrants at the salon. She worked as a teacher in an elementary school downtown, near the Purple Orchid – Second Wave.

Julie enjoyed chatting to Glenda about her work as a teacher, and about the house Glenda and her partner, Billy, were renovating in the northern suburbs.

"You must be so busy – I expect you have no spare time," smiled Julie.

"Actually, I do have some time which I guard fiercely."

"You use that time to rest, do you?" Julie was painting red paint onto Glenda's nails and concentrating hard.

"Not exactly rest," Glenda smiled, "I am an author, and I write children's books."

Julie stopped painting for a moment. "Wow, a famous author! You have been keeping that quiet."

"I wouldn't say famous author. I self-publish my work." Glenda waited for a reaction, and when there was none, she went on. "I have had only limited success. My book is called *Gwendoline Investigates*, and is about an Autistic girl who helps her stepmother solve crimes."

At last count on the website that had published Glenda's book, there were just over 100 copies sold online. Glenda had then tried marketing the books using a company that advertised on the internet. This company would sell her book at a discounted price to their contacts via an email list. She had sold more copies in this way, but for a very small profit.

She had joined a support group for women authors on Facebook and had written about her experiences.

"When I say limited success, it is early days yet," Glenda admitted. "I have sold about two hundred and fifty copies."

Julie smiled at her. "It sounds good to me. Send me a link to your book, and I will look at ordering a copy for my niece. She is six."

Pleased with the potential sale, Glenda left a very generous tip. She caught the train home and that evening, she checked her social media accounts.

A review of the Facebook support group for women authors showed that she had received a comment to one of her posts from an @lulub:

"I just wanted to compliment you on your book. It is one of the best children's books I have ever read. Gwendoline, the autistic child and Pernille, her stepmother, the detective – what child could not enjoy? It should be a bestseller. How are you promoting your book? DM me to discuss further."

Glenda was intelligent, and she liked to think, quite savvy. She was aware that there had been fraud on the internet, but this person seemed so friendly. Also, she thought to herself, let's face it, you certainly need help with marketing the book. What a coincidence that this has come up after discussing the book with Julie that afternoon! Perhaps sales were really going to start looking up.

She sent @lulub a DM and indicated she would like to discuss further.

Almost immediately, a message came back:

"Let me know how many sales you have made so far and how you are promoting your book, and then we can discuss how I may be able to help. Just to give you some background on me, I am a published author – I am with the Kerry Press. My novel is *Breaking Waves*, you might have heard of it. I have contacts in the publishing industry – and I would like to help!"

Glenda felt a spark of cynicism. This sounded too good to be true. However, @lulub had not asked for any money, and what did she have to lose? Her sales so far were hardly going to make her a New York Times Bestseller!

About a week later, she received a message request from someone called Robin Pine. Glenda did not know this person, but knew that @lulub – Lulu – had been looking for people to help her with her writing, so she decided to accept his message.

"Hello Glenda. I have been referred to your work by Lulu Bartlett and have just read your

children's book, *Gwendoline Investigates*. It is a very inspired and clever book. It is educational and fun. A real find. Do you already have someone to represent you? An agent?"

Glenda looked at the name and decided to google it. Who was this person? She found a Robin Pine who was a publishing agent with Stout and Bing, a New York based firm of literary agents. He represented clients who wrote children's books and young adult fiction.

She sat down and thought about this. Why was he contacting her? Did it seem logical that an agent would contact her? However, deep down she knew her book was clever and funny. It deserved recognition. *She* deserved recognition. She could picture it as clear as day – a book signing at Woodhouse, the big bookstore in the downtown area. People queuing up to get her to sign their copy. Then moving on to more book signings in the big cities. Atlanta, Raleigh, Austin and then south to Miami.

She typed back:

"I self-published my book and have been doing everything for myself. I don't have an agent, but I would be interested to find out what that would involve."

An answer came back very quickly:

"An agent would represent you to the big publishing houses and to producers of films and TV shows. This is very important, as these people will not usually speak to indie authors. I

have contacts within the main publishing houses such as Random House, and some large production companies and streaming platforms such as Netflix. I feel your book, if adapted, would make a great Saturday morning TV show for children. We could then pitch future books at the big publishing houses."

Glenda was trying not to get caught up in the excitement she could feel coming from Robin's messages. She had to keep calm.

"What would it cost for you to represent me?"

She wanted to make sure this was a sincere offer.

"I think you should think this through, and not make a rushed decision. You have a high-quality product that I am sure I can work with. I am excited to work with you. But you must be sure you want to go forward. Think it over, and if you provide me with your email address, I will send you over more details of my service and charges."

Glenda gave him her email address and very quickly, an email arrived from Pine@Stout&Bing.com. She went through it carefully, reading what Robin Pine could do for her, and noted that she would pay a retainer of $500. Further fees were contingent upon Robin finding her a publishing or production deal.

The next day, she thought about the email at every break she had from teaching. She decided not to discuss this with Billy, her partner. She had a feeling Billy might tell her to steer clear, and she knew deep down that she wanted to go ahead. She knew her writing was good and deserved a wider audience. It was just so difficult to bring her book to the attention of the public when she had self-published it. If Robin Pine could get her a deal, she would be famous and her work would be shown on television. She didn't want to be told to stop. So, she took out the banking app and wired $500 from her personal savings account to the account Robin Pine had given her, and then sat down to wait to see what he could do for her…

April, 2024

Becky loses her job

Noi dreams of stardom

Chapter 18

Becky becomes curious...

Becky liked her job at Stermer Media. She was the bookkeeper and general receptionist. There were few visitors, and the bookkeeping was simple and none too taxing. Her manager, Bill Underwood, left her well enough alone and she enjoyed sitting in the outer office playing Spotify through her earphones. She usually had time to check out her social media.

Additionally, she had a good salary which she needed as a single mother with a six-year-old daughter. Overall, she felt she was very blessed to have found this job.

She had assumed that Barbara Matthews had been sorted out by Bill and had almost forgotten that incident when a couple of weeks later, the door opened, and a middle-aged man came in. He was red in the face and seemed out of breath.

“Hi, how can I help?” Becky asked.

“I would like to see Bill Underwood,” he panted.

“Certainly sir, do you have an appointment?”

“No, I don’t have an appointment. I came here hoping that he might fit me in. My name is Joel Anthony.”

“I will check if he can see you.”

Becky went back to Bill’s office, and told him that there was a man called Joel Anthony outside waiting to see him.

Bill seemed annoyed. “Tell him I can see him quickly, but I have another appointment. Send him through.”

The meeting lasted less than ten minutes before Joel was back in the reception area – looking angry.

“I should sue this fucking company,” he complained. “Thanks for nothing. He thinks he can fob me off, but he fucking can’t. You can tell that bastard that I will be back, and this time I won’t leave until I get some settlement!”

Becky stared at him, alarmed.

“I’m sorry that Bill couldn’t answer your queries.”

“*Queries*? You must be fucking joking. You tell that fool that without authors using Stermer’s site to publish their work he will be soon out of a job. Why the hell would you treat authors this way?”

With that he stormed out of the building, slamming the door behind him.

Becky sat in a state of shock for a few minutes. Then she went onto the computer and into Google to look up Joel Anthony. He was an author of a couple of non-fiction books on how his family lived by Christian principles in the 21st century. She then remembered the visit from Barbara Matthews. Was this another person that was not being paid their royalties?

She was only a bookkeeper and did not have access to all the accounting programs, but she wondered who was in charge of the royalty payments to authors. She logged into the computer and looked at the various accounts. She looked under the heading Stermer Publishing. There were various sub accounts, including one entitled Royalties. Clicking on this, she could see that there was only one payment that had been made from this account over the last few weeks. This was to Stout & Bing, and was for $50,000. Looking back on the account over the last couple of months, it seemed Stout & Bing received a regular payment each month ranging from $10,000 to $60,000. These were large sums, and would account for a lot of sales.

Later that day, when Bill went out for an appointment, Becky rang the Head Office in Los Angeles and spoke to Rudy who worked in accounts. She had chatted with Rudy before and found him to be very friendly. She explained what had happened and asked him if he had access to the royalties accounts, and also, if he knew who was responsible for making sure royalties were processed. Rudy had a quick look at the account while they chatted, and agreed there was something wrong. He promised to investigate it.

The next day, Becky's phone rang, and it was Rudy.

"Hi Becky. Just to say thanks for the tip off. The royalties are headed up by Bill Underwood in your office. He has to sign to approve payments. It seems that he hasn't signed for the last couple of months. In some cases, royalties are very small, but some authors rely on their royalty payments to live. I passed this on to Steve Cannon, our VP of publishing, and he is pissed off. He has sorted it out, and will be speaking to Bill."

Becky felt nervous, as she had been the one to bring this up to Head Office. "Is this fraud?" she asked.

"No, just incompetence. But Steve said it is this sort of thing that gets us a bad name, so he is pleased I told him."

“Okay. So, all sorted now, and no one knows I rang up interfering.” Becky laughed, but still felt a bit nervous.

“Don’t worry – it’s all sorted, and there is no suggestion you had anything to do with it. I am sure Bill still loves you!”

Becky wasn’t entirely convinced.

Nothing much happened during the next couple of days. Bill still came through the reception and said, “Good morning” in his British accent and then, as usual, locked himself in his office.

The following week was the end of month accounting close period, and Becky was busy with the bookkeeping entries all week, which she sent to Head Office. She was beginning to forget the series of incidents that had her feeling nervous. On the Friday afternoon, just as she was getting ready to leave, Bill rang through and asked to see her in his office.

Bill was sitting behind his very large desk, where arranged carefully was his computer, a few pieces of paper and a picture of him with a younger, very attractive woman. He looked very serious, and did not smile at Becky as he asked her to sit down.

Becky sat and waited for him to speak.

“As you know, this office is a startup and we have not been in operation here long. In this regard, we must be sure that operations are kept to the same standard we have in the Los Angeles Head Office.” He pulled at the sleeves on his shirt, and straightened the paper on his desk. “You will agree, we have to have the highest standards for Stermer Media.”

Becky nodded, feeling sick inside. What on earth was he going to say?

"Considering this, I have been checking some of the bookkeeping entries you have made this month end." Another pause, this time looking at the computer and not at her. After what seemed like an eternity, he turned to look directly at her. "You have made a number of errors in closing the books at the end of this month, which I have had to correct."

Becky was taken aback by this. "I don't believe I have," she spluttered. "I always check my work."

"Not carefully enough it seems!" This was said quite sharply. "What are your qualifications?"

Becky was on the back foot, but beginning to get angry. "You should know my qualifications, you hired me! Now show me where I made mistakes, please."

Bill waved his hand before turning the computer screen around. "Here. You did not bring forward five thousand, six hundred dollars of income."

Becky felt her mouth beginning to gape open. What was he talking about?

She was angry now. "I didn't do that. You are making things up," she blustered.

Bill remained perfectly calm and let her rant on. Then, in the same polite voice, he said, "I am sorry Becky. We can't have someone here who is not thorough in their work. I am very disappointed in you. I am going to have to let you go. I suggest you pack up your things, and I will pay you two weeks salary in lieu of notice."

Becky, near to tears, stood and began shouting at him. "Don't fucking blame me for your shortcomings! It is you who are incompetent! How dare you blame me when you do everything wrong! I'm going to sue your motherfucking ass!"

She was stood leaning over the desk shouting and waving her arms around. At that moment Rodney, the security guard, arrived.

"Come with me, Becky." He spoke loudly. "You need to calm down and leave this office now."

It was humiliating. The people in the main office saw her being led out to the reception by the security guard. She collected her things and was forced to leave. She was then escorted to her car.

Driving home, tears streamed down her cheeks and she banged the steering wheel as she ranted. "I am going to get that bastard!" she shouted. "He's fucking incompetent! How dare he fire me when it was him that was incompetent!"

When she arrived at her friend Mandy's house to pick up her daughter, Kiara, she managed to compose herself enough to go into the house. But when Mandy asked how she was, she burst into tears and blurted everything out.

"Don't worry," Mandy soothed, "you will be able to sort this out. I suggest you wait until Monday and then ring Los Angeles. They will know what happened with Bill Underwood and they will defend you."

Over what seemed like a very long weekend, Becky planned what she would say on Monday, and tried to convince herself everything was going to be okay.

Chapter 19

Noi reaches for stardom

Noi started to follow Danny La Valle on social media. The thought of him filming her book sent shivers down her spine. It was just too exciting!

Two weeks after she had sent the deposit for the PR campaign and rewriting of her book, Robin Pine was in touch again.

"I have good news for you, Noi," he said. "I have had lunch with Danny in Beverly Hills, and he showed interest in a joint project. However, from subsequent discussions and messages it seems that, although he is interested, we are going to have to do a more extensive rewrite than we first imagined."

"A more extensive rewrite? Does he not like my book?" Noi was alarmed.

"He thinks it would make a great project – it is just the whole issue about American audiences. It needs to be rewritten so that they can *really* identify with it."

"I don't know what you mean. I learned English in Thailand growing up, but I also went to English night classes here in America. I speak to Americans all the time and they understand me." Noi was genuinely confused.

"I'm sorry, but that is what he believes – there needs to be a more extensive rewrite for him to consider your book."

Noi sat down and thought for a moment. “If I don’t agree, he won’t film my book?” She was aware that she sounded naïve.

"That’s it,” Robin said. “It is good news in that he wants to go ahead, and he is a famous movie producer. But, he has his standards and in your case, that would include additional rewriting.”

There was silence for a few moments, and then Robin spoke again. “Look, you don’t have to make a decision now, while we talk. I will email you details of the additional rewrite, and you can decide whether you want to go ahead.”

After the conversation ended, Noi checked her emails. Robin had indeed sent her another email – this time he asked for $5,000 for the additional rewrite. 50% was due up front.

Noi felt sick as she did not have that much money. Yet, the thought of Danny La Valle producing her book into a movie was so exciting to her.

She closed her emails down and googled cheap loans. She found it was fairly easy to get a loan of $2,500 if you were a homeowner, as the loan would be secured on your home. Noi and Niran owned their home in the northern suburbs of the city. There was a joint mortgage on the house in both their names. After consulting a couple of banks, it turned out that Saltacres Bank was willing to lend her $6,000, which would cover all the rewriting costs, and would take a second charge over the house. Noi did not want to mention this to Niran, as she felt he would not understand. So, she decided to sign for him as she was confident she could pay the money back when the movie of her novel was a big success. She did not see this as forgery, and as she signed his name, she knew in her heart that everything was going to turn out well.

The money came through fairly quickly, and she wired $2,500 for the additional rewrite to Robin Pine and kept the rest of the money in her personal account to pay over later. Robin assured her she had done the right thing, and that she would be hearing from him soon.

Noi decided to keep this to herself for the time being – it would be a lovely surprise for her friends in the Thai community when her book was made into a movie.

Looking on social media, she saw that Danny La Valle was publicizing a movie he was currently working on called *The Reluctant Pastor*. This movie was set in the Appalachian Mountains, about a woman who fell in love with a religious man. She couldn't wait for it to be released and to go and see it.

Just wait until he is producing my movie, she thought. And she knew this would be just as soon as the rewrite was complete. How exciting!

Chapter 20

Becky – difficult times

On Monday morning, the week after she had been fired from Stermer Media, Becky took Kiara to school and then went home. She flipped open her laptop to look for jobs, but inside, she still felt angry and that the way she had been treated was unjust.

Picking up her cell phone, she dialed the number of Rudy in Stermer's Los Angeles office.

"Wow, you are ringing early, I just walked in," he laughed, referring to the time difference.

Becky decided to be upfront and honest, and told him what had happened with Bill Underwood last Friday.

"I think he blames me for speaking to you."

There was a silence, and for a second she thought Rudy had disconnected. Then he spoke. "I think that is a bit of a stretch, Becky. Look, this is none of my business, and I am going to have to go now, someone has just come to my desk who needs my attention." And with that, he hung up.

Becky sat staring at the phone. A few minutes later she tried to call him again, only to find her number had been blocked.

She then rang the main office and asked for Steve Cannon. His PA said he was busy and asked what it was regarding. Becky explained, and the PA said she would ask Steve to ring back.

Becky spent the morning scrolling on her laptop looking at jobs. She found there were few that paid as well as her last job, and for most jobs she was unqualified. She felt sick as she saw it was not going to be easy to replace her job at Stermer with one that paid as well.

About 11 a.m. when she was sitting at the table working on her laptop, her phone rang, and she answered.

“Can I speak to Becky Arnold please?” a voice she did not recognize asked.

“This is Becky.”

“Hi Becky. This is Julie Moran from Stermer HR. We spoke very briefly when you commenced employment. I want to confirm that we are terminating your employment with us immediately. You were employed on an ‘at will’ basis. This means that either party was free to terminate your employment at any time without notice, for any reason. We will provide two weeks’ pay in lieu of notice, which is very generous. We will write you a reference so long as you accept our conditions of termination of the contract.”

Becky slumped down over the table. She knew she didn’t have a leg to stand on, yet it was all so unfair.

She closed the call off without saying goodbye.

And then the tears came. How was she going to manage? Bill Underwood was an absolute bastard to do this to her! After all, it was he that was incompetent, not her. But how could she *prove* it?

The following days resulted in many rejections for Becky. She was not qualified to be a loan officer. She was not a qualified accountant, so many jobs were closed to her. She had some experience as a bookkeeper, but not sufficient for many employers. Finally, she found a position at the Institute for the Blind and Visually Impaired in the finance office. This was low paid work to assist the accountant in recording fees and outgoings for the school. The salary was approximately 25% less than what she had received from Stermer Media, but at least it would mean she could afford to keep a roof over their heads.

Becky was a cheerful person, and had never experienced real bitterness before this happened. But during her first week working at the Institute, she had come home and made a meal for herself and Kiara and then was sitting watching the TV. During the local news segment, a glitzy evening reception was reported on and, oh no, it couldn't be, that bastard Bill Underwood and the beautiful woman from the picture in his office were captured arriving and smiling for the cameras. The anger and bitterness she felt at seeing his smiling face was indescribable. She vowed at that moment to get him back for what he had done to her. However long it took.

Chapter 21

Jinni

The salon is profitable

As April continued, I remained grateful to Bill and Patrice, for with their help, my business had returned to profitability. The billboard campaign had been successful, and Bill followed this with more advertisements on the podcasts that Stermer Media put out.

In addition, the Underwoods were involved in several charity events in the city. These events were publicized on the local TV station and in the local newspaper, and it was mentioned that Patrice was a co-owner of the Purple Orchid.

It was a good time for the business, and I was beginning to feel more optimistic about the future.

My relationship with Robbie was also going well. She was beautiful and lively and although we had not committed to each other, we had some really fun times together.

I had also spent time with Noi and been brought up to date on her book. Apparently, her agent, Robin Pine, had got in touch with a film producer and director called Danny La Valle who might be interested to film it in Hawaii! It all seemed very exciting.

At this time there were some new customers who had booked appointments and I was chatting to them, trying to establish a relationship. They were full of gossip and loved to talk about celebrities and scandals.

"I think Meghan Markle is finished," said one of the customers. "Bill Simmonds calling her and Prince Harry *grifters* when the Spotify deal ended really screwed them."

"What has she done since?" asked the customer at the next manicure station. "Nothing! They are over."

"There are some good movies out now. Have you seen Shamrock Isle? It is *so* good – funny and romantic."

"Isn't that a Danny La Valle movie?" the next customer enquired.

My ears pricked up at the mention of Danny La Valle.

"Is he an actor?" I joined in.

"No, he is a director and producer. He has had some good movies in the past, but recently not so much. Shamrock Isle is his comeback."

"He has been drinking and partying too much and looks like shit. He hasn't done anything for years before this."

"I read he is a real piece of work who treats women like crap," said another customer, joining the conversation.

"I know he's been married four times, and always to women half his age!"

I was intrigued. "Is he not a nice person?" I asked.

There was silence and then the two American ladies laughed. "A nice person? I doubt that, Jinni. He says he is clean now, but I would take that with a pinch of salt. He has more addictions than you could imagine. Alcohol, drugs, sex…"

I thought my eyes were going to pop out of my head – and he was going to film my friend, Noi's book. She was even more innocent and naïve than me, if it was possible. I made a mental note to have another word with her. I knew, though, that it would likely be futile as she was hardly likely to turn down the chance of a famous director filming her book.

That evening, I returned home from work exhausted and fell asleep in the chair. I was fast asleep when I heard my phone ringing from across the room. I picked up the phone and it was Somchai, my brother. He sounded worse for wear, and I could hear noise in the background as if he was in a bar.

"Where are you?" I asked, as I struggled to come round from my sleep.

He was slurring his words. "I'm at The Black Cat bar." My heart sank. Somchai had spent a lot of time in that bar – drinking too much. It was there that he had started a relationship with Randi. After cheating on his American wife, Barb, he had left his home and set up a new home with Randi. But this had not gone well and he had ended up back with Barb. The trauma of it all had led to Randi attempting suicide.

I couldn't keep the annoyance out of my voice. "What are you doing there, Somchai? I thought you were stopping drinking and had vowed not to go there again."

His voice took on a pleading tone. "I have been so lonely, Jinni. Barb doesn't want me. You know how it is when I get lonely."

I felt sick inside. He was drinking again, and I would almost bet my life on it there was another woman.

"I don't want to go home, Jinni." He was slurring and almost sobbing. "Can I come to you?"

I wanted to say no, but he was my only brother and I wanted to be there for him.

I called him an Uber and paid for it. I got out of bed and was sitting on the sofa in my dressing gown when he turned up. He was drunk and looked very tired and disheveled.

I made him up a bed on the sofa while he told me about Betty, a woman who often went into The Black Cat, and apparently, cared about him. He had been tempted to go back to her apartment, but he said he felt guilty thinking of how much he loved his wife Barb, the mother of his beautiful daughter, Amara. On and on he went until I had tucked him in and left him.

I went to bed troubled. He had fallen off the wagon and was drinking again. Plus, there was another woman in the wings. How Barb put up with him was beyond me. But at the same time, I would do everything I could to protect him.

When I woke in the morning and came into the living room, he had gone. There was a note thanking me for the sofa and telling me he would be in touch later.

It was only then that I wondered if Barb knew where he was last night? I had not let her know, and I wondered if he had told her he had stayed at my apartment.

I was sure she was used to Somchai and his ways. I tried to put it out of my mind as I started another day at the salon, talking to customers and working on their nails.

Due to the stress with my brother, I completely forgot to ring Noi to ask her how things were going with Danny La Valle.

End of April, 2024

Becky attempts to investigate Bill Underwood

Noi sees Danny La Valle – but he does not see her

Glenda is offered a TV deal for her book

Chapter 22

Becky investigates...

The rent was due, and Becky was hard pressed to find it. Losing her job at Stermer Media had been very difficult, and trying to make ends meet on her new salary at the Institute for the Blind and Visually Impaired was near impossible.

Becky would have taken a second job in the evening at a bar or restaurant, but who would have looked after Kiara? As a single mom she did not have anyone to ask.

She sat at the kitchen table looking at her home accounts and thinking up ways to economize. Something burned deep inside her. A feeling of anger and bitterness. She had seen that bastard, Bill Underwood, at a glittering ball only the other week. Why should he be able to live the high life while she had to suffer?

She messaged Patti, who had worked in the offices at Stermer Media. They had chatted and been on a few nights out while she worked there.

Patti came back to her quickly:

"The new receptionist is struggling, and Bill has not spoken to anyone since you left. He comes in and locks his door. There is a rumor he got into deep shit about the Royalties account."

Patti then wanted to talk about her new partner, Greg. He was a musician who played at local venues.

After she finished talking to Patti, Becky pulled up a new page on Google and typed in 'Bill Underwood'. His picture and bio at Stermer Media came up. He had qualified as a chartered accountant in Britain, where he worked for a firm of accountants called Meyer and Co. In 2010, he transferred to their Los Angeles office and qualified as a certified public accountant. He had worked his way up to partner in 2014, working on what was described as 'prestigious' media clients, including Global Pictures Inc.

Here, Becky took a break. She was beginning to feel sick reading it. She had no formal qualifications and knew she should go to night school, but it was difficult with being a single mom. Her lack of qualifications had stopped her getting a well-paying job when she was let go at Stermer. Bill, meanwhile, had qualifications and had been a partner in a firm of accountants with prestigious clients.

She then googled Meyer and Co., Certified Public Accountants. It turned out they had offices worldwide and were one of the top accounting firms in the world. Apparently, they had a media department in Los Angeles with some of the top production companies and studios as clients.

Global Pictures Inc. was a public company headed by Dino Latent, which had produced some very big movies in recent years. Moving on to their website, she recognized at least three box office hits in the last two years. Dino's smiling face was featured throughout the site. He was a famous director and producer that Becky had heard of, and he was reputed to be very rich.

She sat back, thinking. Meyer and Co. were a top firm of accountants with A-list clients including Global Pictures Inc., and Stermer Media was a startup. They had a small, boutique publishing house that had had some success with right-wing commentators and Christian writers. Additionally, Stermer acted as a distributor supplying Christian books to booksellers. There were also the podcasts that they sold to radio stations. However, this seemed a long way from Hollywood.

Returning to Bill's bio, it seemed he left Meyer and Co. in 2017 after three years as a partner, and went to Avalon Media, a company with offices in Los Angeles.

Checking Avalon Media's website, she found that this was the production company of a director named Danny La Valle. She saw that Danny La Valle had made a couple of movies with Dino Latent of Global Pictures Inc. that had made money at the box office in 2013 and 2014. These included *Sunshine City* and *High Desert Living* – both of which were comedies about retirement communities in Arizona that were surprise hits. The third and final film they made together was *Rosy Dawn* in 2016. This had been panned by the critics as being sugary sweet, but was loved by the general public. It had been an enormous box office success. It had made $230 million worldwide, making both Danny and Dino very rich. Surprisingly, Danny then set up his own company in 2017 – Avalon Media. She could not see that the company had done much until 2022, when they had released a film called *Shamrock Isle* which was set in Ireland. This had also been very successful.

So, it seemed that Avalon Media was a relatively small company and had only the one film, *Shamrock Isle*, to its credit.

After six years with Avalon Media, Bill had left to join Stermer in 2023.

“An even smaller company,” Becky said out loud. “Each move is to a *smaller company*.”

Just as she was going to put the light out and go to bed, a message flashed up on WhatsApp. It was from Patti:

“Oh, I forgot. Another woman came to the office this week looking for Bill. He was out at a meeting and she wouldn’t say what she wanted. She said her name was Sheila Kavanagh and she needed to speak to him. He seemed none too pleased when the message was passed on. Don’t know what this is about now.”

Smaller companies each time he moved *and* people looking for him? Who is *this* woman, now? Becky wondered aloud. She was determined to find out.

Chapter 23

Glenda gets a TV deal

In what seemed like very quick timing, Robin Pine came back to Glenda with what sounded like good news. Avalon Media were going to diversify their portfolio and were interested in getting into TV. They had indicated that they would like to produce a children's show, and he felt that her characters could be perfect features. This would involve licensing the characters' names and doing some independent PR to publicize the characters before the show. Robin would go ahead and apply for the licenses, and would do some PR which would involve the local media.

Glenda was delighted, of course, but again this involved a fee. Looking at the follow-up email, Glenda realized that she was now agreeing to lay out a considerable sum of money without a contract. There was the $500 retainer which she had paid, and now he wanted $3,000 for the licenses, and another $2,000 to begin the PR campaign.

This was money Glenda did not have and which she would have to borrow to go ahead. She knew Billy, her partner, would not approve and tell her she should stop now. But the thought of her characters appearing on TV was almost too good to resist. Could she really trust Robin Pine?

She knew there was a Robin Pine listed at Stout and Bing, as she had seen his name on their website. She decided she was being too cynical and she should go ahead and pay. She was only making a few sales by promoting her book herself. How lucky she was to have Robin to guide her.

She also knew who would help her get the money she needed. Picking up her phone, she texted her dad to see if he would meet her for a drink that evening as she had a proposition to put to him. Peter, her father, was always willing to help and he was excited about her book, so she knew he would lend her the money.

Things were looking up, she decided. It would be so exciting when her characters were on TV!

It was hard not to tell people about her TV deal, but she decided to keep it to herself until it was all finalized and she received a contract. Then she would have a big party and invite all her friends around to watch Episode One!

Chapter 24

Jinni

Catching up with Noi

I had spoken to Noi on the phone, so I knew about her book being rewritten to be presented to Danny La Valle.

It was during April that she rang me to say that Robin had had an initial meeting with Danny La Valle, who seemed to like the story. More work was required, though, before he could produce it.

We finally met up for brunch the following Sunday. Noi seemed very excited about having her book produced into a film by Danny La Valle. I asked if she had seen his latest movie, *Shamrock Isle*. Noi said that she had, and thought it was brilliant. She then told me that she now followed Danny La Valle on social media. Taking out her phone, she searched for him to show me his latest post. It seemed he was taking part in an evening discussing current trends in filmmaking with the director Peter Ponsford, and writer Eileen Gunner. This was to take place at a theatre in Atlanta, on the coming Saturday evening. Tickets were on sale for $30 per seat, and there was a link to book.

“I would love to go,” Noi said with a smile.

“I will go with you.” I reached over the table and squeezed her hand. “Let’s stay overnight and spend Sunday sightseeing. We can have a girl’s weekend.”

We bought the tickets and I paid for a hotel and the flight. It would be good to spend the weekend with Noi.

On Saturday, after I closed the Purple Orchid at 4 p.m. we got an Uber to the airport and caught our flight to Atlanta. After checking into our hotel, which was very nice indeed, we went to the theatre for the big event. At first, I was not sure we had gone to the right place. It did not seem as big as I was expecting, and it looked a bit rundown and seedy. There was a small group of people waiting to go into the theatre and milling around in the foyer.

As we joined them, there was a slight stir as a Cadillac Escalade pulled up outside and a man got out. He was a white, jowly man who could have been anything from fifty to seventy years old, it was hard to tell. His hair looked unnatural to me – like he had dyed it jet black. He was wearing a bright blue suit with a shirt that was straining over his belly. I am a Thai lady who likes ladies, but to me, he was a very unappealing man.

A woman stood near us called out, "Danny! Can I get a picture with you?"

I then realized this was Danny La Valle in the flesh. His photos on social media had been filtered that was for sure! He was not very attractive in his pictures online, but the real thing in the flesh was much worse!

Danny ducked his head and walked as fast as he could towards the foyer. A couple of reporters were already there, waiting, and their cameras flashed. He put his hand up and said to whoever, "Not now. I have to get ready for the debate." He then hurried into the theatre.

He seemed rather cold and unwelcoming to his fans. Why had he not gone into the theatre by the back door if he didn't want to meet his fans? Noi and I made our way inside to find our seats. They were towards the back of the theatre, and we sat down waiting for the discussion to start.

"I am sure Danny was just rushing to get ready for the discussion," Noi remarked in his defense.

"He left it a bit fine to get here, didn't he?" I looked at the leaflet advertising the event. "I would have thought he should have arrived much earlier."

I didn't want to say, but I could smell booze as he brushed by Noi and I. He never even glanced at us – two middle-aged Thai ladies. He didn't seem a very likeable character to me.

Well dear, I am not a film buff so perhaps it was just me, but the discussion was beyond boring. How I stayed awake I don't know. Peter Ponsford was a self-opinionated loudmouth, and don't get me started on Eileen Gunner. She was so loud, she didn't need a mic in a theatre. They all seemed to have had a sense of humor bypass.

It was a long night. The theatre was only half full and some people left before the end of the discussion. I wondered if Danny La Valle was as successful a director as I had been told.

Finally, it ended, and we got up from our seats. Noi indicated that she would like to go backstage to meet him. She dashed down the aisle of the theatre to the stage where a minder was tidying up. I ran after her.

"Sorry, if you don't have a backstage pass, you can't go there." The minder sounded bored.

"I would like to speak to Danny La Valle," Noi said proudly. "He is going to produce a film from my book. I am an author. I wrote Summer at the Malami Hotel. I am Noi."

"Yay, right lady." The minder looked fed up. "If you have a pass, you can go backstage. If you don't, you can't. It is a simple as that."

Noi, of course, did not have a pass.

"I don't have a pass. But he knows me. I am Noi, the author of The Malami Hotel books. Just tell him that."

"Sorry lady, unless you have a pass you can't go back there."

With that, the minder moved away from us and left the stage.

We stood staring after him.

We left soon after that. Noi seemed a bit down and ruffled. We got a taxi back to the hotel and went into the bar. It was then that Noi dropped her bombshell.

"I can't believe I wasn't allowed backstage." Noi was now sipping a strong rum and coke.

"You needed a backstage pass, and you didn't have one." I tried to calm her. "I suppose rules are rules. You saw Danny in the foyer. I guess he is busy."

"Yes, but I know he is serious about my book. Why wouldn't he be when it is being rewritten to his specifications."

"Yes, I am sure he is serious." That was what I said aloud but inside, I was beginning to wonder.

"I am paying six thousand dollars for my book to be rewritten in a style he will produce," Noi sobbed.

I very nearly choked on my drink. “What??”

“I am paying for an American person to rewrite my book in a style he will like. I have had to borrow money.”

“Did you say *six thousand dollars*?”

“Yes, it doesn’t come cheap having a rewrite!”

I decided that the best thing to do was to go along with Noi and calm her down. Noi and her husband Niran were not rich people, and that was a lot of money to them. Where had she got it from?

Something in my gut told me this didn’t sound right. But for that evening, I just wanted to keep Noi calm. I tried to talk to her in a placating way, but inside I was already plotting how to follow up on this.

We spent the next day sightseeing as planned, and it was only when we had returned home that I decided to start digging.

I went into Danny La Valle’s social media and saw that it was possible to send him a message. I wrote:

“Hi Danny. I am a big fan of your movies. Are you planning to make a movie in Hawaii about a hotel? Heard a rumor on the grapevine.”

I expected to get an answer to my message one way or the other. However, days went past and I did not receive anything. I was following Danny now on social media, and the subsequent week I saw that he made a post that said:

“So exciting to finally announce the release date for my next project as June 30, 2024. I am working with Peter Ponsford on The Reluctant

Pastor, a Christian film for Avalon Media. We are currently filming in the Appalachians."

There was a picture with the post of Danny La Valle and Peter Ponsford at the debate Noi and I went to. They were both holding forth and looked pompous and arrogant, in my opinion.

There was no mention of Hawaii or The Malami Hotel.

I felt sick to the pit of my stomach. However, when I spoke to Noi, she brushed off my concerns. "My book isn't ready for production yet. It is being rewritten. You will see it yet as a film. It will be Danny's next big project."

I hoped that she was right – but something didn't smell right to me.

Beginning of May, 2024

Keesha poses for a beauty photoshoot

Sheila Kavanagh comes to Stermer Media and meets with Becky

Jenny's BookStop opens next door to the Purple Orchid – Second Wave

Chapter 25

Jinni

Patrice has an idea

Jenny's BookStop opens

At the beginning of May, my two nail salons were busy and growing in popularity. It seemed the beauty salon run by Patrice, who was helped by Clarrie, was also busy.

I was pleased with the way things were going, but it seemed it still was not good enough for Patrice. She asked to meet with me in the coffee bar downstairs when we were closing one Tuesday evening.

She came clattering down the stairs in enormous heels. How she walked in those shoes was beyond me, yet even after a full day working in the salon, she somehow managed to look glamorous and polished. I felt like such a slouch beside her. I was aware my hair needed brushing, and I had no makeup on. My nails looked good though – I never, ever neglected my nails.

She sat down with a coffee, and smiled a blinding smile.

"I haven't stopped all day!" She seemed to relax and stretched her arms above her head. "I can't wait to get home and kick my shoes off!"

Gosh, I thought, she's not kidding!

I nodded. "Yes, it's been a busy day. Glad to see business is taking off."

There was a short hesitation where Patrice sat studying her nails. I wondered what she was going to say, and then she announced, "It is taking off, but actually, I feel we could be doing more. Well, *charging* more. We are a top salon, but our prices don't reflect that. Also, we are not the salon of choice for local celebrities."

I tried not to let my mouth gape open. Goodness! Some people were never satisfied!

"Patrice, this is not Los Angeles. The charges here reflect local prices. We don't have movie stars and millionaires here." I realized I sounded defensive.

Patrice leaned over and smiled. "What about Keesha, who is in that soap opera, Grangemouth? She grew up here and her parents still live here."

My whole face lit up. "I know Keesha. Her family live next door to my brother and his wife. She is a family friend. What exactly are you saying?"

"Could we get Keesha to model for us? Perhaps she could have the 3D nail art and I could apply her make up and we could put her picture on a billboard."

I had to agree it was a good idea – Patrice was very clever, I had to give her that.

"I'll get my brother's wife to come into the salon and we can get her to speak to Keesha."

So, I messaged Barb, my brother's wife, and offered her a discounted Mani/Pedi at the new salon. True to form, she quickly made an appointment. She loves a bargain.

When she came in for her appointment, I quickly turned the conversation away from my brother – who

I knew from recent experience was up to his old tricks of drinking and staying out late – and onto Keesha, who I knew Barb loved to talk about.

"Keesha is such a wonderful person away from the soap opera. She really cares for her mother. Not like my own daughter, Amara. That girl drives me up the wall. She is always busy, too busy to spend time with her mother. I said you will be sorry when I'm gone! Keesha is not like that, and she is rich and famous. Such a beautiful girl."

And so it went on – blah, blah, blah…

Finally, I managed to get a word in, and I asked Barb if she could contact Keesha and ask if she would be interested in being a model for our salon.

Barb was, of course, delighted to act as an intermediary with Keesha.

And so it was that Keesha contacted us about a week later, delighted to act as a model for our salon. She agreed to come in and have a full makeover with Patrice, and have 3D nail art applied by Robbie. Patrice arranged for a photographer to do a photo shoot, and for Jaylace Designs to loan her a stunning dress for the photographs.

It was exciting to arrange and I had to agree, it was a good idea to generate publicity.

Also at this time, the bookstore next door, Jenny's BookStop, completed decoration and refurbishment and had a grand opening. I went with Noi, and we immediately spotted Jenny. To some people she may have appeared eccentric. She had dyed pink hair in dreadlocks, and wore hippie-style clothes. For the opening, she wore a loose, floor-length, floral-patterned dress and brightly colored beads to match her hair. I like eccentric people, so I warmed to her immediately. We agreed we should get together for a chat when it was not so busy.

She had invited a local author along, Eric Ladiv. Eric wrote horror stories which were certainly not my choice, however, Noi and I sat and listened politely while he read from his book.

After, I introduced Noi to Jenny and told her that Noi was an author who had written a book. Jenny was interested to talk to Noi about it, and arranged for her to go into the shop on a day when she wasn't as busy.

I immediately thought, what a great opportunity for Noi! She is going to be very famous. It is simply not true we don't have celebrities in this small city. I will tell Patrice I was wrong when I next see her!

Chapter 26

Jinni

Keesha takes part in the beauty campaign

Keesha was as good as her word and came into the salon the following Sunday to take part in the beauty campaign. She had arrived with her hair piled on the top of her head, in a different look for her. Robbie applied the 3D nail art, Patrice the facial and makeup, and Jaylace Designs had loaned her an outfit which was stunning and very sexy.

"Wow, you look sensational," I said when she was finished.

Patrice had arranged for a local photographer to come in to take pictures. We posed Keesha against the back wall in front of the mural, then sipping a coffee in the coffee shop, and finally, reclining on a sofa.

Keesha immediately sent the pictures to her agent, who messaged back to say he felt they could be used in a PR campaign that would be featured in the newspapers.

We then posted the pictures onto the salon's Instagram.

Patrice had also arranged for a picture to appear on a billboard outside of town. When we had advertised on a billboard previously, it had resulted in a great increase in trade.

It was a very successful day, and Robbie and I celebrated with a cocktail in the downtown area afterwards.

A couple of weeks later, an article appeared in a down-market, online rag about celebrities who had had plastic surgery, titled:

'Life after plastic surgery: shocking exposé of twenty something celebrities who have gone under the knife.'

A picture of Keesha from the photoshoot at the salon appeared in this article. It was a close-up, with her 3D art-covered nails framing her face, which, instead of smiling, wore a sultry, quizzical expression. This was shown side-by-side with a picture of her on the set of the soap opera *Grangemouth*. In this second picture, she had minimal makeup and her hair was straight and long.

"After her success in Grangemouth, Keesha Matthews (26) is rumored to have had extensive cosmetic work done. This includes a boob job and nose and face lift with Beverly Hills plastic surgeon, Dr Ari Moses.

Looking stunning in her latest publicity photos where she poses with 3D nails and exquisite makeup, word on the street is that Keesha is considering a Brazilian Butt Lift."

The article went on in a similar vein about other soap stars, and a country music singer who was only 20 years old.

I flipped to the comments section. My eyes watered reading them – they were brutal.

Maggieonline: Keesha looks older wearing makeup and posing with 3D nails than on the set. It is hard to believe she is 26 she looks more like 46.

Claudballs: She was such a pretty girl – what a shame she ruined her looks with all that surgery and makeup – and what the hell are those nails? Ridiculous!

Minny@home: Is she wearing a wig? Her hair looks as fake as her surgery. And who would want nails like those – only a very rich woman could wear them.

And on and on – none of it complimentary.

It was the opposite of what we wanted. It was cruel and unnecessary.

I was worried first and foremost about Keesha. How would she feel reading this rubbish about herself? Keesha has always been a nice young woman and unaffected by fame, in my opinion. Then – and this was the worst – she had posed to help us out with the salon. Now she was getting all this bad publicity.

I was anxious to speak with Patrice about it. She read the article – and the comments – while I was there.

"Well," she said, "I guess the saying is that there is no such thing as bad publicity, and this puts Keesha in the spotlight. When people see her on the billboard they will know she is advertising this salon."

I looked at her open-mouthed. "But this article is not complimentary to Keesha *or* to the salon. In the comments people are saying she looks much older than she is..."

“I know,” Patrice interrupted, “but the thing is she is in the news and people are talking about her. They are talking about 3D nails and about her makeup. If people are talking, then some will come here.”

It was all beyond me. I guess I didn’t understand self-promotion and PR – I was just worried how Keesha felt and I was determined to speak to her to make sure she was okay.

Thinking back on this sometime later, I realized that I was so anxious about Keesha and the article that I put Noi and her book on the backburner. I didn’t follow up with Noi until much later.

Chapter 27

Sheila Kavanagh comes to town

Sheila Kavanagh sat in her hired Toyota outside some lowly offices and looked again at the app on her cell phone. This had to be it, then. She couldn't believe he worked here. It was hardly impressive. A small business park of dentists and ambulance-chasing lawyers. And Stermer Media.

She finally plucked up the courage to go in and ask to speak to him. She was told he was out of the office. So, he did work here.

What did she want? She was tempted to tell the woman in the office, but knew it had to remain between her and Bill. For now.

Returning to her car, she sat down and prepared to wait. He did not arrive the first day she waited, so she booked into a small motel and decided to come back the next day.

The following day, after waiting a couple of hours, her patience was rewarded as Bill appeared, driving a late model BMW. She waited until he parked and then came and stood beside the driver's door as he got out of the car.

"Hi Bill. Long time, no see." She looked him in the eyes and smiled.

"Sheila." He looked stern. "Please get out of my way. I have no idea why you are here. Any business we had is now finished."

"You must be kidding, Bill." Sheila tried to keep her temper. "No way is our business over. Quite the opposite. I think it is just beginning."

"I don't think so. Any communication between us must now go through our lawyers. Now please get out of my way. I am a busy man, and I have things to do."

With that he pushed Sheila to one side and marched towards the offices.

Sheila stood there staring at him. She felt pure hatred rise up her throat and it was all she could do to control herself and not follow him shouting and screaming. But she knew that would do no good.

She also knew he would have told the staff to ignore her. Despite this, she still went into the office building. The receptionist looked her up and down.

"I demand to see Bill Underwood. Now." She realized she sounded aggressive. "I know he is here. I saw him come in. So please tell him Sheila Kavanagh is not leaving until she gets to see him."

The receptionist saw trouble brewing and pressed a button under the desk. A moment or two later, the woman she had spoken to previously, Patti, came out of the inner office.

"You can't just come in here ma'am and demand to see Bill Underwood. You need an appointment. I can make an appointment for next week, but in the meantime is there anything I can do to help you?"

Sheila went over to her, red-faced and growing angrier by the second. "I lost my job and my good name because of Bill. I need to speak to him about the accusations that he has made against me."

Sheila looked Patti directly in the eyes. “I want to stop him now before more people get hurt.”

Patti looked at her. “Did you say you lost your job?”

Sheila nodded.

Patti indicated to the outside door. “Come outside for a moment.”

They both went outside and when Patti thought no one could hear, she said, “Look I shouldn't do this, but I am going to give you a number of a friend of mine who also lost her job here.”

Patti scribbled Becky’s number down and told her to get in touch.

Sheila went back to her car and quickly sent a message:

“Becky, you don’t know me. But I understand you lost your job at Stermer Media. I also lost my job at Avalon Media and I think we have one person in common. Bill Underwood. Do you want to talk?”

Chapter 28

Patrice thinks back to meeting Bill

Patrice was busy with the salon. She was booked end-to-end every day. So much for Jinni's worries about that article after the photoshoot – she knew it would bring publicity to the salon and it was no surprise there were now even more customers. "Look at the trolls who pick on Meghan Markle," she had said to Jinni. "Look how successful she is. Sometimes bad publicity can turn out to be good publicity."

These were good times, but still there were some odd things going on. When she arrived in the morning to start work, she parked in a lot to the rear of the building. This was shared with the other premises in the regeneration area that were operational now. These included the Institute for the Blind and Visually Impaired, the bookstore and the hardware store. On a couple of occasions, she had noticed a woman watching her. She was an ordinary-looking woman, probably in her thirties, and she would park near to Patrice and watch her get out of her car and walk to the salon. The third time this happened, Patrice had decided that she should confront this woman and ask her why she was looking at her. She turned and walked towards the woman's car. At this point, the woman got out of the car and quickly left the parking lot with her head down. Even when Patrice shouted, "Hey! Please wait, I just wanted to ask you something," it seemed to have no effect, and the woman just left. Patrice told herself to stop being stupid. She must have been imagining things.

But then there was the strange phone call.

One Thursday, she came home and found Bill's cell phone on the island unit in the kitchen. She guessed he must be working in his home office and decided not to disturb him. As she cooked, she heard the phone pinging messages. And then it rang. Without thinking, she answered it. The screen wasn't locked.

"Hi."

There was a hesitation and then a female voice said, "Who am I speaking to?"

"I am Patrice Underwood. Bill's wife. Shall I get him for you?" But before she could say, "Who is calling?" the caller hung up.

Patrice felt sick to the pit of her stomach. This was very suspicious, and she didn't like it at all. Plus, she had been neglecting Bill recently with all the extra work at the salon. She felt that her history with cheating men was about to repeat itself.

She held off on taking the phone to Bill and started to think back to when they met and, actually, how little she really knew about her husband.

She had been working as a makeup artist when they met. She had been freelancing but had a good reputation and got fairly regular work at the major movie studios.

She was just finishing work on a movie when she was told that there was going to be a late-night current affairs program where a makeup artist was needed. The pay was particularly good as someone was needed on short notice. She had been given a number to ring and was pleased that she got the work. It was for one night only.

Patrice had driven over to Burbank where Avalon Media were filming a late-night talk show, where a host was interviewing a Hollywood director about his career in the movie industry. This had been arranged at the last minute, hence the rush to get everyone on set.

She had been shown to a back dressing room and told that the host and the director would be along shortly. The host arrived first, and he was vaguely familiar to her. He was very pleasant, and the makeup session went well.

As he was leaving, he had said that the director was on his way over and she should wait a few minutes.

She mused over who the director might be. She wondered if it was someone famous. When the door opened, she instantly recognized the man who walked in.

He was a middle-aged white man with jowly red cheeks and hair that looked like it was dyed. He looked to have gained weight since he bought his clothes, as his shirt was straining over his stomach and his pants looked too tight. This was none other than Danny La Valle, who looked like he was going to seed.

She remembered that the realization of who it was had made her feel sick. She knew from other people who worked backstage on his movies that Danny had a bad reputation. He drank heavily and was often high on drugs.

Danny sat in the chair and leered at her.

"I'm very lucky today, having you to look after me," he slurred. "I'm in your hands, baby."

Patrice smiled politely and tried to be friendly as she started to apply his makeup.

At first all went well. She was aware he was on something as his pupils were dilated and he seemed high. But it was not until she leant over to put powder on his face that she felt his hand groping her and going up her skirt as far as her panties.

"Stop that right now!" She pulled away. "If you don't behave, I will stop applying the makeup."

Danny laughed. It was all a game to him. His hand was still up her skirt and he didn't seem to care. He was as high as a kite.

Patrice panicked, realizing that they were alone in the room. She moved away from him as if to leave, and then he was on her, kissing her and groping her breasts.

He was panting and telling her how beautiful she was.

"Get away from me!" she screamed as she was fighting him off.

It was only then that she realized they were not alone. Another man had entered the room. She didn't know when he had come in. He was so quiet. He was also very calm and seemed to be taking everything in.

When Danny realized they were not alone, he sat back down in the chair and took a gulp from the glass of water. The man moved over to Danny and stood over him.

“I am not sure we can let you go on if you are high,” the man said, speaking in a British accent. “I am cancelling the session now and I will speak to this young woman to find out what was going on in here. I was witness to some of it.”

Danny started to argue and then slumped down in the seat. He nodded and agreed that he was in no fit state to go on and discuss his movies with a TV host.

The man then addressed Patrice. “Please come with me and we can have a chat. My name is Bill.”

Thinking back to that evening, Patrice felt like she had met her savior. She had never met a more gracious, kind man. He listened to her side of the story, and never once did he query what she said or say he did not believe her. She wondered how long he had been in the room while Danny was harassing her. But she also believed that he knew about Danny and his reputation and that he was wondering what to do for damage limitation.

Bill had taken her to a small bistro near to the studio while they had chatted. She had enjoyed his company very much, even though they were talking about a very unpleasant incident.

She found out that Bill was an executive with Avalon Media. Before she left for the evening, she had agreed to sign a non-disclosure agreement regarding the incident in the dressing room. In return she was to be paid a sum of money, which was basically 'hush' money.

Afterwards, she wondered if she should have held out and argued her side more. If she had, she might have been awarded a larger sum of money. But the money was sufficient to pay for the lease on a storefront in Burbank where she set up her own beauty salon. The icing on the cake, though, was that Bill had contacted her and asked if he could see her again.

They had not dated for long before she had moved out of her studio apartment into his luxurious home in Calabasas. It had been like all her dreams had come true.

What had Bill told her about his past?

She paused stirring the pot of spaghetti, trying to think. She knew he had been married before to an English woman who was also an accountant. That marriage had ended in divorce. He had told her it was amicable. He had no children. He had aged parents back in Britain who he spoke to regularly on Zoom. He also had a sister, Maddi, who had never married and lived at home with their parents in Fishponds in Bristol, England. Patrice had spoken to Maddi a few times, but only once to his parents when she first met him. In that moment, she realized she didn't know very much.

She also knew by having these thoughts she was potentially spoiling things for herself. She had a kind, loving husband and a beautiful home. She was ruining everything, worrying if he was unfaithful.

When she called him to come from the home office for his meal, she decided not to mention the strange telephone call. Instead, she asked him about his day and they sat chatting.

She told herself everything was fine.

Chapter 29

Sheila and Becky compare notes

Becky was excited to meet Sheila Kavanagh. So, she wasn't the only person to suffer at the hands of Bill Underwood! She couldn't wait to hear more.

They arranged to meet at the Highway 76 diner out in the northern suburbs at 7 p.m. and Becky's neighbor had kindly agreed to watch Kiara.

As she walked into the diner, Becky checked Sheila's profile picture again on WhatsApp and looked around. A woman sitting at a booth in the window looked her way and smiled. Becky waved and went over.

"Hi, I'm Becky, and are you Sheila?" When the woman nodded, she rushed on. "I can't wait to chat!" She realized she sounded over enthusiastic and decided to act more cool as she sat down in the booth.

Sheila was not what Becky was expecting. First, she was, to put it bluntly, stunning. Her profile picture did not do her justice. Her hair was styled, her teeth were very white and looked like veneers, and Becky thought, bitchily, she must have had a nose job as her nose was perfect. Even though Becky decided her clothes were not expensive designer brands, she wore a Cartier tank watch and bracelet. She gave the impression of someone who had money. Yet she had gone to Stermer Media looking for Bill Underwood as she said she had also lost her job. Becky was intrigued.

They sat for a couple of minutes appraising each other while the waitress took an order for drinks and left menus.

Sheila spoke first. “It is good we are getting together. I have had a bad experience with Bill, and I understand you have also. Let’s compare stories.”

Becky nodded. “Bill Underwood has ruined my life.” She realized it sounded dramatic, but she meant it.

Sheila seemed very sympathetic. “I understand what it means to have your life ruined by that man,” she volunteered.

After the waitress had taken their orders, Sheila asked Becky to tell her what had happened.

Becky did not need much encouragement. She launched into her story without stopping, and Sheila sat quietly nodding.

Becky ended by saying, “I hate him.”

The waitress came back with their orders, and they sat and ate their food. Becky couldn’t wait to hear what Sheila had to say.

Once they had finished eating, Sheila pushed her plate to one side and took a deep breath.

“Do you mind if I ask you a few questions, first? Before I say anything?”

“Of course not,” Becky smiled. “Ask me anything.”

“You mentioned royalties were being paid to Stout and Bing. Is that correct?”

Becky nodded. “Yes, that was even though other royalties were *not* being paid. It was between ten and sixty thousand dollars a month.”

Sheila waited a moment and then she spoke. “So you feel this was fraud, correct?”

Becky stuttered and felt a bit on the back foot. “Oh no, I didn’t mean to imply it was fraud...”

“Oh, come on,” Sheila said. “Think about it. Why pay only one company?”

Becky was thinking now. “But it doesn’t make sense. If it was fraud, wouldn’t Bill have made sure everyone else got paid so people didn’t complain? If there were complaints, then the account would be investigated.”

Sheila thought for a moment. “That is a good point. But you also feel Bill is incompetent. Did you follow up to find out if Stout and Bing is a real company?”

Becky hadn’t, and was now feeling stupid. She got her phone out and looked Stout & Bing up on the internet. She saw that *Stout and Bing* were a reputable firm of literary agents.

“Stout and Bing are very prestigious literary agents,” Sheila continued. “As you can see, they have an address in Manhattan, New York. Are you sure they were doing so much business with a small publishing house like Stermer?”

Becky looked at her phone and shook her head. “I really don’t know…”

“And as you can also see, they appear to be spelling their name in two different ways. You typed in Stout & Bing, with the ampersand, the *symbol* for ‘and’, and look, the company listed in New York uses the *actual word* ‘and’ – it’s quite clever, and I think it is highly likely that this is fraud.” Sheila sat back and folded her arms. “What do you think we should do about it?”

Becky could now see the difference very clearly, and her head was spinning. This woman was talking over her head. She felt sick. She genuinely had not suspected fraud before.

“But how could a fraudulent Stout and Bing company have been set up as a royalty account and receive regular payments? Surely there were checks within Stermer Media?” Becky protested.

“Bill was the one who checked,” Sheila said bluntly, “and he made sure those payments were paid.”

Becky sat in shock for a few moments.

The waitress came back. “Will there be anything else?” she asked.

“No, no we were just leaving.” Sheila got her card out and indicated that she would pay.

“I don’t know what to think.” Becky was still not entirely convinced. “Bill is senior in that company. Surely he would not cheat a company in which he is a director?”

Sheila laughed out loud. “Why not? Where does he live? Does he have big expenses?”

Becky indicated that she knew where Bill lived.

“Look, I’ll pay the bill and then shall we take a drive and look at his house?”

Becky was beginning to feel a bit uneasy, but also excited. What if Bill was defrauding the company? She knew that carried with it the possibility of a prison sentence. The thought of him in prison was very appealing to her.

They set off in Sheila's hired car and drove into the Southern Hills. Becky remembered Bill had once given out his address to a few people who he had invited to a work-related party at his home. Becky had sent out the invites, so she remembered the address – 1415 Sleepy Hollow Ridge. Sheila put the address into the satnav and they drove slowly up the winding roads of Southern Hills, the lights of the city twinkling below.

As they drove, Sheila began asking more questions.

"Did Bill mention Danny La Valle?"

Becky thought for a moment. "Avalon Media is Danny La Valle's production company. Is that right?"

"Yes, that is correct. Danny founded Avalon Media when he had a big falling out with Dino Latent at Global Pictures. They had been working together for a few years and made some box office hits. There was Sunshine City and High Desert Living, and then Rosy Dawn in 2016, which was the big one. Rosy Dawn was so big at the box office that both Dino and Danny were sitting on a pile of cash, but I think they fell out about sharing royalties."

Becky could see that Avalon Media might have been well-funded with a lot of cash sloshing around.

They were now driving up to Sleepy Hollow Ridge. As they drove along, they saw that the properties were new builds and on huge lots. Number 1415 faced the hills and did not have a city view, but through the gates they could see a beautiful two-story home with enormous glass windows.

"How much would something like that cost here?" Sheila enquired. "If this was in the Hollywood Hills, that would be worth about seven million dollars."

Becky, who was at the moment renting a small two-bedroom apartment, didn't have a clue what a mansion in the Southern Hills would be worth.

"I really wouldn't look at houses like this, but I guess in this city, a lot less than that. Maybe a million?" She had made that up from the top of her head.

"Even so, how old is Bill? Forties? He worked as a manager at an accounting firm and then was at Avalon Media followed by Stermer Media. Where would he get that sort of money?"

Becky realized she had not asked many questions when she worked at Stermer Media. She had no idea how much Bill would have earned. She had earned $50,000 and thought that was a high salary. She had no idea how much Bill would have earned, and had not really thought much about where he might live.

"But he was an executive at Stermer Media," Becky protested. "That looks like an executive house."

"Mmmm." Shelia looked at Becky questioningly. "But are we sure Bill has enough income for a house like that? You say it is worth about a million dollars. He is working for a very small media company."

Becky was shocked. Perhaps Bill was committing fraud. He was not just incompetent – he was fraudulent too.

After looking at the house, they drove back to where they had left Becky's car and Sheila told Becky to contact her if she wanted to follow up with her on this conversation.

"Can we accuse Bill of fraud? There was certainly fraud at Avalon in my opinion. We just need to get evidence. Think how we can get evidence from Stermer."

With that, Becky got out of the car and Sheila drove off. It was only when Becky was driving home that she realized that Sheila had told her precisely nothing about Avalon Media – or her own issues with Bill Underwood.

Chapter 30

Becky wises up

The day after her meeting with Sheila, Becky realized how slow she had been to ask her about her issues with Bill. She messaged Sheila to say they should have another catch up where Sheila could tell her about Avalon Media and why she had issues with Bill Underwood. She felt like a fool sending this message – what had happened to her last night? Sheila had run rings around her!

About 6 p.m. a message pinged on Becky's cell phone:

"Thanks for meeting with me. I believe there was fraud at Avalon Media and much has been covered up. Bill has gone on to another role with no consequences. You should do all you can to find out what happened at Stermer Media, where after our conversation I believe there was also fraud."

Aware that the West Coast was behind in relation to time zone, Becky found the number for Avalon Media and rang, hoping someone would answer.

"Avalon Media. How may I help?" a pleasant-sounding receptionist answered.

"I'm looking for Sheila Kavanagh. Please can I speak to her?"

"Who?"

"Sheila Kavanagh. She is an accountant."

"We don't have anybody of that name here. Are you sure you have the right number?"

"Oh, I'm sorry – wait, I think she may have left." Becky realized she sounded foolish.

"We do not have anyone of that name here, ma'am. I am sorry I cannot help you."

"Bill Underwood, then. Can I speak to Bill Underwood?"

"Bill is no longer with us. He left to go to Stermer Media. You should try them."

The receptionist was polite, but getting tired of Becky and her questions. Becky rang off, thanking her for her time.

She then messaged Patti and asked her if Sheila Kavanagh had been back to Stermer Media.

Patti replied saying she hadn't, but Bill Underwood seemed rattled and in a bad mood.

Who *was* this woman? Becky then went online and started trying to find her on social media. There were several Sheila Kavanaghs listed on Facebook. None seemed to match the woman she had met. They were either too young or too old or looked different. There was one who lived in LA, but she looked dowdy and unattractive and nothing like the woman Becky had met. She tried Instagram and found the same. The Sheila Kavanagh she had met seemed to have no presence on social media. She was beginning to worry that she had been conned.

Next, she looked up Avalon Media and Danny La Valle. There were lots of pictures on the internet of Danny looking worse for wear coming out of

Hollywood restaurants with different women who all looked the same – blondes with large breasts. There was a review of *Shamrock Isle* where it was given four stars. She found an interview with Danny La Valle, where he talked about his life and relationships. In the interview, it said that he had been married four times and was now in a relationship with a younger woman, Holly, who from the way she was clinging to him in the picture, seemed like she hoped to become the fifth Mrs. La Valle. Becky studied the picture – she didn't look like the woman she had met. She read the interview where Danny talked about his struggles with drink and drugs over the years. This had been particularly acute during the years after *Rosy Dawn* had been a box office smash and dragged him into the spotlight. He talked candidly about writer's block and losing the will to go on.

"I was a co-writer as well as director and producer on Rosy Dawn, and felt that I had a story to tell. I know my audience loved this story and I wanted to say so much more, but a terrible depression and anxiety took over me."

Danny went on to say how he had engaged therapists as he had battled his demons. Finally in 2021, he checked into the Betty Ford Centre in Rancho Mirage in California where he was treated for drug and alcohol addiction, and he was pleased to report he became dry and had managed to stay that way until the present.

"When I met Holly in 2022, she became my muse and my everything. I love her with every fiber of my being. She encouraged me to write again and because of her, I was able to write and produce Shamrock Isle."

The article ended by discussing how *Shamrock Isle* had been a big hit at the box office and Danny was now back on form as a top Hollywood director and producer.

So, thinking about what she knew, Danny had money from a couple of box office hits to set up his own company. Money must not have been a problem. But things seemed to have gone downhill from there creatively.

Becky wondered what had happened at Avalon Media and who Sheila Kavanagh *really* was. It seemed that she suspected fraud there – or may have even been involved in a fraud herself.

She wondered if she was getting into something that was over her head.

But her curiosity had been piqued, and this meant that she couldn't stop.

Chapter 31

Jinni

The publicity from the photoshoot continues

After I saw the article about Keesha in the down-market rag, I messaged her and asked to speak to her. She rang me back fairly quickly

"Hi Jinni!" She sounded very upbeat and happy, so this was a good start.

"How are you?" I asked.

"I'm good. Very good. I hear you are going to put my picture on a billboard outside of town."

"Yes, that is true. It goes live next week." I hesitated then went on. "The photo shoot also attracted interest from the media."

Keesha laughed. "Yes, and lots of negative comments!"

I couldn't understand why she was laughing. "I am so sorry."

"Sorry? There is no need to be sorry, Jinni – it is all publicity. Some is good and some is bad. You have to take the rough with the smooth."

I was relieved she didn't seem upset. Yet it all felt so wrong.

The following weekend our local paper, The Tribune, ran the pictures of Keesha with a short article about her career. I looked at the online version of the article where comments were allowed. I clicked on the comments and they were, in my opinion, even worse.

Patty@onenet: Where did Keesha get those nails done? They are ridiculous! How can any normal woman want hands like that!

Benni: replying to Patty@onenet: Who knows? But she looks worse than many women twice her age when they had finished with her.

Poppi: She has had a lot of plastic surgery and looks at least 10 years older than she is!

And on and on it went. There were a lot of comments all on the same theme – Keesha looked old, Keesha had plastic surgery.

I was sure that she had not had plastic surgery. She was a beautiful young woman. I decided to write a comment to put the record straight.

I went under the pen name of **Caringanconcerned** and posted:

Keesha looks a million dollars in the pictures. She is a stunning natural young woman in her 20s. Her makeup has been expertly applied and her hair styled. I love her nails – 3D nail art is new and growing in popularity. I heard she had the makeover at the Purple Orchid salon. They always make people look beautiful.

I posted the comment and waited to see what would happen. Sure enough, people answered my comment – but now with even *worse* comments:

Cassie: A plastic face with goldfish lips – how is that attractive? She has had so much work it is

not true – lift, fillers, lip enhancement – I can see it all. Give me natural any day.

Diane: She was so attractive before she started messing with the plastic surgery.

I wanted to scream – where did these rumors of plastic surgery come from?

Then I saw the comment that really scared me:

Laurie: Well, it goes without saying she would look artificial if she went to the Purple Orchid! Isn't that the place which was nearly closed down for employing illegal immigrants?

Oh no, I had just made it worse by adding my comment! I was at a loss for what to do.

I asked Patrice what she thought.

"Just ignore it for now, Jinni," she advised. "It will blow over and, in the meantime, we are getting publicity for the salon. Of course, Keesha is getting publicity out of it. Don't worry if people are insulting her – she won't care so long as her name is in the paper."

I wanted to take her advice, but I couldn't get the articles out of my head – or the comments. I was worried that the issues around my employing Song, an illegal immigrant, were going to raise their head again.

I was so absorbed with my own issues that I did not see Noi for a couple of weeks. I spent my evenings when I returned home from the salon scouring the online news, to see if there was anything about Keesha and the photo shoot. I assumed that Noi was also busy, and things were progressing with her movie deal.

At least Barb, who had asked Keesha to do the shoot with us, didn't seem angry. She was impressed that Keesha was in the news and also that her picture was on a billboard on the road outside of town.

"She is on her way up. She is going to be such a big star," Barb gushed. "She is very talented and so down to earth."

I couldn't imagine feeling successful if people were talking about me the way they were talking about Keesha, but what did I know? I just hoped it would all blow over soon.

The middle of April, 2024

A reading is planned at Jenny's BookStop

Sheila Kavanagh meets Patrice

Patrice reflects on what she really knows about Bill

Chapter 32

Glenda goes to Jenny's BookStop

At the opening of Jenny's BookStop, Glenda had stopped by and took a copy of her children's book. She had left the book with a note about herself, including her contact details.

She had been delighted when Jenny had contacted her and asked her to drop by as she felt they could do business.

On Monday, April 22nd, after she had finished teaching, Glenda caught the train into the city and went along to the shop with a carrier bag full of several copies of her book. It was a nice sunny afternoon with blue skies, and Glenda felt in a generally optimistic mood.

The shop was not busy when Glenda entered. The original building had been divided into several cozy spaces. There was the main entryway with the tills and a few chairs. Behind this, there were rooms to the left and right featuring literary fiction, crime fiction and biographies. There was also a large space in the center of the building for children's books – this was decorated in a bright yellow and had several tables and chairs for children to sit in and read. Finally, at the rear of the building, there was a space with a podium and chairs where visiting authors could read from their books.

A couple of people were browsing the shelves, and a mother and child were sitting together in the children's area. Jenny came over immediately to greet Glenda.

"Come through," she said warmly. "Sit down and have a cup of tea."

After Glenda had made herself comfortable, Jenny told her how much she had enjoyed reading her book.

"It's paced just right for the six to eight age range in my view," Jenny said.

"I am a teacher at Glenn Elementary and teach that age range," Glenda smiled, happy with the comment.

They chatted for a few minutes about the book and the characters. Then Jenny asked Glenda how she was marketing the book.

It was then that Glenda shared that she had an agent and the book was going to be produced into a TV show for children.

"That is fantastic," Jenny said. "I am wondering if you could do a reading of your book here for us? Saturday afternoons are always popular with moms and little ones."

"I'd be delighted," beamed Glenda.

"I wonder if we could publicize the TV show at the same time? Have you got a date yet for when the show will launch? Which station will air the show?"

There were so many questions, and panicking slightly, Glenda realized that she didn't know that much about the actual TV show.

"Let's fix a date for the reading and I will get back to you with more details about the TV show," she said quickly.

A date early in June was agreed. Jenny told Glenda to bring along several copies of her book which she could sell on the day.

The meeting had been a success, but Glenda realized she needed to speak to Robin Pine. She sent him a message requesting a phone meeting.

Later that evening, Robin rang her on audio WhatsApp and she explained she was going to do a book reading. However, she wondered if she could publicize the TV show at the same time.

"Avalon Media are very impressed with your book. However, as I stated, there was work to license the characters and PR. Today I spoke to them and asked for an update. They would also like to involve Danny La Valle in the production. Danny owns Avalon Media and I presume you have heard of him?"

Glenda thought for a moment. "Isn't he the person who directed Shamrock Isle?" she asked.

"Yes, that is correct. He is a famous Hollywood director and producer. To have him on your project would almost certainly make it an instant success."

A little voice inside Glenda questioned this. Why would he want to be involved in a children's show about a little girl who helped her stepmother solve crimes?

But ignoring the voice, Glenda said, "Yes, I can see having a famous name associated with the program would help sell it. What are the implications of him being involved?"

Robin hesitated a moment before answering. "It would cost more in terms of PR – a small outlay to what you would get back, though. If Danny is involved, we can license the show to a network and get higher royalties. But he would need to be assured that we were publicizing the show."

"What do you call a small outlay?"

There was silence for a moment as if Robin was considering the question. "It would be an upfront payment of ten thousand dollars. A very small amount considering what clout Danny's name would bring the show."

Glenda felt sick inside. *What to do?* This was a lot of money – but she wanted her characters to be in a TV show, and with a big-time director like Danny La Valle having his name on the credits would really help make the show a success.

"I have to consider this," she said. "I will think it over and get back to you."

"Don't leave it too long," Robin warned. "Danny doesn't like to be kept waiting and believe me, there are lots of other projects waiting for him if you are not interested."

With that he ended the call.

Glenda was unsure what to do. She knew her father would loan her the money, but she had already asked for a loan very recently.

The little voice piped up again. Why would a famous Hollywood director want to be involved in a TV show about her characters? It seemed almost too good to be true. Yet Glenda, again, pushed the voice aside. She had read about people who were 'discovered' and had gone on to be famous. Perhaps she was going to be the next one.

She spent a very uncomfortable night tossing and turning, wondering what to do. It was hard to concentrate at school the next day, working with the children. After the school day ended, without having spoken to anyone, she rang her father and asked for another loan.

That evening, she messaged Robin to say she would go ahead – but there was one proviso: she wanted to speak to Danny La Valle to thank him for producing her books into a TV show before she paid the money.

Robin wrote straight back:

"Danny is a very busy man, Glenda. I can ask him, but he may only be able to give you a very small amount of time."

Glenda was adamant, and replied immediately:

"I want to speak to him."

She felt if she spoke to Danny La Valle, she would know for sure that this was all above board and an exciting future awaited her as the author of a book that was to be featured in a TV show.

Chapter 33

Sheila enjoys some beauty treatments

While Becky had sat puzzling over who Sheila Kavanagh was, Sheila had got up early and got breakfast at the IHOP restaurant next to the motel. She loved the pancakes there and sat in a booth by herself eating a hearty breakfast.

She then got into her hire car and drove downtown to the regeneration area. She pulled into the parking lot behind the newly refurbished buildings and walking towards the Purple Orchid – Second Wave, she took the time to look around. The area was still in a state of flux, but some of the buildings were completed and looked beautiful. There was the Institute for the Blind and Visually Impaired where she knew from her enquiries, Becky worked. There was also a cute, hippy-looking bookstore and a DIY store.

The Purple Orchid – Second Wave was a beautiful building that had formerly been a factory. It was painted in shades of purple and white with purple bougainvillea growing up the walls. When she opened the door, she was greeted by the sight and smells of dozens of exotic flowers. To the left of the door was an area where customers were sitting, sipping drinks either waiting for appointments or just chatting. The back wall had a massive mural of a beautiful woman's face with her hand held up showing off her elegant nails. Open tread stairs floated up to the second floor. She almost exclaimed aloud – what a beautiful place!

Walking over to the coffee bar – which also doubled as the reception – she said she was there for her 10 a.m. appointment with Patrice for a facial.

She was told to wait for a moment and Jinni would be with her. Sitting in a chair in the coffee bar, she flipped through the pamphlet offering the services of the beauty salon upstairs.

A few minutes later, Patrice came down the floating staircase to welcome her.

Sheila followed her upstairs to one of the treatment rooms, where Patrice told her to make herself comfortable while she got ready for the facial.

Sheila stretched out on the luxurious bed. It was heated and there was a soft blanket to wrap up in.

Patrice came and sat at the top of the bed and she adjusted the lights. There was some initial conversation about Sheila's skin and the products she normally used.

Sheila had to admit that Patrice was good. She was soon relaxed as Patrice massaged her face.

"I am only a visitor to this area," Sheila said. "I live in LA, but if I did live here, I would come and visit regularly."

"I am also from LA," replied Patrice, continuing with the massage. "I have only lived here a few months. Previous to that, I lived in Encino and had a beauty salon near to the Burbank studios."

"What a coincidence! I also live in Encino," Sheila said. "What was the name of your beauty salon?"

"*Enrapture*," Patrice said, aware that it was a grand name for her tiny salon.

Sheila appeared to think for a moment and then exclaimed, “Enrapture! I know it! I have driven past so many times and have friends who went there. You must have been sad to leave there.”

“I was sad, but I moved here to be with my husband, Bill, who is a media executive. I was lucky that we were able to invest in this salon, and I am happy now with the new business.”

“That is really interesting, about your husband. I used to work in media, too. I worked at Avalon Media, in accounts.”

Patrice stopped then and sat back. “Wow, what a coincidence! That is where Bill used to work! He was chief operating officer until he left to come here to work for Stermer Media.”

“You are not married to Bill Underwood, are you?” Sheila exclaimed.

“I am, do you know him?”

“Yes, I most certainly do. Ask him if he remembers Sheila Kavanagh, and send him my regards!”

Patrice beamed and promised to do so. Soon after, the appointment ended and Sheila thanked her for an excellent facial, saying she would pay downstairs at reception.

When she turned and began to walk down the stairs, there was a secret smile on Sheila’s face. Bill Underwood was in for a shock tonight! She wished she could be a fly on the wall when Patrice told him who had had a facial today!

Chapter 34

That same evening at Patrice and Bill's house

Patrice drove home after her long day in the salon, looking forward to telling Bill that a former colleague of his from LA had been in for a facial. She had the radio on and was singing along. She felt good. She was beginning to enjoy her life away from LA.

Bill was not home when she got back. She went into the kitchen and began preparing the evening meal. She was just preparing pasta when Bill arrived. He looked tired and for the first time, Patrice noticed how old he looked. He had dark circles under his eyes and his skin looked like it needed a rejuvenating facial. Perhaps she should offer him a facial later.

"Have a glass of wine and sit down, dinner is almost ready," she trilled.

Bill poured the wine and sat down at the kitchen island.

"How was your day?" she asked while she cooked.

"Oh, okay I guess," he replied. He took a large swig of wine. "The news commentators on current affairs are going down well and the ratings are good, but the podcasts need someone with more impact to lead them. We are still looking for someone."

Patrice finished cooking, plated up the food and brought two plates over and sat down. They both started to eat and drink.

“Guess what Bill. You are going to love this. Someone came into the salon today for a facial who knows you from LA.”

Patrice noticed that he seemed to stiffen slightly as she said this.

“Is that right? And who might that be?”

“It’s a woman who says she knows you from Avalon Media. Very pretty and well put together. I am sure you will remember her, although she said it was years ago.”

His face was now set as if in stone. “Well spit it out – the name of this woman.”

“Her name is Sheila Kavanagh.” Patrice knew the moment she said the name she had said the wrong thing. Bill’s whole-body language changed. He put his fork down and folded his arms.

“I don’t want you talking to her.” He spoke sternly and loudly.

“Pardon?” Patrice could hardly believe her ears.

“I forbid you to speak to that woman. She is a fake and a fraud and has come here to make trouble.”

Patrice was at a loss for words. What the heck was he talking about? She could see he was deadly serious.

“I’m sorry. You are going to have to explain what you mean. She just came in for a facial as she said she was visiting the area.”

“I am telling you that woman is a fraud. She is wanted by the police.”

“What!” Patrice was now completely shocked. “What has she done?”

Bill took the napkin off the table and used it to wipe around his mouth delicately.

“That woman embezzled a million dollars from Avalon Media. She is very clever and did not leave a trail. It is very difficult to get the evidence to prosecute her. Danny’s lawyers are working on the case as we speak. Once they get enough evidence she will be prosecuted. She has come here to intimidate me into dropping the case.”

Patrice sat staring at Bill. There was so much she did not know.

“How did she take the money? Do you have proof it was her?”

Bill took another long drink from his wine glass and then reaching for the bottle, filled it again.

“She worked for a time in the accounting department at Avalon Media and she took the money to pay for a fake PR campaign. It is very difficult to prove, but the money disappeared from the accounts. I can find where it was paid but proving who owns the account to which it was paid is difficult. I believe she set up a company and an account in a fake name.”

Patrice looked at Bill. “I thought you had cut ties with Avalon Media?”

“I have, but this case is still dragging on and I want to help solve it.”

Patrice swirled the wine in her glass and stared out of the window, going over in her mind what Bill had said.

"But how could she have authorized such a large payment to a fake account? Was it paid in several smaller instalments? I know we must have two people sign for payments over ten thousand dollars at the Purple Orchid, and here you are talking about a payment of a million."

Bill stared her in the eyes.

"Remember, she worked in accounting. Her job was to pay the bills of Avalon Media. It was possible to make the payment as I authorized it as chief operating officer. I had to trust her to make payments. I didn't have time to check everything."

He paused here and looked away from Patrice and down at his hands. "These payments were made to a company called Lorrimar for a PR campaign. It was not the usual PR company Avalon used, but I knew Danny was using a crisis management PR firm to cover up rumors that he was drinking heavily and indulging in Class A drugs. He wanted news reports that he was clean."

"So, the company was legitimate?"

Bill hesitated for a moment and then took another drink of his wine. "Not exactly. The company Danny had contacted was called *Lorimar,* spelled with only one letter 'r'. The payments were made to a company called Lorrimar – spelled with *two*."

Patrice thought for a moment. "But surely the real company would have asked for payment?"

"The thing is," Bill carried on, "Danny had a big row with the woman at Lorimar at the first meeting and they billed Avalon only for a small amount."

"So how was this found out? You say, you agreed it."

Bill shifted uncomfortably in his seat. "It was the auditors who found it when they came in to check the annual accounts."

"Oh my goodness!" Patrice was not an accountant but she knew at the very least this was extremely embarrassing for Bill as chief operating officer. How could he have signed off such large payments without checking? She stared at him.

"Is this why you left?"

Bill did not immediately answer. His face was now bright red and he shifted around in his chair.

"Be honest. Stermer Media is a start-up and they sent you to this God-forsaken place in the Southern States. Were you desperate for a job when you went with them?"

"You don't understand, Patrice," he said. "You have no idea what it is like to be head of accounting with a hundred and one things coming across your desk. Trying to make sure you don't let anything slip through."

Patrice got up and stared out of the window.

"That bitch played me for a fool," Bill went on, speaking loudly now. "I won't rest until I get justice!"

Patrice turned to face him, trying to keep calm.

"This has come as a big shock to me, Bill," she said quietly. "I need time to think about it. I will make sure if Sheila Kavanagh tries to come back to the Purple Orchid, we won't see her. But I have to process what you have told me. Do you understand? It is a lot for me to process."

Bill got up and went over to hug her, but she moved away and walked out of the kitchen. It was only when she got into the privacy of the bathroom that the tears came. This is my Prince, she thought. To put it bluntly, he is everything I had dreamed about. Even if he had signed off on the payments innocently, it seemed very strange that he had not checked that the PR campaign had gone ahead. Thoughts swirled through her mind. When did this take place? Why did she not know anything about it? Was it the real reason Bill left Avalon?

And why had this been covered up? But wait – didn't he say Avalon's lawyers were looking into it? Was there an investigation currently going on and it would be publicized in the future?

And then the most terrible thought crossed her mind which she immediately tried to suppress:

WHAT IF BILL WAS INVOLVED IN THE FRAUD?

Could her Prince Charming really be a fraudster?

It was a very worried Patrice who slipped into bed with Bill much later, hoping he was asleep. He did not turn to her and she lay awake for a long time, staring at the ceiling and wondering if the life she had known was going to fall apart.

The middle of May, 2024

Glenda speaks to Danny La Valle

Patrice reflects

Noi's book is chosen as book of the month at a book club

Chapter 35

Glenda speaks to Danny

Robin Pine was in touch within a couple of days to say he had arranged a meeting for Glenda with Danny La Valle. The meeting was to take place via a WhatsApp video call the following Friday at 8 p.m.

In the run-up to the meeting, Glenda went onto social media and looked at pictures of Danny. She was aware she had never met him so had not heard his voice. She then searched YouTube videos to find anywhere he spoke. There was a YouTube video where Danny was being interviewed by *Ruby*, a podcast host about his film *Shamrock Isle*. She listened to him speaking. He had a deep, resonant voice and he was very articulate in the way he spoke. He described his experiences filming in Ireland and going to a Ceilidh, which he described as a traditional Irish social event which involved dancing and playing Gaelic folk music in the local pub. The music was very cheerful and lively, consisting mainly of jigs, reels, hornpipes, polkas, slip-jigs, and waltzes. He said he found it hard to keep up with the native dancers.

Glenda liked listening to his voice and hearing about the dancing. She wondered if he would really ring her.

At exactly 8 p.m. on the Friday evening, there was a WhatsApp video call from a number she did not recognize. Accepting the call, she saw a man who looked very much like the man in the YouTube video. He spoke:

“Good evening – I’m Danny.”

“Good evening, Danny. I am Glenda.”

There was a pause before he spoke again.

“I like the book.”

Glenda was delighted he liked her book. His voice sounded similar to the voice on the YouTube video, although she couldn’t be 100% certain.

“I produce a lot of movies,” he went on. There then seemed to be interference on the line and his picture disappeared. After a few seconds, he returned and seemed to be speaking, “...filming very soon.”

Glenda started to say, “There has been some interference…” but he talked over her.

“…a lot of projects on the go at once…”

He didn’t seem to be reacting to her comments, and she was worried there was something wrong with the connection on WhatsApp.

He then disappeared again.

She tried ringing back the number, but no one answered.

A few minutes later there was another call from Robin Pine. Robin always made audio calls to her cell phone. She had never seen him.

“Did you speak to Danny?” he enquired.

“Well, yes I did, but…” Glenda started to say.

“It is always a but with you,” Robin interrupted. “What is the matter now? Danny rang you as promised. I told you he couldn’t speak for long. He is a very busy man. Were you not happy with the conversation?”

“I am pleased he rang, however, there were some problems on the line, and I only managed to have a few words with him.”

“He told me that he spoke to you and told you he wanted to produce your book.”

“Yes, yes, he did say something along those lines. Sorry, I was just expecting a longer conversation,” Glenda said.

“I thought this would finally put your mind at rest.” Robin sounded sad. “I am not sure what else I can do to convince you all is in order.”

“It is okay. I am convinced,” Glenda said. “I am looking forward to Danny producing my book into a TV show.”

They ended the call amicably and Glenda wired the outstanding money as requested.

It was only later when she was lying in bed and going over the conversation that she realized Danny had never once mentioned TV shows – he had mentioned movies, which were what he was famous for. She got out of bed and taking her laptop into the study, she sat down and keyed into the search bar ‘Danny La Valle TV shows’. The search came up with Danny’s production company, Avalon Media, and also his personal website. She clicked onto his website and saw that he had several movie credits – but no TV credits. Strange, she thought. But then she convinced herself, maybe he is expanding his repertoire by producing a TV show. She made a note to ask Robin Pine next time she spoke to him and got back into bed. This time she fell asleep almost as soon as her head touched the pillow.

Chapter 36

Patrice reflects

The morning after Bill's revelations about the fraud at Avalon Media, Patrice woke from a disturbed sleep, showered and quickly got ready to go to the salon. She was careful to avoid Bill as she felt she was not ready to speak to him again yet.

In her car driving to the salon, she reflected on how little she knew about the man she had married. He had been her savior that evening with Danny La Valle, and he had been gentlemanly and courteous towards her on their dates.

In the past she had dated men with BMWs and overdrafts. Men who pretended to be rich and then would ask her for a loan. She remembered Mitch, who had taken her to Spago in Beverly Hills. When the bill came there was an embarrassing scene where none of his cards 'worked', and she had to pay for their meals and wine. Then there were the bullshitters who couldn't get their stories straight. One of the best at this was Barry, who told her he was a hedge fund trader and lived in Marina del Rey. When she visited, it was a studio apartment in an older complex several blocks back from the marina. He had explained it away saying he had just moved from New York and this was a short-term rental until he could find his dream apartment. Yet on their first date he had told her he had been working in LA for two years. Total bullshit!!

Her lack of success with men was the opposite of her career as a makeup artist. She had studied professional makeup in Hollywood, and she had enjoyed the course and the process of transforming appearances. She loved applying makeup and seeing a new and often more confident person emerge. She also felt she had a talent for business, and was able to make her small beauty salon profitable in a very short period of time.

However, what she wanted more than anything was for some man to come along and sweep her off her feet. To care for her and love her unconditionally. Her parents had enjoyed a marriage like that. Sadly, her mother had died when Patrice was only seventeen and her father, after a period of mourning was now remarried. She often thought back to the time when she was growing up and of the love her parents had for each other – how her father supported and protected her mother. She wanted this for herself, even though she knew this was not the way modern women are encouraged to think. She kept these thoughts to herself.

Meeting Bill, she had thought that she had finally found the true love she craved. He was a true gentleman who showered her with gifts – flowers, jewelry and champagne. He certainly knew how to be romantic!

She would never forget the first time Bill had taken her to his house in Calabasas. The house was in a secure, gated estate and had breathtaking and unobstructed canyon views. It was so near to the city of Los Angeles, yet the noise of the city seemed so far away. The house was surrounded by the magical setting of the Santa Monica mountains. As they pulled into the motor court, she saw a beautiful two-story residence. Stepping out of the car and into the house, she saw awestruck by the artisanal details, such as intricately designed beamed ceilings, hand-distressed white oak flooring and custom wooden doors. Everything was solid and expensive. Bill had taken her into the dramatic garden room conservatory which provided a beautiful view of the gardens and swimming pool beyond. He had brought them a glass of wine and they had sat looking out on the grounds.

"Do you live here alone?" she had asked.

"Yes, sadly, I am single since my wife left me. However, I wanted only the best for myself. I hope to find someone to share it with in the future."

Patrice could feel herself falling for him. Later, she was delighted when he showed her the primary suite which was accentuated with volume coffered ceilings, a fireplace and a private balcony overlooking the garden. She had taken hold of his hand while they were on the balcony and they had kissed. She had led him back into the bedroom where she undressed him and then herself.

"You are the most beautiful woman I have ever seen," he had breathed when they were both naked.

She had fallen in love with him when they had first made love in her Burbank studio apartment. He was so caring and loving. But that was nothing to this. She was so excited by the surroundings and the British accent that she had to admit it had been the best sex she had ever had.

She had moved in with him in haste, she had to agree. It was only three months after first meeting him that she gave up her studio apartment in Burbank and moved into the house in Calabasas. She now had Maria, a maid who doubled as a cook at her disposal. To come home and have her meals prepared for her was wonderful. No housework, and two gardeners as well – that meant that she could concentrate on her beauty salon 100%.

After a couple of months, he proposed to her, and they had married very quickly. It was a small ceremony in the gardens of the Calabasas house with only a few people present. The sun had shone and it had been the most beautiful day. The happiest of her life, she had felt at the time. Her father and stepmother were the only relatives of hers present. None of Bill's family came from England.

Patrice had been caught up in a whirlwind she had to admit. What had she asked him about himself and his background? Very little!

He had told her that he had been married before. But she knew little about the ex-wife. She was British and had moved to LA to be with Bill. The implication was that she had become homesick and gone home to Britain. Bill had been upset for a while, but was now over it.

She knew very little about his work at Avalon Media. She knew he was chief operating officer with responsibility for the finances, and he obviously bailed Danny La Valle out of difficult situations.

But, she thought, do I really know what he did there?

And then an uncomfortable thought occurred to her – I do not know how much he was paid for the work at Avalon Media. I just *assumed* he was rich when I saw the house and his car and watch and clothes.

Something was pricking at her. When they left LA, she had to sell her salon which was very sad for her. He had promised to buy her a new salon in the new city they were moving to. It took a few weeks for her salon to sell, but it did sell fairly quickly.

Another thought crossed her mind – were there realtors who came to value and sell the house in Calabasas? She did remember one realtor coming to speak to Bill just before they left, but there was no For Sale sign or open house. Bill had told her not to worry herself about it – he assured her that all was okay.

Bill had come to this city and chosen the house here. It was also truly beautiful and she had been so excited the first time she saw it.

But was it really their home? She had never signed any mortgage deed or conveyance. Bill must own the house, she thought.

He had told her that they could employ a maid who would cook and clean, and also gardeners at the new house. Unfortunately, the maid was not available in the evenings to cook their evening meal so they would have to do that themselves. Patrice had agreed to this, as she had agreed to everything Bill had said.

Her beauty salon at the Purple Orchid – Second Wave had more than made up for having to cook their evening meals! And she still had her beautiful BMW he had bought her soon after she had met him.

Bill had been taking flying lessons since moving, with the view to buying a small plane. Surely that said how rich he was.

He is a very wealthy man, she said to herself. Or is he? Is it possible that everything I thought was real is an illusion?

She had been delighted when he had not asked her to sign a pre-nup. He had told her that he was British and British people did not do pre-nups – he trusted that she loved him and that they would grow old together. But looking back, wasn't that a bit strange? He hardly knew her – how could he know if she was trustworthy?

She knew that evening she was going to have to ask Bill questions. Inside she felt stupid and useless. She had always been too trusting and it had got her into so many scrapes in the past.

When she arrived at the salon she said to Randi who was at reception, "Please make a note in the book that we will not accept appointments from Sheila Kavanagh. She is banned from this salon."

With that she began her day in the salon, smiling and chatting to customers while inside her emotions and feelings swirled around like a gathering storm.

Chapter 37

Noi anticipates her movie deal

Noi was keeping in touch with Robin Pine via WhatsApp messages. She had now paid over $6,000 to him for work on the movie version of her book.

She had been keeping this a secret from Niran up to now. However, the first payment was now due on the money she had borrowed. She had to move money around so that this payment went out of her own personal bank account. Doing this, she felt immediately guilty. She had never deceived Niran before, and she felt this was one of the reasons why, despite some imperfections, they had such a strong marriage.

That evening, she went to the restaurant and was in the kitchen cooking as usual. Niran was working front of house. About mid-way through the evening, Mae, the waitress, came into the kitchen and told her that there was a guest who wanted to speak to her.

It must be someone who wants to comment on the food. I hope it is good, Noi thought.

She left her assistant cook, Anan in charge and went into the dining room. Mae had told her the person wanting to speak to her was sitting at the table by the window.

Walking through the dining room, she saw that it was Arpa sitting there, from the book club.

Arpa was all smiles. “Hi Noi, sorry to drag you out of the kitchen. The Pad Thai was delicious, as always.”

"Thank you. I hope you are enjoying your evening. Can I bring you a drink?"

"Not at the moment, but thank you. The reason I wanted to speak to you is I bought a copy of your book from the Purple Orchid last week. I went in for a manicure and Jinni recommended it. She said we should make it the book for discussion in the book club next month."

Noi bowed her head. "I would be honored. Would you like more copies?"

"No, that is not needed, I just wanted to let you know that your book will be discussed."

Noi indicated she was delighted, and then feeling encouraged, she felt like sharing her exciting news. "I have an agent now who is pitching my book to a movie director. Danny La Valle is interested in it."

Arpa looked like her eyes were going to pop out of her head. "Goodness!" was all she could think to say. "Congratulations!"

There was then a short silence when neither could think of anything to say. Finally, Arpa spoke. "I will send you the date we will discuss your book."

Noi returned to the kitchen, floating on air. Her literary career was taking off! She sang to herself as she filled the next orders. There were no worries about paying her loans – she was going to be a famous author. She saw herself on the red carpet at the movie version of her book, and living a life of luxury when the money started rolling in.

She couldn't wait for the book club to discuss her book – and to hear what they had to say about her novel. Life was good and she couldn't wait to surprise Niran with all her good fortune!

Mid-May, 2024

Jenny has an idea for the reading at the BookStop

Patrice consults a private detective

Chapter 38

Jenny's BookStop

It was 5 p.m. and organized chaos in Jenny's BookStop, where Jenny was running around, setting and then re-setting chairs for the evening's book reading. A local author, Bill Edwards, was going to read from his latest dystopian novel. The book readings were going very well, and even though she was still not in profit with her new store, she was happy for the moment that she was almost breaking even.

In a few weeks' time, during the first week in June, she had organized for Glenda to do a reading from her children's book. Glenda had been in that afternoon to discuss the reading, and had told her that there was interest in the book from a Hollywood director – Danny La Valle. Jenny had believed her about this, as her book was a really good read. She was a vociferous reader, so she liked to pride herself that she knew a good book when she saw one.

Jenny had had a few spare moments during the afternoon and had looked up Danny La Valle, as it was a name she was not familiar with. She was surprised to see that he was the famous Hollywood director who had also produced *Shamrock Isle*. She had loved that movie, how could she not have recognized his name? She saw he was now working on a movie called *The Reluctant Pastor*.

Jenny reflected on this and dollar signs started to form in her head. What if she could get this Hollywood director to come to her bookstore? She could put this in the local press and she was sure the local TV station would pick it up.

She was excited at the idea, and it grew over the course of the evening. The reading that evening by Bill Edwards was relatively successful – most chairs were full and people asked him questions. He also sold a few books which he signed.

But, thought Jenny, this was nothing compared to what it would be like to have Danny La Valle here!

The following day she contacted Glenda and they agreed to chat on WhatsApp.

Jenny put her idea to Glenda – she could do the reading, but they could also invite Danny La Valle! This would ensure a lot of interest!

Glenda agreed, and talking, they both became quite excited. Glenda did bring Jenny back to earth by saying that she would expect Danny would want a fee to make an appearance, and they would have to decide if they could afford it.

Jenny was sure they could afford it, and after all, it would be an excellent way to publicize her bookstore.

Glenda agreed to follow up with Robin Pine.

"Do it as soon as possible," urged Jenny. "It would be wonderful publicity for us all!"

Her dreams of elevating her bookstore to the next level dominated her thoughts for the next few days as she waited (not so) patiently for Glenda to get back to her about Danny La Valle.

Chapter 39

Patrice consults a private investigator

Patrice remained suspicious and worried about the visit of Sheila Kavanagh. She had to admit she had been very trusting and had accepted a lot of what Bill had told her up until now, but something about this whole story was off. Wrong. It was too hard to believe, even for a very trusting person.

The stress was getting to her, and she did not know where to turn. She was polite with Bill and they carried on as if nothing had happened. But there were strong undercurrents and Patrice wanted answers.

Sitting at the dining room table, she decided to ask Bill some more questions which she launched into without preamble.

"You told me that you were a partner at Meyer and Co. in Century City. I looked them up and I saw that they are CPAs with a media clientele. A very prestigious firm."

Bill stopped eating and studied her, for what seemed to be the longest time before answering. "Yes, that is true. I was working at their London office and I got the chance to work in LA. That was a fantastic opportunity for a Brit like me. I jumped at the chance."

"Didn't you tell me that Alison, your first wife, was also a Brit?"

"Yes, she is. We got married so she could come with me and get a green card."

"A green card is an immigration document, correct?"

"Yes, that is right. Once you get a green card you can work in the USA permanently."

"So is Alison still in the USA?"

Bill put down his knife and fork and wiped his mouth with his napkin. He then coolly appraised Patrice. "Sweetheart, may I ask why you are asking these questions now? You have never shown any interest in Alison or my career at Meyer and Co. previously. Is this because of that bitch Sheila Kavanagh? She never worked at Meyer and Co. I knew her, unfortunately, when I worked at Avalon Media."

Patrice flushed and spoke more loudly than she had intended. "Of course it is about Sheila Kavanagh! You talked about a massive fraud! What the hell do you expect? I am very worried. Can they implicate you in any of it?"

"Good," Bill said in an emotionless tone, "now you are saying what you mean, instead of asking questions about the past that are no longer relevant!"

He seemed to lapse into a self-reflection and did not speak for what seemed like an eternity.

Finally, he spoke. "Sheila Kavanagh is trying to implicate me in a fraud of her making. Yes, that is true. I am trying to find evidence to prove that it was her that carried out the fraud. The fact she came here and contacted you is despicable. The truth will come out in the end. In the meantime, we should get on with our lives here and try not to let her intrude into our personal world."

“Why is this not in the news? Danny La Valle is a famous director – surely the news media would be interested.”

“Because we are keeping it under wraps until we have evidence!” Bill boomed. “Surely that is evident!”

“But what if she goes to the press? What if she brings you into it? Then your career is ruined!”

Bill sighed loudly. “Patrice! If she puts anything into the media about me, I can sue her for defamation! She cannot do anything – but as she is to blame anyway, I doubt she would go down that route.”

Patrice stood up. She was near to tears and she started to pace the room. “I want this whole thing sorted out, Bill,” she seethed. “It has the potential to ruin both our lives and I want it sorted. Why do you not pay a lawyer to get to the bottom of this? The whole thing is whack! It does not make sense!”

And with that she turned and ran out of the room. She was sobbing and felt impotent. Bill had ran after her, and when he caught her began stroking her hair and kissing her, whispering that it was all going to be okay. She did not reject him, but his advances were not making her feel any better.

It was after that evening that Patrice decided she had to find out for herself no matter what it cost. She went online and found the name of a firm of private investigators that were all women. She was able to make an appointment and to secure the services of Loretta Bromus, a PI who apparently had ten years’ experience in the field.

When they met, Loretta seemed a bit curious about Patrice’s brief. It was, to put it mildly, rather vague.

"Do you suspect Bill of having an affair?" she had asked Patrice outright.

"I don't believe he is having an affair but I am worried he is involved in some shady dealings," Patrice had responded.

Loretta had stopped typing into the laptop and looked her straight in the eye. "Okay. Can you elaborate a little on what you mean by *shady dealings*?"

"Can I be assured of confidentiality if I say this to you?" Patrice fiddled with her rings, nervously.

"Of course. Rest assured you are employing me and I will do all I can to find information out for you, and at all times I will keep what I am told confidential."

"Very well then. Bill is an accountant and was involved with the financial affairs of Avalon Media. This is a company where he was chief operating officer. It is the production company of Danny La Valle, the Hollywood director and producer. I believe there may have been fraud there and a lot of money has gone missing."

Loretta found it hard to hide her surprise. "There has been nothing in the popular press about irregularities at Avalon," she said. "Is this happening while we speak?"

Again, Patrice appeared nervous. "No, that is the thing, and why this is weird. We are talking about a couple of years ago, when Bill was chief operating officer there. He is now with Stermer Media."

She then told Loretta about the visit from Sheila Kavanagh.

"I want you to go to Los Angeles and see what you can find out. Who is Sheila Kavanagh? What happened at Avalon?"

Loretta nodded intently.

"Do you have any contacts that can get that information? Also, Bill and I have only been together a short time and…" Patricia paused, looking down at her rings. She sighed. "I have to admit, I don't know very much about him or his background. Obviously, I know he is British and has been married before. I want to know more about him moving to the States, and also about his first wife, Alison."

Loretta nodded. "I can do this, but it may prove to be expensive finding sources who are willing to talk about Avalon." She turned to her laptop and scrolled for a moment before turning her screen to Patrice. Patrice could see that she would have to pay a retainer and hourly rate for Loretta to go to LA.

"Do it," Patrice said quickly, waving her hand. "I want to know!"

She stopped then, and composed herself. "I will pay your fees – I want to know what happened, but please…" She leaned towards Loretta. "Please be very discreet when looking into Bill's ex, Alison. Bill says she may have moved back to Britain, so it might be difficult to contact her. Whatever you can find out would be brilliant, but please do not alert her to the fact I am looking into her."

Loretta agreed to this and then she accessed a template of a standard contract on her laptop. She edited the details to fit Patrice and her requirements, and asked Patrice to sign online.

Patrice got out her checkbook and paid the retainer – and for five days work in Los Angeles.

They then shook hands and Patrice said, looking her in the eyes, “He is a straight man on the surface. A good man. But I am worried there is a dark side to him. I really need your help.”

After Patrice left, Loretta went onto the internet and searched for ‘Bill Underwood’. A few people showed up, but it was not hard to find Patrice’s husband. He was listed as the chief operating officer of Stermer Media. Loretta viewed his picture. He looked like what she expected an accountant to look like. Clean cut. He was smiling and wearing a suit and tie. Short hair and serious. He was not movie star handsome, and looked to have a receding chin. His hair was just beginning to thin. She studied his eyes. In Loretta’s experience, eyes usually gave people away. She clicked on the picture and blew it up to twice its original size. She then zeroed in on the eyes.

She saw dead eyes. Snake eyes. Looking at his eyes, Loretta became very interested in this case…

Chapter 40

Glenda makes a request to Robin Pine

Glenda had messaged Robin Pine and asked him to ring her. Robin always rang when she asked him, and he was polite and helpful. He usually rang her on an audio call as he was not able to do video calls. Glenda was not sure what his original reason for this had been, but she was not too worried. She was beginning to trust him as time went by.

Glenda decided to explain the reason for calling without preamble. "I am going to do a reading at Jenny's BookStop on June 3rd, and I told Jenny that Danny La Valle is interested in my book and she asked if he would be able to come to the reading and do a personal appearance."

There was a slight hesitation before Robin spoke. "Danny does do personal appearances. It is a very good idea of Jenny to invite him. He would certainly add a lot of clout to your book reading. Hmmm…" He stopped there, apparently thinking.

"You should be aware that his time is very valuable. I see that you have now paid the extra sum we discussed after you spoke to him."

"Yes, I have…"

"However, Danny, as you know, is very popular and would charge for a personal appearance. Is Jenny from the bookstore aware of that fact?"

"We did discuss this..."

"You realize that this is his management that insist on him getting a fee, not me," Robin stated.

"Yes, yes, I understand." Glenda was not sure she dared ask how much it would be, but taking a deep breath, she went ahead anyway. "Can you give me an idea of the cost?"

"I would need to speak to his people. I do not set the price for his personal attendances. "I will get back to you as soon as I hear anything."

Glenda didn't have to wait long. Robin came back with a price within a couple of days. It would cost $10,000 for Danny to attend the book reading and to give a very short talk at the end about the TV show he was planning to make.

Glenda went to see Jenny personally to give her the information. Jenny thought it was a lot of money to pay, however, she realized she was paying for a big-name director and producer to come to her bookstore. She agreed to pay the money.

Robin indicated that the money would have to be paid upfront for Danny to come to the reading. He promised to get a contract from Danny's management company which he would email to Glenda.

The contract arrived very quickly, and was under the name of *Faro Productions*. Glenda was not familiar with this name, but a quick check online revealed that this was a production company Danny had worked with. She forwarded the contract to Jenny, and together they read it through and could find no problems with it. It stated that Danny La Valle would do a meet and greet at *Jenny's BookStop* on June 3rd between the hours of 2 p.m. and 4 p.m. The cost of the visit was $10,000 payable to *Faro Productions*. An address in Los Angeles was included to send the contract. Jenny was asked to wire the money.

It did not explicitly say that he would speak at the event, but they did not think that this was something to worry about.

Glenda signed the contract and they mailed it to the address they had been given. Jenny wired the money, and a couple of days later, Glenda received an email from *Jumpstart Productions,* acknowledging receipt of the contract and money and confirming that Danny would be with them on June 3rd.

At this stage, Jenny jumped into overdrive. She was determined to get as much publicity out of this visit as possible. She posted on her social media a picture of Danny La Valle smiling.

"Jenny's BookStop will be hosting a Reading on June 3 at 2 p.m. by Glenda Ortez of her children's book "Gwendoline Investigates". This book is suitable for all children ages 8 to 12.

We are proud to announce that this book is going to be televised by top Hollywood director/producer Danny La Valle in his "Faro Productions" company.

Danny La Valle will be attending this event in person and will be available for a meet and greet.

Tickets $30 for this event – first come, first served."

Jenny then sent a notice to the Tribune newspaper, asking to cover the event on the day and to include an advertisement in advance.

The local radio station on KAVC98 promised to publicize the event on Jerry Levens commuter show. Jenny even did a phone in with Jerry.

"Hey Jenny – how are you today?" Jerry had a bright voice and infectious laugh.

"Real good and excited that Danny La Valle will be visiting my bookstore!"

"Danny La Valle – now isn't he the director of Shamrock Isle? My wife loved that movie – she cried buckets!!"

"I think we all loved it," Jenny agreed. "Yes, it is the same Danny La Valle who will be coming to a reading of Gwendoline Investigates, a book by a local author that he is going to produce into a TV show."

"Well, we all want to support local talent!" Jerry agreed. "Who is the local author?"

"Her name is Glenda Ortiz. She is a teacher at Glenn Elementary School and is unbelievably talented."

"What is the date of this event? We don't want to miss it," Jerry said.

"June 3rd from two till four o'clock, but you are welcome all day. You can get your tickets from Jenny's BookStop. Thirty dollars, first come, first served."

By that evening, Jenny had 100 enquiries for tickets! She wasn't sure how she would fit all these people in – plus the children accompanying them. But she was going to do her level best.

She then hit on the idea of filming the event and making it available on Zoom for people who couldn't get tickets to see it in person. She found out that if she bought the Zoom Events add-on, she could host a paid event.

Jenny then advertised the Zoom event for $5 per ticket. At this stage sales really took off, and she sold 1,000 links to the event within the first couple of days of the advertisement going out!

Jenny was very happy with the publicity that this event was drumming up for her bookstore, and she felt it was well worth the $10,000 she had paid for Danny La Valle to attend.

She dreamed of other events to be held in the future – each one growing bigger in importance until she had to hire the Newform Theatre to fit everyone in.

Third week in May, 2024

Loretta Bromus visits LA to investigate the background of Bill Underwood

The book club discusses Noi's book

Chapter 41

Loretta visits LA

Loretta Bromus decided to drive to LA. It was quite a distance, but it would mean she had her own car with her and didn't have to hire one. She had spent a week or so investigating Bill Underwood in the office beforc setting off.

He was British, born in Fishponds, Bristol. Loretta had sources in both the US and in the UK. Her UK source agreed to do a search into British records and came back with a report:

"William Earl Underwood was born in 1975 in Fishponds, Bristol, to Carol and Timothy Underwood. They were listed as both being teachers. He had one sister named Madeliene. He attended Bishop Prior School – a private school in Bristol and went onto Aston University in Birmingham where he received a first-class honors degree in Accounting and Finance.

After university he was employed by Meyer and Co., a firm of British chartered accountants in London. He is shown as passing the accountants' exam in 1999, when he won a prize for the best paper on Ethics.

He married Alison Blackmore in 2008 in Bristol. It seems Alison was a work colleague at Meyer and Co.

Almost immediately the trail on Bill went cold in the UK. There was no more information after 2008.

There was an address for his parents in Fishponds, Bristol. There is no evidence that he has children."

Loretta had followed his career path in the US herself.

Firstly, she placed him with Meyer and Co. in their LA office where he stayed until 2017. He had been promoted to partner in 2014. This was a very prestigious promotion with a very good salary to match, yet he left three years later to join the production company of Danny La Valle – Avalon Media. He had stayed with Avalon Media until 2023 when he moved to his current position at Stermer Media.

The life of Bill Underwood was not as straightforward as it appeared from the initial trawl through. Loretta had a source called Joey in LA who was willing to help her, and he had done some investigations of his own. He told her that when Bill was a partner at Meyer and Co., he was employed to do the audit of Global Pictures in which Danny La Valle and Dino Latent were partners. They had had a massive falling out in 2017 and Danny left to form his own company, citing irregularities regarding royalties. Bill had left Meyer and Co. to go with him. This had been reported in the press at the time. However, this falling out was just the tip of the iceberg, and Joey would meet with her to tell her more when she arrived in LA.

As Loretta drove towards LA, she felt fairly sure that this was a case of financial irregularity. She had qualified as a certified public accountant herself, so she understood the intricacies of accounting.

While she doubted that Bill Underwood was cheating on his beautiful wife, she expected to find he did wrong things motivated by greed. In that regard, she had made an appointment with a realtor about leasing a property in Calabasas to try to find out more about the property where he had lived.

Meanwhile in LA, Joey had been trying to get people who had worked with Bill to talk. He had had some success at Meyer and Co. and someone called Penny had agreed to talk to Loretta. She was not worried about being paid for her information.

Joey went on to say that it was much more difficult to find people who worked at Avalon Media with Bill to talk. Joey had rung her and they had chatted.

"I feel that everyone who worked at Avalon was given hush money, made to sign non-disclosure agreements. Besides Bill, there were only three other staff there – Sheila Kavanagh, Kevin Jones and Brett Zimmerman.

Kevin Jones will not speak to me – under no circumstances and for no amount of money.

I tried to track down Sheila Kavanagh and found out she lived in the Hollywood Hills. However, it seemed she had left there about a year ago with no forwarding address. The trail ran cold at that point. It may even be that Sheila Kavanagh had left the country.

Brett Zimmerman also used to live in an apartment in the Hollywood Hills. When I visited, his girlfriend Zoe answered the door. It seems he left her with a lot of debt and she is really angry. She has agreed to talk as she knows some things about Avalon. But she wants money for speaking – a lot of money, so it is up to you if you want to go ahead."

Loretta was intrigued and said she would like to speak to Zoe if Joey could set something up.

Loretta had found out through her enquiries that Bill's ex, Alison, had not in fact moved back to her native Britain. She was still living in LA, in the San Fernando Valley. Loretta was intrigued by this. Bill's second wife had been told that his first wife was no longer in the States. Why was that? Did Bill have the incorrect information?

Once settled into her motel in the San Fernando Valley and after eating dinner, Loretta decided to have an early night ready to start her enquiries the following day.

Chapter 42

Loretta meets Alison

The following day very early, Loretta drove out to Tarzana in the San Fernando Valley where Alison Underwood now lived. The house was an end townhouse in a community that looked to have a swimming pool. It was within walking distance of a metro station and was just minutes from shopping and dining. Yet it was very ordinary after the life Alison would have enjoyed with a man who was a partner in a firm of accountants.

Loretta parked opposite and waited to see who came out of the house. She didn't have to wait long. A tall, handsome, tanned young man came out first and got into a van with Barry's Pool Care stenciled on the side. Shortly afterwards, a heavily pregnant woman came out and started walking towards the metro. Loretta quickly got out of her car and followed her. She was fairly sure this was Alison Underwood. She had mousy hair tied back and wore eyeglasses and was carrying a shopping bag and her purse. She was heavily pregnant and not walking very quickly.

Loretta caught up with her and struck up a conversation.

"Lovely day today – almost too nice to be going to work!"

The woman turned and smiled. "You don't say," she said in a British accent.

"Don't I know you?" Loretta asked. "It's Alison, isn't it?"

"Yes, it is!" Alison seemed quite taken aback. "But I just can't seem to place you…"

"You are an accountant, I think?" Loretta interrupted. "I used your firm last year. I just can't remember when."

"Is this when I worked at Gold and Arin in Pasadena? I've moved now and work downtown at Kennedy Peabody. It's less of a commute."

"Yes, that's right!" Loretta smiled. "Kennedy Peabody. I will take a note of that for when we need an accountant again. Will you still be there though?" She glanced at Alison's stomach.

Alison's whole face lit up then. "So excited about the baby. We have been blessed."

"When are you due?"

"I have six weeks to go," Alison beamed. "It's a girl. Barry and I can't wait! This is our first baby."

"I am so pleased for you," Loretta smiled. They had arrived at the Metro station and stood on the platform waiting for the train.

Alison seemed encouraged to talk about the baby. "I thought I couldn't have children when I was married to my first husband. We are beyond excited."

The train was full when it arrived and someone gave Alison a seat. Loretta stood in the aisle, but there was no more conversation.

Loretta got off the train at the next stop and caught another train back. Getting into her car she drove a short distance to the Fifty-Nine Diner on Ventura Blvd where she had arranged to meet Joey for a breakfast meeting. Joey would bring Penny, a former colleague of Bill Underwood who was keen to talk.

Chapter 43

Breakfast meeting at the Fifty-Nine Diner

The Fifty-Nine Diner was an authentic 60's diner, complete with bright décor, posters and a juke box. Joey was sitting in a booth at the back when Loretta went in. A woman who looked to be in her early thirties and was wearing a smart, Ann Taylor dress sat with him. They were both eating the steak and eggs breakfast.

Joey introduced the woman as Penny Green – a former colleague of Bill at Meyer and Co.

Loretta ordered herself steak and eggs and for a while, they all sat eating.

After they had finished eating and had chatted for a few moments, Loretta turned the conversation around to Bill Underwood. She explained that she was a private investigator looking into his past.

Penny seemed happy with the explanation and indicated she did not want to be paid for her information.

"I worked with Bill on a number of occasions when I worked at Meyer and Co.," she said. "What exactly do you want to know about him?"

"Was he a partner at Meyer and Co.?" Loretta enquired.

"Yes, he was promoted to partner in 2014, and then he left in 2017."

"Would this be unusual for someone promoted to partner to leave so soon?" Loretta asked.

“Yes, I would say so. I guess that is what you want to know about?” Penny asked. “You do realize that I cannot go into specifics about particular clients. I am bound by a code of ethics. I am prepared to talk about a former colleague, but I want assurance that my name will not be brought into any report and I will remain as an anonymous source.”

“Yes, I understand and we will not use your name in any report, we can assure you of that. On that basis, shall we go ahead?”

Penny nodded.

“We understand that Bill left Meyer and Co. to go and work at Danny La Valle’s new production company, Avalon Media. This was formed when Danny and Dino Latent parted ways at Global Pictures.”

Penny smiled and dabbed at her lips with a napkin delicately. “Ah, I thought so.”

Loretta and Joey both nodded and indicated she should go on.

“As you know, companies listed on the stock exchange have to have a team of outside accountants come in each year to check their accounts and give a report to the investors in the company on whether the accounts presented the financial position fairly. Meyer and Co. were employed to check the accounts of Global Pictures – the company owned by Danny La Valle and Dino Latent.”

Loretta and Joey indicated that they knew this.

“Was Bill the manager on this account?” Loretta asked.

"Yes, he was. I worked on this account from 2012 to 2017 when Bill left Meyer and Co."

"That is a long time," Joey commented. "What was it like to work with Bill?"

"In 2014, Bill was promoted to partner. As you know, partners in an accounting firm are the owners of the firm. This was a very big promotion for Bill. A manager at an accounting firm has to be technically excellent – able to review accounts and make adjustments. Bill was able to do this..." she paused a for a moment. "*Proficiently.*"

Loretta noted the use of the word proficiently.

"So, you do not think Bill was excellent?"

"No, I don't," said Penny, flatly. "He was thorough, he would check our work and the accounts very carefully, but no, he was not excellent. But the real issue was when he was promoted. A partner is required to do very different things to a manager. A partner must go out and get new business for the firm. This involves having a network of contacts and going to the country club and schmoozing chief executive officers of big companies and persuading them to use Meyer and Co. as their accountants. The actual accounting work is left to a manager once you get promoted to partner."

Joey was listening intently and he nodded. "That seems to make sense. What you are saying is Bill was proficient as a manager but not proficient as a partner."

Penny shifted awkwardly in her seat. "I feel that may have been the case."

She tidied the cutlery before going on. “Global Pictures were his flagship client. You can read about them in the LA Times and other newspapers if you want. What I am saying is public knowledge. In 2016 they had a big hit with Rosy Dawn…”

“Yes, we know about Rosy Dawn,” Loretta said, “and the fact that it took millions at the box office and not long after, Danny La Valle and Dino Latent decided to part ways. There were rumors that they had fallen out about royalties. We know Bill went with Danny who then formed his own production company.”

Penny nodded. “Yes, all that is true. There were arguments about royalties and who should have the cash. Bill signed off the accounts for Global Pictures as the independent accountant to say they were presented fairly. Yet just after that, it was found that there was some money missing.”

Loretta and Joey looked at each other. “I don’t remember reading about this in the newspaper,” said Loretta.

“There were strong hints that there might have been fraud if you go back and look at the newspapers at this time. However, they were quashed by Steve Rogerson, the senior partner of Meyer and Co. who brokered a deal regarding sharing the royalties between Danny and Dino which they were both happy with. You can’t quote me on this, but there was a lot of gossip at the time as Bill had been very busy and not approachable to the team working on the accounts.”

Loretta had her cell phone out and was looking on the internet. She was quiet for a few moments.

“You will see the reports if you look in the papers late 2016 early 2017,” Penny indicated.

Loretta was clicking on her phone and she found a headline in the Daily Trends from December 2016 which she read out loud:

“Shocking allegations of disappearing royalties in Dino Latent and Danny La Valle feud”

A well-placed source in Los Angeles has told the Daily Trends that superstar directors, Danny La Valle and Dino Latent are embroiled in acrimonious discussions regarding the royalties for “Rosy Dawn”.

“Rosy Dawn” was a favorite with fans in 2016, grossing just over $200 million at the box office. The embattled directors Danny and Dino are reportedly locked in intense discussions to sort out how royalties should be shared.

Our source told us that Dino is the more senior director and believes that he should have the bigger share.

Danny was seen by our source having lunch with his agent at the Beverly Hills Hotel. At this lunch he was reportedly overheard telling his agent, “I want this sorted as soon as possible. This is fraud and I am being cheated out of my share.”

Loretta placed her phone on the table. “Was this just Danny saying things in frustration? Or do you feel there were financial irregularities?”

“Well, I did a search and there has never been an official fraud investigation into Global Pictures,” Joey said.

Penny smiled. "No, there was never anything official. There were rumors about money being missing and Danny being cheated out of his share."

Loretta leaned over the table. "Come on, Penny. You worked on the account, you knew whether there was fraud or not. You have my word that anything you say will remain confidential. As you can see, I am not recording this conversation."

At first Penny said nothing. Loretta had figured out, though, that by coming here Penny had something to say and if they gave her enough space, she might say it.

The waitress came by and filled their coffee cups.

After the waitress left, Penny finally spoke. "Okay, there were slightly more than rumors. When I first started working with Global Pictures it was only a small production company and didn't have very good systems to record cash and royalties. Every year we told them they should set up proper systems. When Bill was a manager, he was involved in talking to them about this. We were always ignored. But as I say, they were only a small company so it didn't seem to matter.

In 2016, when Rosy Dawn was a big hit, it came back to smack them in the face! But the big issue was that by this time Bill was a partner, and in my view, not coping well with his new responsibilities. We reported back to him that there was a lot of money floating around and it was not being kept securely. However, for whatever reason, he didn't treat it as urgent. He then signed to say the financial accounts were presented fairly without doing a full check."

"So, you feel it could very well have been negligence on Bill's behalf rather than fraud?" asked Loretta.

Penny shrugged. "Whatever it was, Dino Latent came to see Steve Rogerson, the managing partner, very soon afterwards. Steve interfered and brokered a deal between Danny and Dino, and then soon after, Danny left to set up his own production company – with Bill as chief operating officer."

Loretta thanked Penny for the information. She now knew Danny had left under a cloud.

Chapter 44

The book club discusses Noi's book

Margaret Peabody had run the book club in the northern suburb of Petersfield for the last five years. The book club had a diverse set of members, which reflected the population of Petersfield. This included a couple of members from the Thai community, Alpa and Mae.

Members picked the titles for the books to be read in turn. They were given a month to read the chosen book, and then they had a coffee morning at Margaret's house where the book was discussed.

Alpa had suggested that they read the two books in the *Malami Hotel* series by her friend and local author, Noi.

There were eight members at the meeting, including Alpa and Mae.

Margaret asked Alpa to give a brief overview of the books before they called the meeting open to discussion.

Alpa described how the books were about a hotel in Hawaii – they told the stories of the guests who visited the hotel and the shenanigans they got up to whilst on vacation.

After she finished, there was a brief silence.

Margaret waved her hand. "Anyone like to volunteer to go first?"

Kathy Avery spoke first. "I want you all to know that although I haven't got any proof they were actually on the Mayflower, that my family have been in the USA since that time. We are therefore acclimated to the culture and language of this great country." She stopped there and smiled at everyone. "For someone to come here as an immigrant – am I right, Noi is an immigrant from Thailand?"

Alpa nodded and smiled.

"To come here as an immigrant and write a book in English. Bearing in mind that English is not her first language! Well, this is something we should applaud, do you not think?"

She then put the book down on her lap and proceeded to applaud. Everyone else joined in making suitable noises.

Alpa nodded. "Noi did come here as an immigrant, but is now fully fluent in English after taking night classes."

"What an achievement!" said Harry Cohen, beaming at Alpa. "I can't string two words together in Spanish despite vacationing in Mexico for the last 30 years! The thought of living in Thailand and being able to write a book in English is so impressive."

Alpa was beginning to get embarrassed for Noi. She knew Noi was not a native speaker of English, but that should be overlooked while they discussed her book, surely?

"So, did you enjoy the book?" Alpa blurted, looking around the room. There was an awkward silence.

Mabel Grimes, who was a retired librarian, spoke first. "I do not want to take away from the achievement of writing in English, but I felt it was not very original. Those stories have been told over and over again. In fact, I felt much of it was very similar to the Love Boat. I am sure everyone remembers the Love Boat – that TV series from the 1980's, except this is set in a hotel on land."

Harry nodded. "Yes, we can't expect a masterful command of the English language from a Thai immigrant, I know that, but I did feel I had read or seen on TV much of it before. The stories were not original."

Wilma nodded. "It is very much, he said, she said. I like stories that are more subtle and engage the reader in different ways."

Alpa wanted to leap to her friends' defense.

"You may not think it is original, but it is well written. Mae and I are Thai and we can read and write well in English. We don't feel we could write a full novel, but we could write. In addition, other people are impressed with Noi's work. Noi has told me a major Hollywood producer is interested to make it into a movie."

The silence that followed that outburst seemed to last an eternity. Finally, Margaret spoke. "Can we know more about this, Alpa?"

"Certainly." Alpa was nervous now that all eyes were on her. "Noi has a literary agent, Robin Pine, who has contacted Danny La Valle, a Hollywood producer. Danny is interested in making a movie out of Noi's book."

Margaret and Wilma exchanged glances.

"Danny La Valle is a famous Hollywood producer," said Wilma. "We all know Shamrock Isle, I am sure. Are you certain this is who will produce the movie?"

Alpa could feel her face getting hot and red. She felt they were patronizing her friend, but didn't know what to say.

"All I know is what Noi has told me," she blurted. "She is very excited."

Harry spoke carefully and slowly. "I believe looking at this book that she self-published it. I cannot see the name of a publisher."

"Yes, she did self-publish," Alpa said. She could feel herself blushing.

"It is very unusual for someone who self-published to have a literary agent. Did she contact an agent after she had self-published? You see, a literary agent usually contacts publishers."

"*Or* movie producers." Alpa felt defensive now. "And the literary agent contacted her."

Harry continued very slowly. "Please ask Noi to be sure that she is speaking to someone who is legitimate. By that I mean, does she know that this person is a reputable literary agent?"

Alpa was staring at him, at a loss for words. "He told Noi he was a literary agent, why would he not be reputable?" Sometimes she didn't understand Americans.

"Please ask Noi to check his credentials and also to make sure that he really is able to secure a contract with Danny La Valle," Harry urged.

Alpa realized she looked stupid and her mouth was gaping open. "Okay," she finally said, with a heavy nod.

After the meeting ended, Alpa and Mae left together to catch the train back to their homes.

"Those people are racist," Mae said. "I hadn't thought about it before, but now I can see they are. They think because we are Thai we are not as good as them."

Alpa agreed. "I will ask Noi to check out her agent's *credentials* as they called them, but why should he not be reputable? I want to ask Jinni what she thinks about this, too. She knows a lot – she is a businesswoman."

"I agree, I'll call in at the Purple Orchid tonight."

With that the two friends arrived at the station, said goodbye and went their separate ways.

Alpa sat on the train, messaging Noi:

"How are you? The book reading of your novel went well this morning. Just wondering how you met your agent, Robin Pine?"

Noi was quick with a reply.

"He contacted me through a Facebook site for authors. Why do you want to know?"

Alpa took a deep breath and typed:

"The book club just wondered if he is reputable?"

No answer. Alpa worried that Noi was offended.

"Noi are you there? I just wanted to give feedback from the book club."

"Why do they ask these stupid questions? Of course he is reputable! He knows Danny La Valle who is going to make my book into a movie."

Oh dear, there was no shaking her. She believed in Robin Pine and there was no way she was going to change her mind.

Alpa felt she had reported back what the book club said but inside, she felt slightly sick. She often did not understand American ways, but there was something about this agent and the lucrative movie deal that did not make sense. She decided to have one last try.

"I am pleased that you have an agent and a movie deal, I just want to be sure that all is okay. Have you signed a contract with Danny La Valle where he offers you a sum of money for your book?"

This time there was no response. Alpa thought she might have gone too far, but at least her conscience was clear. She had tried to say something. She knew Noi would never accept it, but there might be fraud involved here. Alpa wanted to protect Noi, but at that moment she did not know how she could do this. She would have to bide her time and see what happened.

Chapter 45

Jinni

The book reading and other concerns

I found out about the book reading at Jenny's BookStop from Jenny herself, who popped round to ask if I would display a poster advertising the event.

She put the poster onto the reception desk and as I read it, I gasped. Glenda, who was a customer at the Purple Orchid, was going to read from her book, *Gwendoline Investigates*. I knew she had written a children's book, so that was okay. But it was the next announcement – and the picture – that floored me. Danny La Valle was going to come to the reading as he was going to produce a TV show of Glenda's book!

What?!

My word the man must be busy, I thought. He was filming the *Reluctant Pastor* according to his social media, had promised to film Noi's book, and now he was also filming Glenda's book!

A little voice inside told me that this was highly unlikely, and there was something very off here.

I told Jenny I would display the poster, and I spent the rest of the day thinking about the event. Of course, I had seen Danny La Valle at the boring debate in Atlanta. But that was in a theatre. True, not all the seats had been sold, but he still filled about half of a theatre. It seemed fantastical that he would fly out here from LA to attend a reading of

Gwendoline Investigates at an unknown bookstore in a small city.

But what if I was just being a cynic? Perhaps he did have the capacity to make all these programs.

The following day I was surprised by a visit from Mae, a lady I know in the Thai community. She arrived at the Purple Orchid in the Walks district, just as we were closing and asked if I would like to join her for a drink as she had something she wished to discuss with me.

We went to a small bar not far from the salon and sat nursing two beers. We chatted pleasantly for a few minutes about life in the USA and our families back in Thailand, and then Mae told me about a book club meeting she had been to yesterday where Noi's book was discussed.

"The book club members queried if Noi's agent was reputable," Mae said.

My heart sank. I had been thinking the same thing! But I felt it would be disloyal to Noi to discuss my suspicions behind her back.

"I will speak to Noi," I assured Mae. "She is in constant contact with her agent. What do the book club members suggest she do to make sure the agent is legitimate?"

Mae didn't know, which wasn't very helpful.

"Okay," I said. "Shall we look it up on the internet?"

I got my cell phone out and typed into Google. Several answers came back, including 'look for professional credentials', and 'get the contract in writing so that there is no misunderstanding as to what the agent will do'.

"I will speak to Noi and ask her if she has a contract in writing and if her agent has professional credentials."

Mae seemed happy with that, and we turned the talk to other topics including a Thai festival to be held in June in the downtown area.

The next day I bought two tickets to the book reading. I then rang Noi and told her about it.

I could sense she was as shocked as I was that Danny La Valle was coming to the city.

"Perhaps you should discuss this with your agent," I said. I wanted to bring up her agent delicately. "I wonder if he represents Glenda as well as you? If not, does he know who represents Glenda and how they were able to persuade Danny to come and speak at the book reading?"

Noi agreed. "I will speak to him now," she said, ending the call.

I hoped that I was being paranoid and all would turn out well in the end. I must admit, it would be interesting to go to the book reading and to see Danny La Valle again. Although, I hoped he wouldn't be as boring as the last time I saw him! With that, I turned my attention back to the salon and to working on customers' nails.

Last week in May, 2024

Loretta speaks to Zoe who knows what happened at Avalon Media

Jenny receives an unsettling letter

Chapter 46

Zoe speaks about her boyfriend who worked at Avalon Media

Loretta had organized with Joey to meet with a young woman named Zoe, whose boyfriend Brett Zimmerman, was a former employee of Avalon Media. She had been given an address in the Hollywood Hills, which turned out to be a townhouse in a condo complex. Loretta had no doubt rents would be high in this area, but it was not as grand as she had imagined.

She parked in the visitor's car parking area and walked along a walkway until she came to number eight. She knocked on the door.

The door was answered by a very beautiful woman with perfect features, long blonde hair and a light tan. "Hi, are you Loretta?" she asked, and when Loretta nodded, she ushered her in with a smile. "I'm Zoe – come in."

Loretta crossed the threshold into the townhouse, and after walking down a short corridor went into a large room which was the living area including kitchen. It took her breath away. She had never in her life before been in an area that was so untidy or so dirty. Coffee cups and used pizza boxes were left on the coffee table and scattered on the floor. Papers were strewn around and it looked like Zoe had got undressed and left the clothes where she stepped out of them in piles around the living room. The kitchen looked greasy and dirty with dishes piled high on the counter tops. The curtains were closed (as were the windows she suspected) and the room had a hot, airless feel. If there was air conditioning, it was not turned on.

“Sit down,” said Zoe brightly, seemingly oblivious to the mess. “Can I get you a drink?”

Loretta sat on the greasy, dirty sofa and declined a drink. Yuck, this place was disgusting. What a slovenly mess.

Zoe sat opposite her and launched forth. “I am in a mess here. Brett left me with no warning and then I find out he is up to his ears in debt. I might be evicted from here for nonpayment of rent. I am an actress and resting at the moment. I certainly hadn’t budgeted for having to pay for all this. Normally I wouldn’t speak to a private investigator, but needs must. I must make it clear though, I want money up front to talk.”

Loretta looked at her. How could someone so beautiful live in a mess like this, she thought. But there was one consolation, at least she didn’t beat around the bush. They agreed a price after some negotiations. Zoe was quick to point out that all the staff had been paid hush money so Brett would not be able to speak, but as his girlfriend, when he had been indiscreet enough to tell her, she felt she was not covered by any such agreement.

After the money changed hands, Zoe asked what Loretta wanted to know.

"Tell me what you know about Brett working at Avalon," Loretta said. "What did he do and did he earn a good salary?"

Zoe thought for a moment. "Are you familiar with Danny La Valle? He started the company in 2017 when he had a big falling out with Dino Latent. Bill Underwood was in charge of the office. Brett was supposed to liaise with the public relations company and also do some public relations himself.

I met Brett in 2019 and we moved in here soon afterwards. He earned about two hundred and fifty thousand dollars at Avalon, which was a lot of money to say that Danny wasn't involved in any projects. After he filmed Rosy Dawn with Dino, he didn't make another film for years. I guess at first Danny was in demand for interviews, but by 2019 he wasn't as popular. So, there wasn't much to do in terms of..." here Zoe passed before continuing. "Well, official public relations, if you get my drift."

"Sorry," said Loretta, "I'm not following. What do you mean *official* public relations?"

Zoe laughed. "Danny was completely off his head on drugs and alcohol. He was a mess. But he was also a very rich man thanks to his movies – Rosy Dawn in particular. Are you familiar with Hollywood, Loretta?"

Loretta didn't appreciate her patronizing tone. "I am sure you are going to tell me."

Zoe laughed. "In Hollywood people can smell money from a mile away and if you are rich and an idiot, they will soon find ways to part you from it! It was like play time in the sweetie store at Avalon Media! They all took advantage of Danny. All four of them. There were big salaries, cars, jewelry – you name it. They all had their fingers in the till."

"Wasn't Bill Underwood the chief operating officer? Shouldn't he have stopped it?"

Zoe looked at Loretta like she was simple minded. "He was the *worst* offender. He agreed to the big salaries, signed off on cars and, I was told, in the case of Sheila Kavanagh, plastic surgery."

There was silence for a moment. Loretta was making notes on a small pad.

"I guess you are saying Danny was off his head due to substance abuse and didn't know what was going on?"

Zoe smirked. "Correct. And you see Danny also had his own problems. Partying with young girls, if you get my drift, and buying illegal substances. All things that, wink, wink, Brett had to cover up."

She paused again for effect. "It wasn't until Danny checked into rehab and came off the drugs and alcohol that he was well enough to even look at his business."

"That was when he made Shamrock Isle, I believe," said Loretta.

Zoe nodded. "Things really started going off here when he finished filming and did a review of the accounts. That was when Danny and Bill called Brett into a meeting and accused him of paying himself extravagant expenses. They said he put claims through for dinners in Beverly Hills at Spago and places like that with public relations people, and they said they had checked the dates and that he was lying about meeting people on those days. He had also claimed for a weekend break in Mexico at the One & Only. Geez, I knew that was a fraud as I went with him!" She chuckled to herself. "He also bought clothes at Loro Piano in Beverly Hills and charged them to the company. What a laugh!"

Loretta wasn't sure why this was supposed to be funny, but she smiled.

Then Zoe dropped her bombshell. "They then went on to accuse Brett of cooking the books. It was a joke really, as Brett had nothing to do with accounting. It seemed a million dollars was missing, and could not be accounted for. If anyone should have been implicated, it should have been Bill Underwood. He was the accountant – but he was sitting with Danny firing people."

Ah, thought Loretta. The missing $1 million.

"Bill told Brett he was going to do an investigation, but in the meantime, they were terminating Brett's employment. This related mainly to his spending Danny's money as if it was his own on food, clothes and vacations. He had no choice but to sign a non-disclosure agreement and accept a termination payment. If he had not accepted it, then they would have refused to write him a reference."

Zoe then went on. "After that, things went really bad here. It took Brett a while to get another job and he was not very happy. It was lucky I was working on that movie, The Long Passage to Brentville at the time. Have you heard of it? I played Jennie."

Loretta hadn't, but nodded politely.

"After that finished, we started running out of money. That bastard was running up credit card debts…"

This was just the beginning of a long rant.

Loretta let her carry on for a while, and then brought her back to Avalon. "What do you know about Sheila Kavanagh?"

Zoe thought for a while. "Wasn't she the accountant? Well, she had her fingers in every pie, too. Have you seen her? Like I said, she has had so much work on her face, all paid for by Avalon Media." She paused for a moment. "Mmm, I believe she was fired too, but my understanding, from Brett, is that they refused to give her a reference so she has never been able to find another job."

Goodness, thought Loretta. What a mess!

After she had finished the interview, Loretta left to go back to her room to write up her findings. It seemed that what Bill Underwood had told Patrice may very well be true. There was $1 million missing but it seemed he was involved in helping Danny look for it.

Chapter 47

Jenny receives an unsettling letter

The publicity for the book reading with Danny La Valle attending was going well. Jenny had already sold 40 tickets to the live event and 100 tickets to watch the event online via Zoom. She was excited about how well everything was going.

She had a seat behind the counter in the BookStop, where she often sat when the store was not busy to check on the inventory or her social media. Today, she had decided to check on Danny La Valle. He hadn't posted anything today, but there was a post on Instagram from a couple of days ago. She knew it was Danny La Valle as it had a blue tick. There was a picture of a mountain range and the caption read "Really excited guys about the filming of "The Reluctant Pastor" with Peter Ponsford in the Appalachian Mountains. The stunning scenery takes my breath away." Jenny thought for a moment. The Appalachian Mountains weren't too far away from here, so he wouldn't have too long a commute.

About 11 a.m. the mailman came into the store and smiling, said he had a letter for Jenny.

Taking the letter from him, Jenny said, "Wow, that looks official." She wondered what on earth it could be.

When she opened it, she saw it was from Danny La Valle on an Avalon Media letterhead. It read:

Dear Jenny,

You have placed advertisements stating that I will be present at "Jenny's BookStop" on June 3 to do a Meet and Greet with customers who will be charged a fee to attend. I would never charge to do a Meet and Greet and will not be attending this event.

I have asked my attorney to follow up by sending you a Cease-and-Desist Notice.

Please remove my name immediately from all advertising material.

Danny La Valle

Jenny, at first, could not believe her eyes. She read it again. What on earth was this? Glenda had assured her that Danny La Valle would come and she had believed her.

She laid the letter on the flat surface of the reception counter. She then took her cell phone out and took a picture of it. She then sent the picture to Glenda via WhatsApp with a brief message.

"What is this?!"

Jenny guessed that Glenda would be teaching, and sure enough, an hour or so later her cell phone rang – it was Glenda. She was spluttering and not making a lot of sense. "What the hell is that?!"

By this time, Jenny had looked on Danny La Valle's social media account and saw he had made another post. This was a similar notice, but this time addressed to his fans stating that the advertisement saying he would be at Jenny's BookStop was false.

Jenny directed Glenda to look at Danny's social media.

"I presume you have also got this message?" she asked.

Glenda wasn't making a lot of sense. "No, I haven't," she finally said. "But I wouldn't, all my communication goes through my agent, Robin Pine."

"I suggest you ring him now and ask him what the heck is going on," Jenny said. "There is no way this is a mistake or a mix-up. It is perfectly clear that he is not coming." She could feel tears welling up and when she spoke, her voice broke. "He is accusing us of…fraud!"

Glenda was getting very nervous. "Don't get ahead of yourself. I will call Robin as soon as I finish teaching today."

"Please do, and get back to me as soon as possible. It looks like I am going to have to announce that this event is not going to take place. To say this is embarrassing is to put it mildly."

Jenny was very near to tears and shaking as she sat back down behind the counter. A customer came over to buy a book, and she found it difficult to stop her hands shaking as she rang up the purchase. She tried to smile and remain bright, but inside she felt a sick dread. What on earth was she going to say to the people who had bought tickets? She knew without a doubt that she was going to have to refund people's money.

After closing up the shop and heading home, she checked her cell phone for messages from Glenda. Nothing as yet. But later, at about 11 p.m. a message came through:

"I have just spoken to Robin Pine. He says that Danny will definitely be coming to the reading

and to wait until tomorrow when a message will arrive to say that the letter was a mistake."

Jenny doubted that that was true. The following morning, she went into the BookStop and sure enough, when the mail arrived there was an attorney's letter with a cease- and-desist notice.

Jenny photographed it and sent it to Glenda. She knew deep down that she would never get her money back, and that same day she made an announcement on her social media that the book reading was cancelled, and the money people had paid for tickets would be refunded.

Standing at the counter in her new shop, Jenny felt sick. She knew the backlash from this would be much worse than the loss of revenue, and she asked herself for the thousandth time, how could you be so stupid?

30 May, 2024

Loretta meets with a realtor in Calabasas

Becky hears more news from Stermer Media

Jinni wonders who Danny La Valle really is

Chapter 48

Loretta meets a realtor in Calabasas

Loretta had obtained the address of the property where Bill and Patrice lived in Calabasas from Patrice herself. She had been able to put in a public records request on the property to the County Assessor's Office. From this, she was able to find who owned the property, the property value, liens and tax information, etc. From the records, it was clear that Bill Underwood had never owned the property. The property appeared to be owned by a Ronald Zoltan. A search of this name showed that the property was currently available to lease through Ronald Zoltan's real estate firm. She had rung to make an appointment to see it.

Loretta met the agent, Missy Guber, at the real estate office. Missy began immediately with a sales pitch for the property. "It is a beautiful property with many upgrades..." Missy launched into a full description, aided by a glossy color brochure which she showed to Loretta.

Loretta smiled and nodded and then she spoke. "I must be honest with you, Missy. Although I would love to lease that property if I could afford it, that is not the real reason I came in today. I am a private investigator and I have been asked to do a confidential investigation into Bill Underwood, a British man, who I believe rented that property."

Missy's smile faded, and at first it seemed she was not going to cooperate. She then turned to her computer and started to type. "The name is Bill Underwood, correct?"

Loretta nodded.

“Can I ask why you are interested in Mr. Underwood?”

“It’s a divorce investigation,” Loretta replied.

“Okay, so the wife is looking for assets. Well, this was not owned by him, it was leased to Avalon Enterprises. The signatory for Avalon was Bill Underwood. The property was leased to Avalon from October 2019 to September 2023.”

“Did the company pay the rent? Were there any issues?” Loretta asked.

“The file shows no issues,” said Missy. “Rent was always paid and the property left in good condition.”

Loretta was writing on a small pad. “I presume I can get information on Avalon Enterprises from their company 10k?”

Missy was looking closely at the file. “The company is registered in the Philippines.”

That shocked Loretta. “Are you sure?” she asked.

Missy turned the computer screen so Loretta could see the registration details. She then turned it away from her.

“The only other information I can give you is that the rent was paid in cash up front. This is fairly normal in real estate transactions of this nature.”

Loretta knew that if this was the case, then there would have been few other enquiries about the company. The investigation got curiouser by the minute.

She thanked Missy for her time and drove back to the motel. She was just about to get in touch with Patrice to fill her in, when her phone pinged. It was a message from Joey saying he had found a person who worked with Bill Underwood at Meyer and Co. who was prepared to talk to her on condition of anonymity. A meeting was set up for that same day in the early evening. The person was a man named Greg.

Chapter 49

Meeting Greg

Loretta met Greg in a coffee shop just off Wilshire Boulevard. Greg was a very thin and tall man in his early forties. He was sitting in a booth sipping a coffee when Loretta arrived.

He seemed quite devoid of emotion and spoke in a monotone voice. However, it was clear that he knew Bill Underwood having worked with him at Meyer and Co.

"Why do you want to know information about Bill?" he asked.

"It relates to potential personal issues with his family," Loretta replied vaguely.

"Oh, I see." Greg studied her closely. "Well, I can't say I am surprised. Okay, fire away, what do you want to know?"

Loretta said she was interested in his former wife, his work at Meyer and Co. and why he left there to work for Danny La Valle.

Greg looked at her and then started to speak.

"I thought I knew Bill well when we both worked at Meyer and Co. We both worked long hours and on some of the same clients. Bill was married to Alison at the time. She was British, like him, and had come to America to be with him. Bill was crazy about Alison, but this didn't stop him leaving her alone while he worked long hours. Bill thought love equaled money. The richer he was, the more she would love him. Alison had found work at a small firm in Pasadena and they bought a house there. I remember going to the house-warming party. It was a house in a beautiful neighborhood that needed a lot of work. Alison did some of the work herself, and oversaw some of the other work. Do you want to know more about Alison?"

Loretta nodded, making notes.

"Alison was lovely, a real sweetheart. But she was in a foreign country married to someone who neglected her for his work. As I said, Bill loved money and felt the money made up for him being at work most of the time. So as far as money went, they were blessed. The house was beautiful, they both drove Mercedes and Alison had a wardrobe full of expensive clothes. I believe the long hours only got worse after Bill was made up to partner. But this was when it was also difficult, as it seemed no matter how many hours he worked, he couldn't keep up."

"Would this be normal for a new partner? A partner is an owner, correct? Therefore, Bill would get a share of the profits of the accounting business."

"Well, first it is not normal and second, yes, he would have got a share of the profits. It seemed Bill found it difficult to bring new business in and to keep on top of the clients he already had."

"Did he confide in you?" Loretta asked.

"Not exactly. We always got on well, but now he was a partner he was senior to me and we could not chat as we used to. But it was obvious from his demeanor that something was really wrong. He seemed anxious and irritable.

There were some issues at Global Pictures, which was his biggest client. Dino Latent and Danny La Valle had a big falling out. Typical of creative types, Dino thought he was the most important and should have the biggest share of the royalties from that hit movie, Rosy Dawn. Danny had the same thoughts! So they argued constantly about money and the share of royalties. In the end, Danny left the company and Bill went with him."

"Do you think there was any fraud involved in the split?" Loretta asked.

Greg was silent for a moment and eyed her curiously. "None that was ever talked about openly. There was never a fraud investigation or prosecution, but there was gossip." Here, Greg stopped and rearranged the cutlery.

"What sort of gossip?" Loretta encouraged.

"Well, it might just have been evil gossip, but there was talk of there being some money missing. But there was never any proof of any wrongdoing and in the end, Dino kept ownership of Global Pictures and Danny set up Avalon Media…"

"With Bill Underwood as his financial adviser," said Loretta.

"Yes, that is true. I stayed on at Meyer and Co. for a few years, but it was obvious I wasn't going to make it to partner so I also left and went to West Coast Cable as Finance Director. I kept in touch with Bill, though.

During this time, Bill fell apart emotionally. I think this is what you want to know? He had been busy with work, pulling down a very big salary and so as far as he knew, that was what Alison wanted. Well, it turned out it wasn't!"

Greg took a break here and took a sip from his now cold coffee cup. "One day Bill went home early to a scene that sounds corny but must have been hell to experience. He saw the pool guy's van in the drive. There was nobody out at the pool, which he thought was strange, so he went into the house. Going up the stairs he could hear noises from the bedroom – and yes, you guessed it, when he opened the door there was Alison and the pool guy naked in bed."

Greg stopped so Loretta could take this in. He then went on.

"There were terrible rows after this. From what I understand, Bill told her he would forgive her if it stopped immediately. But Alison told him she didn't want to stop. And she told him the thing he really couldn't understand – she told him she didn't want his money. She said Barry, the pool guy, had more love and affection in his little finger than Bill had in his whole body. She told him she felt he was like a robot."

"I presume there was a divorce then," said Loretta.

"Oh yes, Alison just wanted Barry and not Bill. They had just finished the house and had to sell it to pay for the divorce. It was a very ugly divorce as Bill did not want to give her any of his money. After all, it was Alison who had committed adultery, not him! That is what he said."

Loretta could guess what was coming. "So, they spent a lot of money on attorneys then?"

"Of course I would not pry into his affairs, but yes, I get that impression. The house in Pasadena was sold and what was left was divided up between them."

"Bill was pretty devastated then?"

"He was very bitter! He said no woman would ever take him for a ride again. He was sorting his money out so nobody could get their hands on it."

"Do you still see Bill?" Loretta asked.

"He moved out of state last September, and I haven't seen him since. To be honest, I didn't see much of him before then, after his divorce. We were both very busy with our jobs, and you know how it goes."

"Sure," said Loretta, nodding. "So, you feel he was very bitter about his divorce?"

"Extremely," nodded Greg. "He is an accountant through and through and to lose that much money to someone who was – pardon my language – fucking around behind his back was particularly difficult for him."

Driving back from the meeting, Loretta was beginning to gain a picture of Bill Underwood. A man who was failing as a partner at Meyer and Co., failing in his marriage to someone he loved and failing to keep his hands on the money he had made – a devastating thing for someone who worshipped money. She felt this only scratched the surface though, and there was so much more about the man that was still to be revealed. She messaged Patrice to arrange a time to talk.

Chapter 50

Stermer Media investigate

Steve Cannon, Vice President of Publishing at Stermer Media, was a well-fed, balding man in his early fifties. He had, in his own view, worked hard to earn the corner office in the company headquarters in Los Angeles. At first, when Rudy from Accounts had been to tell him about the royalties account, it had just been an annoyance. Authors and agents not getting paid their royalties was bad news for Stermer. It could mean that they would lose valuable authors to other publishing houses and that was the last thing he wanted. He had put Bill Underwood in charge of the account and it seemed he had not signed off on all the royalties for the last couple of months.

Steve had arranged a Zoom call with Bill where he had shouted and used threatening language. Bill had sorted the account out very quickly after that and everyone received their royalties, including back pay.

Steve had thought that was an end to it, until he received the management accounts. Even after the corrections, it seemed there was something very wrong with the account. Stermer accountants budgeted the amount that would be paid for royalties each month from orders for books they had received. Before the corrections, the amount paid out for royalties more or less equaled the amount Stermer had budgeted to be paid out. However, after payments had been made to the authors who had complained they had not received payment, the amount paid exceeded the amount Stermer had budgeted to pay by about $50,000. It was almost as if someone was being paid when no orders had been received.

Steve had asked Rudy to do a thorough check of the account.

Rudy was meeting with him today to go through the result of his check on the accounts.

"The difference relates to the payments to Stout and Bing," Rudy explained.

Steve looked at him. "You do know that they are one of the most prestigious literary agencies in New York?"

Rudy nodded. "Sure they are. Well, Stout and Bing are, but the payment was made to *Stout & Bing* – they might seem the same, but they are not the same. Different spelling."

Steve was intrigued. He opened his laptop and went into the royalties account. "Show me." He slid the laptop over to Rudy.

Rudy drew the laptop near to him and began to scroll through the payments. "Here," he said, turning the laptop around to face Steve.

Steve could see a payment had been made to 'Stout & Bing'. He clicked on the payment and could see that the contact for the account was 'Robin Pine'.

"Robin Pine is an agent at Stout and Bing," Steve said. "I've met him. He has some very high-powered clients. Are you saying he doesn't have an author who we publish?"

"Exactly! But the *Robin Pine* we paid works for a different agency. See the spelling – it is different. The real agency spells their name with the written word 'and'. We paid a company who instead, spells their name with an ampersand."

Steve's face was starting to turn puce. "What type of fuckery is this?"

Rudy stared at him. "It seems like fraud to me."

"Fucking hell! Go away and find out how much is involved and then come right back to me. Do not mention this to anyone until we are certain how much is involved!"

The next day, Rudy was back with a short report. "There have been payments to that suspect Stout & Bing for the last three months. In total, we're looking at a hundred and twenty-five thousand dollars. The money was wired direct."

Steve looked like his eyes were going to pop out of his head. He was clearly furious. His first instinct was to get Underwood on the phone to find out what was going on. But then something told him to hold his fire. Instead, he thanked Rudy for the information, and told him to keep what he had found quiet for the time being until he could carry out a full investigation.

As soon as Rudy left the office, Steve rang the auditors, Meyer and Co., and asked to speak to Graeme Moore, the partner in charge of the Stermer account. After a brief discussion, it was agreed that Meyer and Co. would send an auditor to Stermer to investigate the payments out of the royalties account.

Half an hour later, he had left the office and was driving to the Warehouse restaurant in Marina del Rey where he was due to meet his wife for an early dinner. As he drove, he fumed and swore to himself. This had to be that thieving British bastard Underwood – he was in charge of the fucking account. Fucking Brits! You couldn't trust them with anything! But then his logical side took over and he queried why an executive with Stermer Media would want to jeopardize his whole future for $125,000. Then the most horrible thought of all occurred to him – maybe there is more. Maybe the bastard is ripping us off for millions! He also knew that royalties had to be set up on the account by an accountant, Glenys, before they could be paid. Underwood had more of an oversight role. So maybe he was jumping to conclusions. Glenys would never defraud the company, he was sure. She was a grandmom and a sweet old lady. He would never suspect her. And so on and so on – the thoughts swirled round in his head.

It was not a happy man that was shown to a seat overlooking the yachts and the sunset at the Warehouse where his wife sat reading the menu and sipping on a cocktail. In fact, as he sipped on a Mai Tai, Steve felt murderous, yet through it all he kept a huge, rictus grin on his face and made small talk with his wife.

Chapter 51

Becky hears more news from Stermer Media

Becky couldn't deny that things had been difficult financially since Bill had fired her, for what she felt were questionable reasons. She was a single mom, and had very little support. To say she had had to tighten her belt was putting it mildly. Some days she barely ate so that Kiara could eat well.

She was, however, having to accept that this was her life now. Sometimes, in the morning when she arrived at work and was parking her car, she saw Bill's wife get out of her fancy Mercedes and walk towards the Purple Orchid beauty salon. The woman always looked expensive and well groomed. Life sucked, it really did.

Today, she was just parking when her cell phone pinged. It was a message from Patti, at Stermer Media:

"Did you ever find anything out about Bill Underwood? It sucks here. The big boss came out from LA last week and spoke to us all. If we don't increase business by 50% over the next few months, it seems like this office might have to close.

Also, we have the auditors in, checking the accounts. It seems there might be fraud. They are not saying where there is fraud – but rumors are it could relate to the publishing house."

Becky read and re-read the message. Perhaps they did listen to her after all when she left. She had to admit though, she had found out nothing about Bill Underwood. Her meeting with Sheila Kavanagh had ended up with her telling Sheila all about herself and getting nothing back! She messaged back to ask about the fraud, but Patti didn't have any details.

She did, however, know Robbie who did the 3D nail art at the Purple Orchid from a yoga class she used to go to. She might know Bill's wife and perhaps Bill himself. She might find out more from asking at the salon.

She couldn't afford the 3D nail art or even a normal manicure, but she decided to go along to the Purple Orchid during her lunch break and order a coffee. She asked the receptionist if Robbie was in that day, and said she would like to speak to her. After a few minutes, Robbie came out of the salon and came over to see her.

After they had chatted for a moment or two about the yoga class and the new salon, Robbie sat down on the chair opposite Becky.

Becky lent forward and said, "I would love to have my nails done but am struggling at the moment. I lost my job at Stermer Media and am working at the Institute for the Blind and Visually Impaired for a much lower salary. I didn't come here though to beg!"

Robbie nodded, obviously puzzled about what this was about.

"Does Patrice Underwood work in the beauty salon here?" Becky enquired.

"Well, I think it is a bit more than that. She is a part-owner in the business with Jinni. Do you know Patrice?"

"No, but it was her husband I worked for at Stermer."

Robbie was starting to get a bit nervous about where this was going. "I think he is an investor in this business, but it has nothing to do with his work at Stermer Media, so far as I know..."

"I think he is incompetent or worse… he could be committing fraud," Becky blurted out.

"Wow!" said Robbie. "That is a pretty serious accusation, Becky! Do you have anything to back up what you just said?"

Becky looked nervous and started twisting a ring round and round on her little finger. "I was visited by someone who worked with him in LA, a person named Sheila Kavanagh, who was certain he was committing fraud at his last job and when I questioned something he had done at Stermer, he fired me. Also, I have been told by someone I worked with at Stermer that there is a fraud investigation going on as we speak."

Robbie didn't know what to make of all this. "Look Becky, I know you are upset, but Bill doesn't really have anything to do with the day to day running of this salon. I think the best thing is to go back to the senior management at Stermer Media with your worries."

With that, she stood up and smiling, said she would have to get back to her next customer. She added that she hoped Becky would come into the salon again and have a manicure with her soon.

Becky was red in the face and feeling like a fool, she got up and left the salon and walked back to the Institute for the Blind and Visually Impaired.

Robbie, however, was slightly titillated as she returned to her next manicure, and made a note to herself to tell Jinni and Patrice at the end of the day.

Chapter 52

Jinni

Who are Bill Underwood and Danny La Valle

At the end of another long and busy day, I was getting ready to leave when Robbie called me over, and explained she had something to tell me. She also said she would like to speak to Patrice.

The three of us sat down in the coffee shop area of the salon.

Robbie began by saying, “Something very curious happened at lunchtime. Becky, who is a person I used to know vaguely from yoga, came in and asked to speak to me. She was very upset that she had lost her job at Stermer Media and wanted to speak to me about Bill Underwood.”

“Do you know of someone called Becky who used to work with Bill?” I asked Patrice.

Patrice shook her head.

Robbie went on. “She implied – and this is why I want to tell you Patrice – that there may be wrongdoing at Stermer Media. Fraud. She also said that a woman named Sheila, I think she said, had visited her from LA to say there was fraud in LA when Bill worked for Danny La Valle.”

I looked at Patrice. She looked sick.

“Do you mean Sheila Kavanagh?” she asked.

“Yes, that sounds right. Do you know her?” Robbie said.

Patrice looked at her hands for a moment before speaking. "Not exactly, but she came here for a facial and said she knew Bill in Los Angeles."

I spoke then. "Hold on a minute. If this is not true it is slander! Bill's reputation is on the line here, Patrice."

Patrice looked very uncomfortable.

"I didn't know Bill worked for Danny La Valle," I said.

"Yes, he worked for Danny when I met him and left to go to Stermer Media. He ran Danny's financial affairs."

"Hold on a minute," Robbie said. She went over to reception where there was a poster. "Danny La Valle was supposed to be coming to the BookStop next door to a reading one of our customers, Glenda, is doing of her children's book. But…" She paused for a few moments, searching her thoughts.

I finished for her. "It has been cancelled as Danny La Valle is not coming. Jenny at the BookStop is going to refund the money we paid for tickets."

We all sat for a moment thinking about all this information.

"My friend, Noi, has written two books which she self-published. She has been contacted by a literary agent who told her that Danny La Valle is going to produce a movie of her books."

Patrice and Robbie looked at me and no one spoke.

"Stermer Media owns a boutique publishing house," Patrice volunteered. "However, they are a Christian, right-wing company. I can't imagine anything they are involved in would be fraud."

“Noi published her book through Delta Online,” I said, going over to the counter and checking on the spine of one of Noi’s books that were there for sale.

Upset, Patrice stood up and began to pace back and forward. “Something is very off here,” she said, choking back tears. “I hope I am being paranoid.”

I went over to her and hugged her. “Please go home and ask Bill. We might all be imagining things. Come back tomorrow when you have talked to him and we can see more clearly what is involved.”

My gut instinct told me that Patrice knew more than she was saying. It was with a heavy heart that I caught the train home to my apartment in the northern suburbs.

Who were these strangers that we had let into our lives?

Who was Danny La Valle? Why offer to come to the BookStop next door and then cancel? Or did he even offer – was what Glenda and Noi believed about him true, or an illusion? Also, and more importantly – who was Bill Underwood, the investor? Was he a rich man, or was he also another, elaborate illusion?

"A great deal of intelligence can be invested in ignorance when the need for illusion is deep."

Saul Bellow

June 1, 2024

Patrice speaks to Loretta

The fallout from the cancelled visit to the BookStop

Chapter 53

Patrice speaks to Loretta

Driving home after speaking to Jinni and Robbie, Patrice felt anxious and distressed. She had not read the report that Loretta had sent her yesterday. This was because she and Bill had been to a dinner downtown with a man who had a very influential podcast, and Bill was hoping he would sign with Stermer Media. Bill had been professional and charming and she hoped she had backed him up by being the perfect partner. She had been too tired when she got home to read anything. She now wished she had read the report before talking to Jinni and Robbie.

When she arrived home, Bill was not home yet, so she put a pre-made lasagna into the oven. She then sat on a stool at the kitchen island and read Loretta's report.

So much of it backed up what Bill had told her.

She knew from painful experience that he was the fixer for Danny La Valle. After all, she herself had signed a non-disclosure agreement and received hush money.

It was also true that there was $1 million missing and no one knew who had taken the money.

However, some of it was a surprise.

Alison was still living in Los Angeles and had left Bill for the pool guy! It seemed this had broken his heart. She was now pregnant by the pool guy. Bill never talked about Alison – she wondered if he knew she was pregnant.

Also, the house in Calabasas was rented and he had paid cash for the lease. But when she looked back, Bill had never told her he owned the house and she had never asked him for any details. She had never questioned anything. Perhaps, she mused, she wanted to believe so much that she didn't want anything that would spoil her dream.

The stories that he was not good at getting new business for the firm, Meyer and Co., were surprising. She knew that he had been taken on to develop the business in this city for Stermer Media. She wondered how he was getting on with this. The dinner downtown the other night had seemed to be a success.

There were also the rumors and suspicions around Global Pictures and the argument between Dino and Danny. The fact that Bill was involved with this client and then abruptly left Meyer and Co. to join Danny at Avalon Media worried her. Plus, there was the $1 million missing at Avalon. And now there was this Becky, saying there were rumors about fraud at Stermer Media.

Patrice sat and mused for a moment about Bill's career. It seemed everywhere he went, there were rumors about financial mismanagement. This was not looking good.

Patrice had to admit she did not know a lot about his background, but it seemed he came from a middle-class family in England. His parents were both elementary school teachers. Although well educated, they were not wealthy. Bill had been expected to mix with chief executive officers and rich individuals at the country club. Perhaps this did not come naturally to him?

When she had first met him, he seemed to be doing a good job as Danny's 'fixer' where there was no touting for new business involved. Yet there was then the worrying situation of $1 million missing, and now he was back in the situation of having to tout for new business.

She rang Loretta after reading the report to ask for her take on it.

"Bill has made money during his career as an accountant," Loretta explained, "but he has also lost money. A prolonged, acrimonious divorce being the main site of his financial losses. The house in Pasadena had to be sold to finance the divorce and pay the lawyers. I can find out more about this if you wish, as I can get hold of the court filings."

"Yes, I would like to know the details," Patrice said. "He never mentions Alison. The only thing he has said is that she went back to Britain, and it seems that is not true."

"We can also look at his current financial situation," Loretta said. "Did you sign a pre- nup?"

"No, I didn't," Patrice said. "I was so in love with Bill I never thought about it."

"I think especially as you have not signed a pre-nup it is very important to find out more about his current financial situation. I can do that."

Patrice said to go ahead and thanked her for the work she had done. Then she said, "What I don't understand is if there is a million dollars missing and accountants are looking into it, why is there no resolution?"

"Yes, that is very interesting," Loretta replied. "We definitely need to follow up on that. Quite some time has gone by and you would think they would have been able to find out where the money is by now."

Patrice agreed. "I don't know much about accounting and money, but it does seem strange. Also, who is this Sheila Kavanagh who came for a facial? Where does she live now? What does she know about what happened at Avalon?"

Loretta promised to look into it. They agreed she should go ahead and ended the call.

Later when Bill had returned from work, Patrice tossed a salad and when they were sitting down eating it with the lasagna and a glass of red wine, she felt the urge to ask more questions.

"How are things at Stermer, Bill?"

"Everything is fine. Busy, busy, busy," he replied with a smile.

"Is the expansion into this area going to plan?" she asked.

Immediately she knew she had said the wrong thing. His face clouded over.

"Why would you ask a question like that, Patrice?"

"Do you know someone called Becky who says she used to work with you at Stermer?"

Bill's face was going red and he put his knife and fork down. "What are you talking about, Patrice? Has that woman been to your salon?"

“Apparently, she spoke to Robbie and said you let her go. She also talked to Sheila Kavanagh.” Here Patrice paused, feeling angry vibes from Bill. “Fraud was implied.”

Bill was now quite clearly agitated. “And you believed her did you, Patrice? Is that how much I mean to you? You believe any gossip in a stupid woman’s salon?” He stopped momentarily to compose himself. “Let me tell you who this Becky is you are talking about. She used to be on the reception at Stermer Media and I allowed her to do some basic bookkeeping. She has no accounting qualifications, but I gave her a chance to make some accounting entries into the books.” He stopped again and looked Patrice straight in the eye. “And you know what, Patrice, she fucked it all up! She did it all wrong and turned a profit into a loss!” He was clearly furious. “It took me hours to sort out the mess she made. Yes, I let her go. The gal was incompetent!”

Patrice didn’t like the reference to a ‘stupid woman’s salon’ or the word ‘gal’. But to be fair to Bill, it might well be a disgruntled former employee out to make trouble.

“Okay, I know people can turn nasty when they lose their jobs. But here we have two people. Sheila Kavanagh and now this Becky. How many more are there, Bill?” she asked.

“And you care, do you?!” he yelled. “You were happy to take Danny’s money, weren’t you? You have been happy to live in my homes and you have never questioned me before about my work and where the money comes from. Why now? What have these two gals said to make you like this?”

Patrice was close to losing her own temper. "I want you to know Bill that I work very hard. Yes, you financed my business, but I work hard to make it profitable. I feel very worried how angry the mention of these two women makes you. I hope they are just making things up. I really do."

Bill got up from the table and marched out of the room to his study, where he slammed the door. That was the last time she saw him all evening.

Much later when she was in bed, he came and slid into the other side. He had his back to her and no words were exchanged.

Patrice knew that he was covering up something – but what he was covering up and how serious it was remained a mystery to her. She knew Loretta could find out more, and she knew she had to share whatever this was with Jinni. After all, Bill had invested in Jinni's business.

Patrice now had Alison's address in LA. Her next move would be to go there and meet Alison. The first wife's view would be very helpful.

Perhaps there is no such thing as true love, she thought. I thought I had met a true gentleman who would love and care for me for the rest of my life, and maybe life is just shit and such a person doesn't exist. A feeling she had never experienced before rolled over her – it was a feeling of bitterness and anger at herself for being so trusting and accepting.

Chapter 54

The fallout at Jenny's BookStop

It was the cease-and-desist notice from the attorney that upset Jenny the most. It was so unfair. She had not wanted to deceive anyone. She had believed Glenda when she said Danny was going to produce her children's show. How could she have been so naïve and trusting?

She had returned the money that people had paid for tickets, and put a notice out that the reading was cancelled. How embarrassing the whole thing was. Then a woman turned up just as the bookstore was closing for the evening.

"Are you Jenny?" she asked. "The owner of Jenny's BookStop?"

Jenny nodded. "How can I help you?"

"My name is Rosie Banks and I am a reporter from Daily Trends, an online newspaper."

Jenny had never heard of Daily Trends, but then she did not read the newspaper online.

"We have been contacted by a person who wishes to remain anonymous, but who says you were selling tickets for a personal meet and greet with Danny La Valle, but have now cancelled."

Jenny bristled. "That event is cancelled. You are correct and anyone who bought tickets have had their money refunded."

Rosie nodded. "I know you have refunded the money. But I am wondering – did he cancel or was this fraud? Was someone pretending to be him to take money from you by false pretenses?"

Jenny spoke, probably too quickly. "Of course it was fraud, somebody pretending to be him. I believe the author who was going to do the reading has also been taken in by this fraud. She believes she has a literary agent who knows Danny La Valle."

Rosie immediately got a pad and pen out and asked for the name of the author and the agent. She also asked for contact details for the author.

Jenny then decided she should speak up. "I acted in good faith! I am the victim here! I truly believed that the author, Glenda, was going to have her book produced by Danny into a TV show and I was excited to have him come to the bookstore to promote it. I used to be a fan of his, but it is so cruel how he treats his fans. He sent me an official letter telling me he does not do paid Meet and Greets. He should put a notice on his social media saying I acted in good faith – there has been a fraud here."

Rosie continued taking notes. "You feel Danny should acknowledge that there has been a fraud here?"

"Yes, I do," spluttered Jenny. "This has very likely damaged my business."

Rosie then asked if she could take Jenny's picture. Jenny agreed to this and posed alongside a bookshelf in the shop.

She then gave Jenny a card and left the BookStop.

A couple of days later, Jenny received a WhatsApp from a friend telling her to go online and read the Daily Trends.

Going to her laptop, she brought up the online site for Daily Trends. Even the site itself was garish and loud with bright colors and memes of women with large breasts and big hair. There was one big headline article followed by a number of smaller articles.

The screaming headline article had the text, "Finally Justice is Done" and contained a picture of a man. Clicking on the article, she saw it referred to a pedophile monster who had lived in Austin, Texas for ten years and worked at an elementary school – until he was detected a couple of days ago by an intrepid reporter and was now returned to prison.

Jenny scrolled down the articles, each more sensational than the last.

Finally, she found it. The article was about tenth in the list.

"Fake A.I Danny La Valle causes a storm in a bookstore – Rosie Banks reporting"

Under the heading was a large picture of Danny La Valle looking pensive and holding a book. The picture, which had been airbrushed to within an inch of its life, showed a smiling Danny looking at the camera. He appeared to have no wrinkles or grey hair and his face was chiseled.

Clicking on the article she saw it began:

"An Artificial Intelligence (A.I) deepfake scam has ruined a bookstore owner's dreams of a Meet and Greet with a Hollywood Producer that would have made her shop famous."

There was then a large picture of Jenny stood in her bookstore with the caption:

"Ambitious bookstore owner, Jenny Pascal in her store."

There was then a paragraph about how Jenny had purchased the bookstore in the regeneration district and had dreams of it being the biggest bookstore in the region.

It stated she had agreed to pay Danny $5,000 to do a meet and greet in the bookstore in the hope of making it famous.

Jenny could not remember saying anything along those lines to Rosie.

The article then included a short interview with Glenda Ortiz, the author of *Gwendoline Investigates*. Glenda had stated that she had spoken over the phone to Danny La Valle who was happy to come and do a meet and greet at the bookstore. She was excited that he would be producing her book into a TV show for children. She had spoken to him through her literary agent, Robin Pine.

It was then reported that the Daily Trends had tried to contact Robin Pine – the famous New York literary agent who worked with the renowned firm, Stout and Bing. He had released a statement to say that he did not represent Glenda Ortiz and had never represented her.

Danny La Valle had been contacted and through his representative he had stated that he had never charged for a meet and greet.

A technical analyst had looked into the telephone call and had stated that it was possible, using A.I technology, to take words that a person had said and record them. It would then be possible to convince someone they were actually speaking to the real person.

It seemed some people who had bought tickets were also contacted and they stated the money had been refunded, but they were angry that they had been invited under false pretenses. Blah, blah, blah.

However, if this was not bad enough, comments were allowed on the article and there were 317 of them. Oh my word, thought Jenny reading them.

Fun@themoon: How can people be so stupid and yet remain in business? Did that woman really think a big important producer like Danny La Valle would visit her little bookstore?

MissHeggerty: $10,000 for a big important producer to come to her store! How could anybody be so stupid as to believe that? Danny is close to being a billionaire!! It would be like pocket change to him.

MrDarcy: People are incredibly stupid and naïve. Delusions of grandeur on the part of those two idiots. It makes me wonder honestly about the intelligence of some people.

And so it went on. Comment after comment stating that Danny La Valle was a big important man and it was so stupid to believe he would come to a meet and greet in a little bookstore in a small city in the Southern States.

Jenny felt immediately angry. She felt like writing a reply to each of the comments, where she said, who would this person be without his fans? Nobody! He should care about his fans! But then she felt sad and the tears came. Perhaps she was an idiot to believe a Hollywood producer would come to her little bookstore!

She was sitting at the reception desk with tears rolling down her cheeks when Jinni and Noi walked in.

Jenny hastily blew her nose and dried her eyes, and tried to act normally.

“Hi,” she said. “Can I help?”

“I think actually we can help you,” Jinni said.

Noi then spoke up. “I also thought Danny La Valle was going to produce my books into a movie.”

She was silent for a moment as Jenny took this in.

“I have paid Robin Pine, who I now know is a fake, money I don’t have that I have had to borrow. This was money for PR, and rewrites for an American audience. Niran, my husband, doesn’t know I borrowed this money and I dread to think what will happen when he does.”

At this stage her lip trembled, and the tears came.

Jenny rushed around the counter and standing in her shop in front of shocked customers, she hugged Noi and the two of them stood together as they sobbed.

Chapter 55

Noi faces uncomfortable truths

Noi always read the news online. It was the first thing she did in the morning when she woke up. She loved the gossip magazines and reading about celebrities. One of her favorites was the Daily Trends. Sure, it had a lot of rubbish in it, but it could be very informative too, she felt.

Today as she had scrolled through the Daily Trends and had seen the article about Danny La Valle, she couldn't believe her eyes. She read it once, then she read it twice and then she felt sick to the pit of her stomach. This had to be made up. Jinni had messaged her to say she had got tickets for the book reading that Danny La Valle was going to attend, and they were both going to go. Surely this was made up?

She immediately got her cell phone out and rang Jinni to ask if she had seen the article. Jinni hadn't, and promised to read it and ring her back.

It was possible to forward the article, so Noi forwarded it to Robin Pine, with a request he contacted her immediately.

This couldn't be true! She got out of bed and started pacing around. She knew she had to take the children to school, so she had to behave normally.

She had gone into the bathroom and set the shower running. While in the shower, she had begun to placate herself by thinking about Danny La Valle. Perhaps this Glenda person had been mistaken. She knew Danny produced movies with plots similar to her book, but she had never known him to produce a children's book. Perhaps this woman had been mistaken and the fake Danny had contacted her. Surely it must have been the real Danny who Noi had been in touch with. But even as she thought this through, the sickening thought occurred to her that actually, she had never spoken to Danny La Valle. When she and Jinni had gone to Atlanta to hear him speak, he had been too busy to talk to any of his fans. She had accepted the word of Robin Pine that Danny was going to produce her book into a movie.

After drying herself from the shower, she looked at her cell phone. There were no messages. She looked at the message she had sent Robin Pine. She had received nothing in response. He was usually very quick in replying. A sick feeling had almost overwhelmed her.

There was a message from Jinni that said, "Please call. We must speak."

She went back into the bathroom and, locking the door, called Jinni. It was a painful conversation.

"This article has to be made up. What do the Americans say? Fake news," Noi said.

"Are you sure it is fake news? I don't mean to get down on you Noi, but are you sure?"

"Of course I am sure. Would I have given money to people who I thought were fakes?"

"The agent you spoke to was Robin Pine, correct?" asked Jinni.

Noi agreed that Robin Pine was his name.

"How do you know he is reputable?" Jinni urged. "Have you checked out his background and credentials?"

Noi became agitated. "You are as bad as Alpa. Just because the book club don't believe in him, doesn't mean he is not real."

"Alpa mentioned this to you, did you check it out?"

Noi became very angry at this point, and began shouting and spluttering.

"In the article, it says Robin Pine is affiliated with a New York agency called Stout and Bing," Jinni interrupted. "Why don't you ring there?"

There had been more spluttering and shouting.

"Come to the Purple Orchid later today. Can you come about 1 p.m.?"

Noi agreed to that and then wiping her tears, came out of the bathroom. Niran had been standing outside the door, and was looking furious. "What the heck have you been doing in there?" he demanded. "Shouting and carrying on. Who are you talking to?"

Noi decided to ignore his rants, and went to make the children's breakfasts. Their behavior was beyond belief, shouting and falling out and refusing to eat.

She found it hard to keep calm and had ended up shouting.

"Shut up the pair of you – and if you don't eat now, there is nothing tonight – no reading of a story, no TV, no nothing!"

"Nana lets us do what we want!" yelled Anong.

"We'll see about that!"

She had shooed them out of the kitchen, got them into their shoes, gave them their lunch boxes and driven them to school. She turned the radio up and tried to get them to sing along.

The morning had been spent at home cleaning and doing the laundry and avoiding Niran.

At 1 p.m. she had driven to the Purple Orchid. Jinni had just finished with a customer and they had gone to the back room. There, Jinni opened her laptop and typed 'Stout and Bing, New York' into a google search.

A firm of literary agents in Manhattan came up. One of the agents was indeed Robin Pine. He had been involved in the publication of some very successful novels and was a graduate of Cornell University.

Jinni then rang Stout and Bing and asked if she could speak to Robin Pine.

"Who may I say is calling?" asked the receptionist.

"I am calling on behalf of one of Robin's clients – the author of the Malami Hotel."

"What is the name of the author?"

"Noi Asnee."

"Just a moment."

There was silence for what seemed like an eternity and then the receptionist came back. "Mr. Pine does not have a client with the name Noi Asnee. Are you sure that you have the correct number and name?"

Jinni had thanked her and ended the call. The look on her face was of concern and pity.

So, who was the Robin Pine who Noi had spoken to?

It was at that moment that Noi first realized she had been conned. She leaned forward and put her head in her hands. She cried and cried and cried until the tears wouldn't come any more.

She had been conned out of money that could have been used for so many other more worthy things – to refurbish the restaurant, to redecorate the house, for the children's college funds, for a vacation. Not only had she been conned, but she had *borrowed* the money to give to the conman. Now she had to repay that money.

When the crying had stopped, Jinni had taken her hand and told her that they were going to go next door to speak to Jenny at Jenny's BookStop.

"Think how she must feel," Jinni had said. "It is her shop, her business that is in the news. So many people know that she has been involved in a fraud. Just when she was starting to build her business up, this happens."

So, walking together hand in hand, they had gone next door to the BookStop…

Chapter 56

Glenda refuses to believe in fake news

No matter how often she read the article in the Daily Trends, Glenda could not get her head around it or believe that it was true.

So many thoughts went through her head as she tried to find a rationale for the article.

Robin Pine might not have told his colleagues at Stout and Bing he was her agent. He was keeping the relationship under wraps until the TV show launched. She wondered if that was commonplace in the world of literary agents?

There was always the danger that if the fact that Danny La Valle was going to produce her book into a TV show became public, someone else might steal her ideas and produce a similar show.

The relationship between Glenda, Robin and Danny was to be kept top secret! That was one explanation.

She had read an interview in Daily Trends where Danny La Valle had stated he was a "private" person. He didn't like to have his personal affairs in the public arena. He talked about his daughter, Arriana, who was now 21 years old and a sophomore at university. She was to be protected at all costs from the public eye.

So perhaps Danny wanted to keep his relationship with her, Glenda, secret. She had spoken to him. How could she have spoken to him if he didn't know who she was?

Also, she had read that Hollywood celebrities had management who looked after them. Perhaps his "people" did not approve of him coming to the bookstore for the fee they had agreed and he was too embarrassed to admit that was why he was not coming.

Glenda felt that Danny was in her corner. He loved her book and he was going to produce a children's show.

No one had said anything the first day at school after the article appeared in the Daily Trends, although Glenda felt some people wouldn't meet her eye. It was on the second day that the principal called her to a meeting. Dr. Carlos Petite was a tall, ungainly man with a shock of black hair. He was not unkind, but he could be very blunt with his comments.

He asked Glenda straight out about the article in the Daily Trends.

"It is not publicity we would seek for this school, Glenda. Do you feel there is truth in what was said?"

Glenda spoke indignantly. "There is no truth in what was said. I have spoken to Danny La Valle and he intended to come to the event. I will sort this out and get back to you."

"Please do," Dr. Petite said. "These rags are a menace and we must do all we can to prevent fake news."

Glenda was determined to prove that she was right, and she drove home that evening thinking how she was going to do that.

Arriving home she was greeted by Billy, her partner, and it was not a pretty sight. He was sitting up at the kitchen island and he looked very angry. He had the Daily Trends up on his laptop.

"What the fuck is this?" he demanded. It was rare for Billy to use profanity, so Glenda knew he was very angry.

"It's just gossip. It's made-up rubbish!"

"You are *quoted* in here Glenda! You spoke to the reporter and told her that your agent was Robin Pine. That's what it says!"

Billy was scrolling down the article. "Here – Robin Pine is my literary agent, says Glenda Ortiz, and he introduced me to Danny La Valle, who will be producing a children's TV show of my book!"

He looked her straight in the eyes. "How come I don't know anything about this?"

Glenda was embarrassed and she felt close to tears.

"I wanted to surprise you," she said. "I only wanted you to know when my show was on television."

Billy looked at her in horror. "There is no show. The whole thing was a con. A fraud. You don't seriously think you are going to have a show on TV do you?"

Glenda didn't speak. Hot tears were welling up in her eyes. But something deep inside her told her that she was right and Billy was wrong. She was going to prove this.

"I am going to have a TV show," she said.

"You are a fool if you believe that." Billy stared at her. "Surely you know that you have been conned?"

"I have not been conned and I will prove it to you!" Glenda was in tears now but deep down she was determined to prove that she was right and he was wrong.

The beginning of June, 2024

A number of people go to Los Angeles

Patrice meets with Alison

Loretta follows up on the missing money

Glenda requests a meeting with Danny La Valle

Chapter 57

Patrice meets with Alison

The following Saturday, Patrice caught a flight to LA and left Clarrie in charge of the beauty salon. She had Alison's address and she was banking on the fact that as an accountant, Alison would work during the week and not on weekends.

She caught an Uber from the airport to the address in Tarzana. The townhouse looked well-kept as Patrice walked up the path. She had decided to surprise Alison and was now very nervous that this would pay off.

When she knocked on the door it was answered by a very handsome, suntanned young man wearing sweats.

"Hi, are you Barry?" she asked.

He nodded and seemed taken aback. "And you are?"

"My name is Patrice Underwood. I am the wife of Alison's first husband, Bill. I would like to speak to Alison about Bill."

"Just a moment, wait here," he said and closing the door, he disappeared.

Patrice stood on the step for what seemed like an eternity. She could hear traffic thundering by on nearby Tarzana Boulevard. If there were birds in this neighborhood, their song would be tuned out by the sound of the traffic. A man walked past with his dog, probably heading to a park. He smiled and nodded.

Finally, the door opened and a woman stood there. She was heavily pregnant and wearing sweats. Her hair was pulled back into a ponytail and she wore eyeglasses.

"Hello Patrice," she said. "I am Alison." She had an English accent, just like Bill. "Just wondering why you wanted to see me?"

"Please can I come in and explain?" Patrice felt she was almost pleading.

Alison stood to one side to allow her to come into the townhouse. Even so, the entry way was so small that Patrice felt herself brush against Alison's pregnant stomach.

The living area was open to the kitchen and doors opened out onto a small terrace. It was clean and tidy, but very small.

Alison indicated that Patrice should sit down. Barry was in the kitchen and he called out, "Would you like a coffee or a cup of tea?"

Patrice said she would like a coffee and there followed an awkward silence with Patrice and Alison silently eyeing one another up and down. They were very different, that was for sure. Patrice was beautiful and very well groomed. Even though it was morning, Patrice was wearing full makeup and had styled her hair. She was the 'unapproachable beauty'. Alison on the other hand, was more the 'girl next door' type of pretty. Her nails were not manicured and she wore no makeup. But her laugh was infectious and she radiated warmth.

Barry busied himself with making the coffee, but tried to break the silence. "We knew Bill had married again, Patrice, but we did not expect to meet you. I hope there are no problems between you and Bill."

Patrice spoke up then. "Bill and I have been married for nearly two years. I married him after knowing him for a very short period of time. He literally swept me off my feet. I found him kind, considerate and a real gentleman. I would have followed him to the ends of the earth."

Patrice explained about moving from Los Angeles, and Bill's new role with Stermer Media and the investment in the Purple Orchid.

"We were very happy, until very recently when some strange things have happened. People from his past have turned up and there have been allegations of…" here she stopped and looked down.

"Go on," Alison encouraged. "I think you are going to say… financial irregularities? Is that correct?"

Patrice nodded, tears not far away now. "I realized when this happened how little I know about Bill. I can't believe I married someone without knowing about their background, but I did and now I am worried that I don't know the man I married."

Barry and Alison looked at each other.

"Have you confided these feelings in Bill?" asked Alison.

"I have, but he is very reluctant to talk. He also tells me it is other people who are to blame – and I don't really know what to think." At this point, Patrice broke down in tears. "He is not the man I thought he was! There is so much that is coming out about his business dealings that is frightening."

Alison seemed genuinely concerned about Patrice's distress.

"If you feel it will help you to understand, I can tell you about my relationship with Bill and why we ended up divorcing. You are right that there may be some shady dealings in Bill's past and he will be reluctant to share them with you.

But first, how did you meet Bill, Patrice?"

This was awkward as Bill had paid Patrice for her silence. "It was when I was working as a makeup artist on a talk show and Danny La Valle was a guest." She had decided that wasn't a lie, it just wasn't the whole truth.

Alison nodded, although deep down she knew Patrice wasn't being 100% truthful with her. She also had a feeling that Patrice had got in over her head with Bill. She would talk to Patrice, but she guessed that Patrice was a gold digger looking for a rich, older man. Oh dear, she had picked the wrong person with Bill! She was finding out now, too late, how Bill was a clever, weasel of a man who would make sure he held on to his money.

"Sit and enjoy your coffee, Patrice, and I will tell you about my relationship with Bill."

Chapter 58

Alison's love story

In between sips of her tea, Alison began to talk about her relationship with Bill. It was a long time since she had really talked about him, and she found it brought back conflicting emotions when she talked about him now. She started at the beginning when they first met.

"I met Bill when we were at university in the UK. He was a lovely, quiet person who was always kind. He did not drink or smoke or do drugs. He was a serious student, who usually attended lectures and seminars. He might not have been the most exciting bloke but I didn't want excitement, I wanted someone who would be my best friend – and that is what we were, best friends. I could tell Bill anything and vice versa. He knew all my secrets and I knew all his.

After university, we both went into accounting and worked at Meyer and Co. in London. Bill won a prize in the accounting exams and impressed the partners with his technical ability. I was much more of a plodder. I passed my exams, but I was never outstanding.

We lived together in London, and after a year or so, Bill took me to meet his parents in Fishponds, Bristol. Bill had a much older sister, and his parents were elderly. They were both teachers and the conversation was about how Bill had already passed them by in terms of earning ability. They were nice, but I got the feeling he was not particularly close with them.

After Bill had qualified, he was given the chance to work in the Los Angeles office of Meyer and Co. Everyone wanted this opportunity but only one person per year was chosen. There was no way he wasn't going to go, so we decided to get married so I could follow him.

Even though we were married it still took a while for me to be able to get papers to go to the USA. In fact, it was not until Meyer and Co. got a green card for Bill. We lived apart for two years. During this time, we spoke all the time and I made a couple of visits to LA.

When I first moved here it was blissful. We were finally together! Bill had by this time secured a promotion at Meyer and Co. and was now a senior manager. I was able to find work with a small firm in Pasadena, but I had to take exams again to qualify as a CPA.

At first, I was so happy to be with Bill that I did not notice how he had changed. He had always worked hard, so that was no different. I still did not see much of him although we lived together again. I was busy studying for the CPA exam and I guess I was tired when we were together, but even so, I started to notice that we did not talk when we were together. There was no real communication. I asked questions and he just grunted responses.

Bill wanted us to buy a house, and we agreed Pasadena would be the place to buy for us. Housing was very expensive, and the house we bought was a fixer upper in the beautiful Brigden ranch. The area was so gorgeous – the streets were lined with oak trees and there was an incredible view of the San Gabriel Mountains. There was a lot of work to do –

both inside and out. As I worked less hours, I was in charge of renovations.

We lived in the house while it was renovated. Bill was never there, working increasingly long hours. He was promoted to partner in 2014. As you know, partners own the firm and share the profits.

It was during this time that he changed. We had always been careful with money, after all we were both accountants so knew how to put a budget together and live within our means.

We had always had a joint bank account, but at this time he opened a new account where I presume, he started paying in the payments he received from Meyer and Co. I did not have access to this account, and every month he moved money over to the joint account to pay the bills. He became more secretive and did not discuss the bills with me.

He also bought a new Mercedes, a new wardrobe of expensive suits and started going to an expensive salon in Beverly Hills for haircuts and, believe it or not, manicures.

He bought me a Mercedes and told me I should go out and buy new clothes on a credit card he gave me. The card was in his name.

I had to look the part as the partner's wife! But don't forget, I am an accountant too, and it seemed to me we were spending more than he earned. However, as I didn't know what he earned anymore it was difficult to say for sure. It didn't stop me discussing it with him.

He told me that he had been given an advance on his partner's equity. This was not convincing to me, as I knew that to be accepted as a partner in an accounting firm, you had to pay money into the partnership! Not the other way round!

At this time, he had a client, Global Pictures. He spent many hours there, as he said there were issues with their accounts. This was when the secretive phone calls started. He would get in late and I would warm him some food and sit with him. His phone would ring and he would excuse himself so he did not have to speak in front of me.

One day, he was in the bathroom, freshening up before eating, and had left his cell phone on the kitchen table. It rang and I picked it up. I spoke to a man who said he was Danny and he wanted Bill to ring him back asap as "he was in deep shit".

When I relayed the message to Bill, he was furious, yelling at me about answering his phone. It was only later that the penny dropped that I had been speaking to Danny La Valle."

At this point, Alison stopped speaking. Both women sat quietly as they wondered what it was that Danny wanted and what he meant by "in deep shit".

Chapter 59

Alison talks about the end of her relationship with Bill

Alison had been open with Patrice so far, but now as she got into talking about the events leading up to the end of her relationship, she seemed more emotional and got up and walked over to the window. She was silent for a few minutes, and then she returned and sitting down, continued her monologue.

"I knew one or two people who worked with Bill. Karl was a good friend, and we saw Karl and his partner, Jess, for dinner at this time. Work was never discussed, but I followed Karl when he went to the bathroom and waited outside. I asked if he knew if there were any problems at Global Pictures. He wasn't willing to tell me anything, well not that evening he wasn't, but later, he made up for his silence.

It seemed that very quickly Global Pictures were in the gossip magazines with stories of arguments between the two owners, Dino and Danny. Millions of dollars in royalties from their movies were in dispute. The whole thing was a mess.

I wanted to talk to Bill about it. I knew that Global Pictures were his client and that he must have views on what was going on. It was at this time that it became obvious that Bill did not see me as a friend or as someone he wanted to confide in. He would brush off any questions with flip answers such as "And you believe gossip magazines now?" It was incredibly frustrating.

The next thing I knew, Bill was leaving Meyer and Co. to go and work with Danny at a new company Danny was setting up called Avalon Media. The whole thing stunk! It was obvious to me at least that there had been some wrongdoing and that it was being glossed over for the public."

She was silent for a moment. "Did Bill discuss his decision to leave with you?" Patrice asked.

"No – he told me after the fact, when it had been decided he would go to Avalon. There was no discussion. No asking what I thought. It was a done deal."

Patrice could see that this would be difficult for Alison.

"Plus," Alison confided, "he now became even more secretive. I was given money each month to pay the household bills, but there was no discussion about how much he earned at Avalon. I did ask, but he told me not to worry, that he was earning plenty."

She was now obviously upset talking about Bill. "I was in a foreign country away from my family and I felt that my husband was no longer my close friend. There was so much that was secretive. Plus, it was very unusual for anyone who had been promoted to partner at Meyer and Co. to leave so quickly. In my mind, I felt he was somehow tied into the arguments between Danny and Dino at Avalon. Especially as he went to Avalon with Danny."

Barry came over then. "Do you feel you should take a break, Alison?" he asked. "This is obviously upsetting for you, and you have to think of the baby."

Alison squeezed his hand and smiled. "I am fine. I have nearly finished now."

She went on. "I rang Karl and asked to see him. Bill had now left Meyer and Co. Karl was prepared to talk as he said he was concerned about Bill. It seems he was involved in the fallout at Global Pictures. Dino and Danny were shouting and making accusations. Dino said that there was money missing and that is when Danny brought Bill into it. He said Bill had checked the accounts and he had said everything was fine. Karl didn't know everything about the arguments, but he feels Meyer and Co. were able to cover things up and get Danny and Dino to make an agreement. Part of that agreement was that Bill would leave to work for Danny."

Patrice stared at Alison. "Does no one know about the arguments? Was there a fraud that Bill was involved in? I'm not an accountant, but it sounds to me like he left under a cloud."

"He certainly left under a cloud. But I was stonewalled by his firm, his colleagues and Bill himself. I am not sure if it was incompetence or if he was involved in some underhand scheme."

Patrice sat silently taking all this in. She waited for Alison to go on.

"When Bill began working for Danny, things got worse. He worked very long hours and I barely saw him. Sometimes when we were together, there were strange phone calls that Bill always took in private. His secrecy and our failing relationship made me want to confide in somebody. At the time, I was working part-time as I was busy taking charge of the refurbishment on the house. Part of this involved having a pool built. Barry's firm built the pool and Barry was involved in the maintenance.

When Barry used to come to service the pool, we started chatting and having a laugh together. Barry was everything Bill wasn't. He was warm, funny and caring. I fell head over heels in love.

I know this sounds like a cliché, but one afternoon Bill came home early from work and caught Barry and I in bed together. He was absolutely furious. He gave me an ultimatum. He told me that I should end the relationship or it was the end of our marriage. I chose Barry."

"Bill must have been devastated," Patrice said.

"He was. He talked a lot about money and how he had given me an expensive home and possessions. He didn't understand that meant nothing to me – I wanted love."

There was a heavy silence, as both women contemplated what love really meant to them.

Then Alison dropped the bombshell.

"Bill was not prepared to divorce amicably. We had a contested divorce as I wanted my share of the house, and some money from him. After all, he had been the main breadwinner. He refused to move out of the house in Pasadena, so I moved in with Barry. We stayed first in an apartment he was renting in Reseda. After we had employed attorneys and began discussing how our assets should be divided up, it became particularly nasty. I had told you that Bill had a private account where he received his salary and I did not know what his salary was. The figures he presented were shocking. The house in Pasadena was valued at two million dollars but there were various notes for the purchase and refurbishment for one and a half million dollars. He had minimal investments and he said his salary at Avalon was a hundred thousand dollars. This was low for a chief operating officer, as I am sure you know. In addition, he had taken personal loans and borrowed money to buy the cars – his net worth was about zero."

Patrice felt sick – this was the man she had thought was wealthy. "I guess this was all a fabrication, so he didn't have to give you anything?"

Alison nodded. "The divorce was a nightmare. He couldn't hide his pension, but he hid any other asset he might have had. Danny backed him up about the pay at Avalon and he could provide evidence of the loans. I got my attorney to check money overseas, but Bill is very clever. My attorney found nothing. In the end we settled and I got the house in Pasadena plus a share in his pension and some cash he had. When I sold the house in Pasadena, I cleared four hundred and fifty thousand dollars out of it and used that as a deposit on this townhouse."

Patrice felt anger for Alison. "You feel he cheated you, don't you?" she said.

"You bet he cheated me! The man is a master of creative accounting and if I was you, I would get something in writing now. What do you know about what he earns?"

Patrice felt inadequate and stupid. "I don't know," she admitted.

"What investments does he have? Are you a joint owner in the house you live in?"

"I know, I know. I have been stupid," Patrice sighed. She then talked about Bill helping her get set up in her beauty salon business. “I one hundred percent trusted him.”

Alison took hold of her hand and looked her in the eye. “If I were you, I would stop trusting and start looking out for myself from today.”

It was good advice, but it didn’t stop Patrice crying on the plane on the journey home. What a fool she had been.

Chapter 60

Loretta makes a second visit to Los Angeles

It was the missing $1 million that intrigued Loretta. How could so much money be missing and yet nothing seemed to have been done about it?

She had flown back to LA, hired a car, and was the first person to arrive at the offices of Avalon Media on Monday morning. She went to a small coffee shop in the lobby of the building while she waited for the staff to arrive. She had a long wait. After waiting for what seemed like forever, the receptionist in the lobby told her that someone had finally arrived at 10 a.m. Her credentials were checked out very carefully and a security guard even patted her down! Finally, she was allowed in the elevator to the 4th floor. Exiting the elevator, she walked into the reception area where a tall, slightly stooped man was waiting to meet her.

“Hi,” he said. “I am Kyle Janus, the Finance Director. How can I help you?”

Loretta explained that she was a private investigator employed by the wife of Bill Underwood. His wife wished to have more information about what had happened at Avalon Media before he left, and in particular, if he was involved in a fraud investigation.

Kyle indicated that Loretta should go into his office. He asked to check her license after she had sat down.

“There is an investigation into missing money, you are correct there. A firm of professional accountants are looking into it for us." He eyed Loretta curiously. "You say Mrs. Underwood is interested in the investigation?"

"Yes," Loretta replied. "She wishes to know if her husband is implicated."

Kyle hesitated for a moment. "Does she have information that would be helpful to the investigation?"

"She may have some information when she knows more about the investigation," Loretta said.

"You must understand, I will need to clear this with Danny," said Kyle.

Loretta agreed to this and they exchanged numbers so Kyle could get in touch. She didn't have to wait long. Kyle gave her the name and number of an accountant who was looking into the missing money and said it was fine for her to contact him.

Loretta followed up quickly. The accounting firm were Purcell and Associates, and the contact was Dave Purcell. They were a small firm with offices on Sunset Boulevard. Dave agreed to meet with Loretta at his office later that day.

The offices were in a shop front that had seen better days and were slightly rundown. This was a surprise to Loretta. She had expected better, but she tried not to judge.

Dave Purcell was a middle-aged man whose hair was receding. He had a paunch and his shirt strained over his stomach. He had pulled his tie off and his shirt was open. He came out to reception to greet her, and puffed and panted on the way back to his office.

Entering his office, she could see that the furniture was chipped and dated. Dave's desk was untidy and piled with his laptop and various papers, plus the remnants of his lunch.

"Sit down, sit down," he said, indicating an old chair in front of his desk. "Now I understand your client is married to Bill Underwood?"

"Yes, that is correct. She is interested to find out more about Bill's employment at Avalon."

"Is this a divorce investigation?" he asked.

"No, it is not a divorce. My client wants to become more familiar with her husband's financial affairs."

Dave smiled. "Of course. I get it, and how can I help?"

Loretta explained how she had been informed by former employees that there was a large sum of money missing from Avalon. This had occurred while Bill was the chief operating officer. She wanted to find out more about the money and whether there were any implications for Bill in its being missing.

Dave asked if Loretta's client had discussed the money with Bill. Loretta said Bill had implicated another member of staff and said it related to an account with a PR company. The company was called Lorimar, but the money went to another account altogether – *Lorrimar*, spelled differently with two r's.

"Yes, that is correct, we have found that a number of payments were sent to this fake company. However, the fake company was not registered in the US. The company is registered in the Philippines."

This surprised Loretta. “The Philippines?” she queried.

“Yes, that is right,” said Dave. “We could find out the names of the owners, but the company is protected by data protection laws and other legislation.”

“Who are the owners?” asked Loretta.

“They are listed as two Americans – Robin Pine and Lulu Bartlett. Have you heard of these people?”

Loretta, making notes, had to admit she hadn’t heard of either of them.

“Please follow up with your client, to find out if she has heard of them. Also, there are other affiliated companies. Stark Press, which is a publishing company and Stout & Bing, a firm of literary agents. Together they employ a number of people to work for them in the Philippines. However, due to the data protection law, we can’t find out much about them.

Additionally, we have served notice on the company for return of the monies, and we have been informed that the company has insufficient funds to do so. We were sent a copy of their audited accounts which would suggest this is the case.”

Loretta was scribbling on her small pad. “So, the money went to the Philippines and then Robin Pine and Lulu Bartlett moved it on somewhere else? Where do you think it went?”

Dave smiled. “That, Loretta, is what we all would like to know. Money went to the Philippines. From there the trail goes cold. We would be grateful for any information.”

“And at no time was Bill Underwood involved?”

"Bill authorized the original money transfers, however, it cannot be shown that he had any involvement with the company receiving the money in the Philippines. We have never been able to contact the individuals Robin and Lulu who were listed as owners."

"Can you show that Bill was negligent in authorizing the transfers?" Loretta asked.

"That is ongoing at the moment," said Dave. "Can we keep in touch? Can you ask your client about the names I gave you and see if she can shed any light on it?"

Loretta promised to stay in touch and they ended the meeting.

Later in her motel room, she typed up the second part of her report and sent it to Patrice to ask if she had heard of the people and companies that Dave mentioned.

Chapter 61

Patrice has a Zoom call with Maddie – Bill's sister in Fishponds, Bristol

Patrice had set up a Zoom call with Maddi, Bill's sister. She had spoken to Maddi with Bill on Zoom a few times in the past. On two occasions his parents had joined Maddi on the call. His father had early onset dementia, and it was hard for him to talk on Zoom. She realized she had not spoken to his parents for over a year now. The truth was, Bill did not often speak to his family, and as far as she knew he had not visited them since she had known him.

Maddi was older than Bill and in her early fifties. Dowdy and plain, she worked at home, for Patrice believed, a call center answering complaints. She had never married, which was not a great surprise to look at her. Bill's parents were in their late seventies and Maddi also doubled as a carer for them.

Patrice had never been to Fishponds where Bill's family lived. It was a suburb of Bristol, about three miles north of the city center. The houses were mainly Victorian terraces and the Underwoods had a large Victorian house near to the shops and bus routes. Patrice had once commented that it sounded "charming" and Bill had laughed and said it was more like inner city squalor.

Maddi was sitting in the dining room when the Zoom camera came on. She wore eyeglasses and had her hair cut in a short bob. She wore no makeup and had a plain, pale face. Patrice wondered if she could do a make-over on her. Then she pulled herself up short. Stop being bitchy, she thought.

The dining room curtains were closed and the house had a dank, gloomy atmosphere. Maddi looked depressed and smiled only briefly when she saw Patrice.

"To what do I owe the pleasure of this call?" she asked in her British accent.

Patrice felt she sounded condescending and snooty, but thought this was probably just her way as a British woman.

"Hi Maddi, how are you?" Patrice had a false smile on now.

"As well as can be expected, caring for both parents day in and day out." Maddi affected a false smile. She didn't enquire about Patrice or Bill.

"I just wanted to have a chat and find out how things were with you and Bill's parents." Patrice realized it sounded lame.

"Well dear." Maddi stared into the camera. "Much the same as ever. Mum and dad don't go out much now. Mum is in a wheelchair and I sometimes wheel her over to Page Park in Staple Hill with dad walking alongside. She still likes to come shopping and we go to the Sainsburys supermarket in Emersons Green. Other than that, they stay here and watch TV."

"And how is your job, Maddi?" Patrice asked.

"Again, much the same as ever. Not much going on there. I don't live the high life like Bill in the States."

Although she laughed to cover it up, Patrice could feel the bitterness in her voice.

"I hope that Bill and I can come back to visit you all real soon." Patrice knew it sounded hollow.

"Yay, right." Maddi was still staring at her through the camera.

"Actually," Patrice started, getting down to the real reason for the call, "I wanted to know a little bit more about Bill's life before I met him. I feel that as we don't live near, I can't come around and ask to see pictures of him growing up with his family. I would really love to come and visit you, but Bill has been so busy at work that it has not been possible so far. I was just curious."

Maddi peered at her as if she was an idiot and then sighed heavily. "Bill is always busy, making the big money from what I have heard.

I am not sure what I can tell you. Bill and I had a very normal childhood. Our parents were teachers here in Fishponds. Bill was always the clever one and he got a scholarship to a private school. He excelled there and was able to go to university where he studied to be an accountant. I was the dull, plodding one and I didn't go on to university.

After university in Birmingham, Bill moved to London, so he has not lived with us here since he was eighteen. I, on the other hand, never left home and have lived here all my life.

I worked as a bookkeeper for a number of years and then as our parents got older, I became their carer and now do this work online from home.

What did we do growing up? Well, we used to have days out in Weston-super-Mare on the beach and we would go away to Devon and Cornwall in the summer for a week's holiday in a caravan.

Our parents were good parents and were always there for us – now I am always there for them."

"Did you go to church?" Patrice enquired.

"Oh, are you a religious person? Well, at Christmas and Easter we went to All Saints Parish Church, but we were never regular churchgoers."

It seemed to Patrice that Maddi answered questions but did not respond by asking about her.

Maddi then lapsed into a long monologue about her parents' health – which appeared to Patrice to be poor. Her father had dementia which was predicted to get worse. She wondered how much longer she could care for him at home. Meanwhile, her mother had diabetes, was now clinically obese, and also had arthritis and spine problems which meant she could not walk. Additionally, her mother had age-related macular degeneration, which meant that she was going blind. She struggled to read a book now and Maddi had to read to her. Their lives were cruel and full of pain. The end would be a blessing in Maddi's view.

Patrice ended the conversation feeling that they should have visited more and perhaps she should ask Bill about a visit in the future. She felt depressed for the rest of the day, Maddi was so downtrodden and dreary. His parents were, reportedly, sick and near the end of their lives. Yet Bill never talked about his family. It seemed he had dismissed them in his mind when he moved to the US. He was now living the good life in the States and had forgotten the people who raised him in Great Britain.

Maddi's plain, sad face haunted Patrice for the rest of the day. She wondered about Bill. It spoke volumes that he did not go back to visit them. She had considered him to be so kind and loving, a true gentleman. In truth he was cruel to the family that had raised him, cutting them off for all intents and purposes and never returning to see them.

It was a very sad and painful situation.

Chapter 62

Glenda is determined to meet with Danny La Valle

After talking to Billy and Dr. Petite, Glenda had become very angry. She reasoned that she was a bright, intelligent woman – well aware of cons and frauds on the internet. After all, she had spoken to Danny on a video call! Of course It was him!

She sent a private message to Danny's Instagram account in which she asked Danny to confirm he was going to televise her children's book. No answer.

It was at this point that she did something foolish. She clicked on the article in the Daily Trends. It seemed other people were still reading it, as there were now over 1,000 comments. She clicked on the comments section and immediately wished she hadn't.

Bookaholic: If Glenda Ortiz is a teacher, we have to pray for our children. How can someone so stupid be in charge of our children's education?

Egghead: As if a big famous Hollywood producer would produce a TV show from a book by a total unknown. Some people are so arrogant.

Mountainwoman: Danny La Valle is filming his new movie near my home in the Appalachian Mountains. I have seen him and the crew. He waved and smiled when I drove past him going to the grocery store. He is a rich producer and anyone would know he wouldn't be involved with a Meet and Greet at a tiny unknown bookstore.

Bigfanclub: Glenda is ugly. Why she would think Danny La Valle would want her is mad. The woman is crazy.

Glenda became furious after reading these comments. It was appalling that the Daily Trends did not censor comments, she felt. The last one she had read was particularly cruel and off topic. Also, why wouldn't Danny La Valle produce her book? Her book was good. He would be lucky to have the chance to produce her book.

She was so incensed she could not sleep. She tossed and turned all night, disturbing Billy. It did not help that they weren't speaking, either. About 4 a.m. she gave up trying to sleep, and going into the kitchen, she sat at the counter and fired up the laptop. She looked at the cost of cheap flights to Los Angeles and booked the earliest she could find.

At 6 a.m. after a quick shower, she drove to the airport. Once there, she text the school to say she was sick and having a day off.

It was a short flight to Los Angeles, and when she arrived, she paid an Uber to take her to Sunset Boulevard. She had looked up the address of Danny's production company, Avalon Media, on his website. Going into the building, she was met with a receptionist on the first floor.

"How can I help?" asked the receptionist.

"I would like to meet with Danny La Valle at Avalon Media. Please can I go through to the office?"

The receptionist eyed her up and down.

"Do you have an appointment?" she asked.

"Not exactly, but he knows me," Glenda said. "I am sure he would wish to talk to me about recent, um, developments."

"Mr. La Valle is not in the office today," the receptionist said. "Plus, he does not see people without an appointment."

Of course, Glenda could have kicked herself, didn't one of the comments say he was filming in the Appalachian Mountains? How stupid she was!

"Can I speak to his PA?" she persisted.

"You cannot speak to anyone at Avalon without an appointment. What I would recommend is that you get in touch with the office online and make an appointment."

"But I am here now!" Glenda was getting angry. "Please can I speak to someone – I feel there has been a terrible mistake. Say my name – Glenda Ortiz – they will know who I am."

"Very well ma'am," the receptionist said. "Just wait over there and I will speak to someone."

Glenda stood back from the counter, but noticed that a very tall, burly man had come into the room. He was wearing a security guard uniform. He nodded at her and at the receptionist.

The receptionist was speaking quietly on the phone. She then called Glenda over.

"Can you outline your business with Avalon, please."

"I want to clear up the misunderstanding about my book, Gwendoline Investigates. There was an article in the Daily Trends that said Danny would not be appearing at a meet and greet at a bookstore to promote my book. I wished to discuss this with him."

"One second please." The receptionist picked up the phone. "Wait over there."

More whispering into the phone. The security guard stood in front of the elevators. Glenda stood, like a naughty child, in the corner, straightening her top and smoothing her hair. Her breath was coming in short gasps and she was trying to regulate her breathing. This was ridiculous, she told herself. There was probably less security at Fort Knox.

Finally, the receptionist called her over.

"If you wish to follow up on your book and the meet and greet, you may contact Mr. La Valle's attorney. If you let me have your email, I can send through details of how to get in contact with him."

Glenda was shaking. "Please, let me speak to someone in the office. I have spoken to Danny about this and I know it is all a mistake."

"That is not going to be possible, but as I said, if you give me your email address you may contact Mr. La Valle's attorney."

Glenda lost it at this stage. "I don't want to speak to the fucking attorney! Can you not hear me? It is all a mistake!" She was really yelling now, and she was leaning over the reception desk.

She felt a hand on her back and she was aware that the security guard was directly behind her. "Come along, ma'am," he said. "It is time to leave now."

Gently, he turned her so she faced the outside door, and holding on to her, he moved her outside. It was not true to say that he frog marched her, but it felt like it, and in Glenda's eyes it was just as humiliating.

Once outside, she knew she could not go back and she had not got the name of the attorney. She stood there shaking with the dreadful realization that Danny La Valle did not know her and was as much a victim as she was. Someone had played on her desire for people to read her book and had conned and cheated her. The cruelty was beyond anything she could even begin to comprehend.

My book is good, she told herself over and over. Children who have read my book have said they love it. I have sold a few hundred copies on the self-publishing website. Why wouldn't a Hollywood producer be interested in it? Anybody would have believed what I believed. Wouldn't they?

She had checked out Robin Pine and she saw online that he worked at a literary agency in New York. She now knew though, that she had to try to speak to him through this literary agency. This person had denied knowing her, according to the Daily Trends.

Standing in the street outside the offices in the shade of the building, she googled Stout and Bing, New York. She then rang and asked to speak to Robin Pine.

"Who may I say is speaking?" said the receptionist.

"It is Glenda Ortiz, one of his clients. The author of Gwendoline Investigates."

There was silence for a moment and then the receptionist spoke. "Mr. Pine does not represent anyone of that name. You are mistaken. I cannot put you through to him."

This time Glenda did not argue. She ended the call and with her back against the wall, slid down until she was sitting on the sidewalk with her knees raised.

She had been conned. There was no TV show and no PR. She had made a fool of herself in front of her partner, her father, Jenny at the BookStop, the people in her city and the whole world in the Daily Trends.

People passed, going in and out of the building giving her strange looks. She put her head in between her knees so she did not have to look at them. She sat for what seemed like the longest time. Then she stood up and paying for an Uber she made a promise to herself – she would get revenge on whoever had done this to her.

June 3rd, 2024

Loretta hears from Zoe

Patrice faces her demons

Jinni meets with Patrice

Chapter 63

Loretta hears from Zoe

Loretta was back home and enjoying a nice long lie-in on Sunday morning when her cell phone pinged with a message. It was Zoe, asking her to ring as soon as possible.

Zoe seemed excited. "I caught up with Sheila," she explained. "I put out that I was looking for her, and she got in touch."

"Great," said Loretta. "What is happening with her?"

"You know Lord Peter Walker, don't you?" Zoe asked.

Loretta had vaguely heard the name, but had to admit she was not that familiar with him.

"He is a media sensation in LA. He just starred in Dino Latent's dark comedy, Love in Dark Times. Handsome, rich as fuck and has just inherited a fucking castle in Scotland. A distant relation of the royal family. Man, he is something."

Loretta was frantically googling as they spoke, and pictures came up of Lord Peter Walker – one in which he was wearing a kilt and striding around Scottish moors, and in another he was in shorts and T shirt, walking on the beach in LA. She had to admit he was a handsome man. She had not watched the movie he had starred in, but knew that it had been a media success.

Zoe was getting carried away with herself. "Well, it turns out that Sheila had, through her contacts, heard that he needed someone to do the accounts for his production company. She applied and got an interview. Apparently, they hit it off straight away, but get this." Here Zoe paused for effect. "Danny La Valle would not give her a reference. He said that she had to speak to Bill. When she spoke to Bill, he was not willing to help her either. What a pair of slime balls! So she lost the job!"

Loretta could see that this would be devastating for Sheila. "Can she not demand a reference?" she asked.

"Well, she could, but the implication was that it would be poor and she still wouldn't get the job."

"Thanks for finding this out, Zoe," Loretta said. "Should I assume that Sheila is still unemployed?"

"She has now left LA to go travelling," Zoe said. "I tried to ask her to contact you before she went, but she was not interested. She is starting south of here and going to go to the Philippines where she knows some people and she intends to stay a few months. She is hoping that either the issues with Danny and Bill will blow over while she is away or she will find somewhere better to live."

Loretta asked if Zoe could let her have Sheila's contact details. Zoe sent this through and Loretta thanked her.

Loretta tried to get in touch with Sheila immediately after the meeting with Zoe was over. It took a while for Sheila to respond, though. When she did, she sent the following text:

"You say you work for Patrice Underwood, Bill's wife, and you want to find out about Avalon Media. Let me tell you this, Bill Underwood is a

fraud. He was taking Danny La Valle's money all the time he worked for him. Danny was off his head on drugs and booze so had no idea what was happening to him. Bill took full advantage. He is a slime ball. I did as Bill told me and was paid a very nice salary. However, I did not defraud Danny out of any money and that is the honest truth. They now refuse to give me a reference so I am fucked, basically. I am going travelling and want to forget about the whole miserable time working at Avalon Media. Please don't contact me again."

Loretta never did meet Sheila, who left the next day to go travelling. However, she noted all this to report back to Patrice. The reference to the Philippines she found particularly interesting. She had no doubt Sheila had profited enormously during Danny's episodes with drink and drugs.

Lord Peter Walker was well off without her, she thought as she typed up her report.

Chapter 64

Patrice has more questions for Bill

Bill and Patrice no longer shared a bed. Patrice had moved into a smaller room along the corridor. Now the weather was warm, Bill rose early each day and swam a few lengths in the swimming pool.

He was a good, strong swimmer and the swimming cleared his mind.

Today, as he was toweling himself dry, Patrice came out with a coffee for him. She was avoiding his eyes and was about to leave when Bill spoke and asked her to sit down.

“Can we talk please, Patrice?” he asked. “This silence is killing me.”

Patrice sat down. “What do you want to talk about? From my point of view, I have so many questions, Bill,” she said.

“I feel you have been listening to gossip and you believe this over what I have told you. We were so happy together until you listened to idle gossip. It is breaking my heart.”

“Is it gossip?” Patrice asked. “Okay, let’s sit down for five minutes and we can go over what I am concerned about.”

They moved over and sat down at the outside table, each holding a coffee cup.

Patrice sighed. “I almost don’t know where to begin. Okay, let’s start at the beginning. Why did you leave Meyer and Co., Bill? The truth.”

Bill rolled his eyes. "Why are you asking this now, Patrice? When we met you were happy to accept me for myself. There were no questions about my past. Yet it seems that place I invested in, the Purple Orchid, is a hive of gossip and you were so quick to become embroiled in it. To doubt me, your *husband*. Have you no idea how hurtful that is to me? I, who have always loved and trusted you. Have I ever asked you questions about your past?"

Patrice started stuttering. "There has been no need. There are no rumors about me. I just want to end the rumors about you, Bill. To have the truth from you."

Bill took a sip of his coffee. "End the rumors? Patrice, you can end the rumors yourself. Tell these people you don't believe them. That is all it takes to end the rumors."

He looked at her. She looked away.

"Have you heard of Tall Poppy Syndrome?" he asked. She shook her head. "All poppies should be the same height and if one is taller everyone wants to cut them down to size. This is not Hollywood, Patrice. This is small-town America. Small- minded people. You are a beautiful, multi-racial woman and I am a successful media executive. We stand out – we stand taller – and people want to cut us down to size. The only way to deal with such rubbish is to rise above it and refuse to listen and be intimidated."

Again, Patrice was silent. She turned her coffee cup around and around and studied the pattern on it.

"Okay," she finally said. "I see what you are saying, but it does not make sense with what happened here. The people who are saying these things are people who used to work with you. Sheila Kavanagh, who worked with you in LA, came here and spoke to me. Becky, who worked with you at Stermer, spoke to me. These are not just idle gossips, they are former colleagues. From two different places. If it was just one colleague, I could overlook it, but two colleagues from two different places? That is what is troubling me."

Bill nodded. "Both women with axes to grind, as I explained to you. For goodness' sake Patrice, what is wrong with you?"

There was another silence, and then Patrice spoke. "I went to LA and talked to Alison."

She saw the color come up on Bill's cheek and a muscle start twitching. "*Pardon*?" he said. "You did what??"

"I wanted to find out about her. You said she had gone back to England, but that isn't true, she is living in Tarzana in the San Fernando Valley. She told me a lot about you and the divorce."

Bill was furious now. "How fucking *dare* you?" He was shaking with rage. "You two- faced, scheming bitch! Going behind my back. Why? Why do that? I notice you didn't care about Alison when we first met and you wanted to live in my house and become my wife. Haven't I always given you everything you have ever asked for?" Tears started to roll down his cheeks. "Look at this house, I gave you this. The beauty salon, the car, the clothes, the jewelry. You were happy to take all these things but *now* you start to question me?

You visited Alison behind my back. You don't know anything about Alison. For your information, Alison is a two-timing, underhand bitch. She was screwing the pool guy while I was at work, earning money so she could live in a beautiful home. Don't you realize she hates me as I hired a good attorney and I made sure she didn't get her hands on my money."

He stood, and turning his back on Patrice, made his way towards the house. He had answered none of her questions and now appeared heartbroken. For a moment, she felt a pang of regret. Perhaps she should have kept quiet and her perfect life could have gone on. This was only a feeling she had for a moment, because she knew there was something really wrong and she had to find out what it was. Getting up, she also walked into the house. It was so beautiful that even after living there for several months, it still took her breath away. But she had to be strong, even if it meant that her days living there were numbered. She took her cell phone out and messaged Jinni to arrange to meet with her at closing time that day.

Chapter 65

Jinni

Meeting with Patrice

The nail and beauty salons had closed for the day, and Randi was cleaning when I sat down with Patrice in the coffee shop area.

This was not the same woman who had designed the beauty salon and organized the grand opening in March. This was a worried woman, and it also worried me a great deal. Patrice spoke first.

"I'm sorry I didn't come and speak to you the day after our last conversation. The truth is, I went to LA to speak to Bill's ex-wife, Alison. I have also had a private investigator looking into his affairs."

This took me aback. "I see," I said. "You will appreciate that this is very worrying for me. Bill agreed to be an investor in my business and since this happened, and you opened the beauty salon, business has been better. I have felt some relief from anxiety about money. In fact, I feel this new building is doing exceedingly well. These rumors about Bill that are circulating are not what I want to hear. I hope that your visit and the PI helped to put an end to the rumors."

Patrice then told me everything she had found out – and believe me, it was not what I wanted to hear. In fact, it was extremely disturbing.

"So," I said, "let me summarize – he left Meyer and Co. and Avalon, most probably under a cloud. Plus, there is money missing from Avalon. He has fired someone at Stermer who is saying there is fraud there. He has been involved in an acrimonious divorce that has left him broke."

"There is more," said Patrice. "When my private investigator visited Avalon Media, they asked if I had heard the names Robin Pine and Lulu Bartlett. Wasn't it Robin Pine who rang Noi?"

"Yes, she was first contacted by Lulu Bartlett who put her in touch with Robin Pine. Why?"

"Those are the names of people who own a company in the Philippines. This company is fraudulent, and money was sent there from Avalon Media."

"When Bill worked at Avalon?" I wanted to be sure.

"Yes, that was the case," said Patrice.

"Are they real people or just made-up people?" I asked.

"The real Lulu Bartlett is an author and the real Robin Pine is a literary agent, but neither has anything to do with the company in the Philippines. The people in the Philippines are con artists pretending to be other people."

I felt sick and spoke angrily. "How can this have happened? Are you saying that you think Bill might be involved with the fraud coming out of the Philippines?"

I realized I shouldn't have spoken so hastily. Patrice broke down in tears. She got a tissue out of her purse and wiped her eyes. We sat in silence for a few minutes, then Patrice spoke.

"At the moment, I have no idea what Bill is capable of. There is so much in his past that is shady and underhand. I have been such a fool! I accepted what I saw in front of my eyes without checking it out. I saw his job with a media company, the expensive car, the beautiful house with staff to cook and clean, but I was too shallow to look and find out what lay beneath."

I could see that she was distraught and I knew it was neither the time nor the place to question.

I reached over and took her hand, and we sat quietly. I wondered what was going to happen. Deep down I thought resentfully, what on earth did Carole Parks do to check Bill out before she recommended him as an investor? I knew there were some difficult conversations we were going to have to have in the near future, but for now I could feel Patrice's pain and I knew not to push any further.

My gut instinct told me that Robin Pine taking money from Noi was too great to be coincidence. It was beyond cruel if it was him who had taken money from my friend and goodness knows who else in the community.

When we left that evening, we locked up and said goodnight and I walked to the train with a heavy heart.

June 4th, 2024

Noi, Glenda and Jenny meet and go public

Danny La Valle makes a big decision

Chapter 66

A meeting is planned

The fallout from the cancelled meet and greet had been immediate. Jenny's BookStop was a new store, only recently opened. Previous to the article in the Daily Trends, the bookstore had been ticking over, but yet to breakeven. Each month there was a loss, but this was less as time went by. Yet it seemed that after the article in the Daily Trends, it had become famous locally! It was amazing how many people had visited to browse the books for sale. Jenny would never understand what motivated people to come and visit when there was a scandal involved. However, she was happy for them to come and to sell them books!

"Do you stock Gwendoline Investigates? asked one customer. She did, but she was completely sold out!

She had been furious at Glenda for getting her involved in the fraud. After Noi had visited her, she had rung Glenda and Glenda had point blank refused to believe that they were involved in a fraudulent scheme. Since then, Jenny had ignored her.

That evening, she rang Glenda again. At first, Glenda seemed embarrassed to speak to her. Then before Jenny could speak, she rushed in apologetically.

"I have been such a fool, Jenny. I should have realized that I was being conned, but I wanted to believe so badly. This Robin Pine character knew which of my buttons to push. I know now that it is possible to use A.I to generate a fake voice and image. I know I wasn't speaking to Danny La Valle." She stopped there as her voice was shaking.

"It is absolutely disgusting," Jenny agreed. "Also, to do this to an author who is proud of their work is ..." Here she stopped. She was at a loss for words.

"I want to do something," Glenda said. "I feel we shouldn't just let this go. We should find out who these people really are and sue their asses."

Jenny agreed. "We should take it forward. There is another author who you may not know called Noi. She is a Thai lady who wrote a book about a hotel in Hawaii. She was also contacted by Robin Pine and Lulu Bartlett and guess what – Danny La Valle was interested to make her book into a movie."

"At a cost I'll bet!" said Glenda.

"Yes, she has borrowed money she tells me. Noi and her husband own a Thai restaurant and although it does okay, they cannot afford to lose the sort of money she has paid those fraudsters."

"We should meet up and decide how best to go ahead," Glenda went on. "We should involve Noi."

Jenny agreed that it would be a good idea. "And Jinni," she added, "from the nail salon, she is a very good friend of Noi and came in with her to talk about what happened."

"Okay let's do this," said Glenda.

It was only then that Jenny remembered she was ringing to find out how she could get more copies of Glenda's book to sell in the store!

Chapter 67

Jinni

Noi is invited to the meeting

I wasn't surprised that Jenny wanted to meet up to talk about the fraud. I was pleased she had involved me, even though I had not been involved personally. I also wanted to involve Patrice, so I suggested we had the meeting at the Purple Orchid – Second Wave at closing time in the coffee bar area. Noi had arranged for cover at the restaurant so she could come to the meeting. I knew things were very difficult for her. When Niran found out he was absolutely furious. The fact she had borrowed the money too, was a very serious thing in his eyes. It threatened the restaurant if she was unable to pay the money back.

We met up after we had closed the Purple Orchid that evening. There was myself, Jenny, Glenda, Noi and Patrice. Patrice also brought a new person I had not met before into the meeting. This was the private investigator, Loretta.

We sat in the coffee bar nervously sipping ice water. I desperately needed a Thai rum, but I stopped myself. I needed to be sober for the meeting. Patrice took charge of the meeting, asking everyone to introduce themselves. After introductions, each person explained to Loretta about the book fraud.

Loretta was very interested, taking notes.

"So let me get this correct – you were contacted by Robin Pine – you did not contact him?"

Noi and Glenda agreed this was correct.

"He asked for money, correct?"

They both agreed, and then Loretta asked them how they sent the money to him.

"I was asked to wire money," said Glenda, and Noi and Jenny agreed.

"Can you explain a bit more about what you did?"

"Sure," Glenda said. "Robin asked me to wire the money using Western Union. He asked for a digital transfer using their mobile app. It was really easy. I took out an account online with Western Union. I just went into "send money" and I chose "Wire Transfer" and then I put in the details Robin had given me."

"What details did he give you?" Loretta enquired.

"He had a bank account number for me to pay the money into. The name of the company he said to pay to was Lorrimar. This was a company that he did business with that provided PR for film companies."

"Was the bank account in dollars?" Loretta persisted.

"Yes, I didn't do an international wire transfer."

"Was this the same with you, Noi, and with you, Jenny?"

Noi and Jenny had both wired funds to Robin.

Noi added that Robin had told her it was the only method for her to send money and he said it was the quickest.

Loretta sighed. "Please can you let me have the bank account details you wired the money to and I will follow up. I hope that the account is legitimate but sadly, scammers will often ask you to wire funds because once you have wired the money there is usually no way for you to get it back."

Glenda got her phone out. She went into the app and gave Loretta the details.

I got the feeling that Loretta felt that they were very naïve to believe this person and send him money.

Patrice had been silent and she looked very uncomfortable. "I feel you need to make this public, to warn others," she said.

"We have already done this in the Daily Trends where there was an article on the fake Danny La Valle. The comments on that article were brutal! People were not exactly sympathetic," Jenny said nervously. "Yet amazingly, my shop has been so busy since then with people wanting to visit and browse."

Patrice nodded. "I was thinking about authors in particular. This is incredibly cruel to anyone who has written a book. It is giving people false hope as well as cheating them out of their money." She stopped for a moment to compose herself. "It is so wrong."

Glenda spoke up. "I agree. Any author believes in their work and to feel that someone is preying on that to take money under false pretenses is, as you say, very cruel."

"I don't care if people think I am naïve", Noi added. "I think there are a lot of people like me who would have snapped the hand off someone who offered to publicize their book."

"I still have contact details for Rosie Banks, from Daily Trends," said Jenny. "Should we contact her to do a follow-up article? It might encourage more people who have been conned by these scammers to come forward."

I thought it was a great idea. "Also, one of my customers and friends, Ellie, works at the university and knows how to do research. We could ask her to get involved," I said.

"And Loretta, you must continue to try to find out more about the money and where it went," said Patrice. "We don't know the size of this con yet. Are there just a few people involved, or is it a really big con involving hundreds of indie authors?"

We each agreed that these were good ways to take this forward.

After the meeting, I caught the train home deep in thought. What had been unsaid, of course, was that Bill Underwood knew Danny La Valle. Was Bill part of this con? It sickened me to even think this, but there was a possibility.

I slept very poorly that night with bad, vivid dreams. In the morning, I caught the early train and put the radio on when I arrived at the Purple Orchid while I got ready to open the salon. I liked the commuter show with Jerry Levens. I hummed along to the songs he played and then he announced:

"A local media company, Stermer Media, are celebrating today. They have just signed a major podcaster and activist, Ronald Carter, to produce a series of shows for them here in the South. Ronald will need no introduction to many of you. He has had a podcast in the top ten for the previous five years and has a massive following on social media. Twenty million followers on Instagram. He is a voice to be reckoned with. Here to talk about the signing is an executive from Stermer Media – Bill Underwood."

I stopped arranging the flowers in the foyer and my mouth gaped open.

I then heard Bill holding forth in his British accent.

"We are beyond delighted, Jerry, this is amazing news for Stermer. Yes, my lovely wife and I met with Ronald at Capri restaurant downtown. We also know him from the church where he is a very active member... Blah, blah, blah."

So, it seemed that Stermer were not doing as badly as feared, or more likely, Bill had been able to turn things around at the last minute. It seemed for the time being his investment was safe, but what other things were there brushed under the carpet that might come to light? I shuddered to speculate.

June 7th, 2024

Niran is resentful

Ellie becomes involved and starts her research

Bill lays his soul bare to Patrice

Chapter 68

Niran is resentful

Niran was, he liked to think, an even-tempered guy. He very rarely lost his temper. He was able to take the rough with the smooth. He loved his wife Noi and his two children and they were the center of his universe.

If his family had been the center of his universe, the restaurant had been his baby and it had grown in a fairly modest way and was now profitable. It provided a living for Niran and Noi and the two children. However, margins were tight. He always had to be careful. The way he priced the meals and the amount he paid to the staff who worked in the restaurant had to be plotted out very carefully. Even a small error on what he charged could tip them over for the month and the restaurant would make a loss.

Despite these tight margins, he had been able to put a deposit down on a small home in the northern suburbs and pay a mortgage each and every month.

In addition, for the last three years he had been able to take his family on a vacation to Hawaii and they had stayed at a small hotel. It had been a lovely, family-oriented time where they had laughed and spent time together swimming, walking and sunbathing.

Now when he thought of that vacation, he felt anger such as he had never felt before. Noi had used that vacation time – that precious time – to write her ridiculous books. The Malami Hotel was the location she made up – the setting for several stories around people who were visiting Hawaii. He had not read the whole book because it was so boring. He had stopped reading at Chapter 2! The story was not interesting. Anybody could see this.

Not only had Noi written the book and self-published it, but she believed a Hollywood director wanted to produce it into a movie!

The woman was crazy. He could feel the anger building up inside him, searching for an outlet.

Today as he sat on the back stoop of his house drinking his morning coffee, he felt like lashing out and hitting someone.

The crazy woman. He was shaking as he went over this in his mind. The crazy woman had PAID for someone to rewrite her book so it could be produced into a movie.

The crazy woman had taken out a second loan on the house to pay for her crazy fantasies.

He got up and slowly went into the kitchen. Noi was busying herself making breakfast for the children who had not come downstairs yet. He was shaking with rage.

"I can't bear to look at you!" he yelled. "How could you have done this? You are a crazy woman and I just don't know how I can go on living with you!"

Noi had her head down and tears were pouring down her cheeks. Niran only spoke to her now to shout at her and call her names. She hoped it would blow over, but deep down she was frightened for their marriage.

"The children will be here in a moment," she chided. "Hush and we can talk later. I will get a job to pay the money back."

"And where are you going to get a job?" shouted Niran. "You work in the restaurant, remember? The restaurant you threatened with your stupid borrowing of money!"

Noi left the room and running upstairs, told the children they were leaving immediately. There was much moaning and complaining as both children were hungry and wanted breakfast. However, they went with their mother – without their lunch boxes – and they stopped at Tastee Doughnuts for breakfast. As she stood in line for their order, Noi saw a sign that said there was a vacant position in the shop selling doughnuts.

After dropping the children at school, Noi returned to say she would like to know more about the position. It was part-time – mornings only, six days a week. Noi decided to apply. Going home she filled out the forms online.

A couple of days later as she and Niran were getting ready for bed, Noi told him she wanted to tell him something.

"I have a job at Tastee Doughnuts that I will be starting next week. I will be working there in the mornings from seven to eleven. You will have to do the children's breakfasts and take them to school. I will work there until I have paid back the six thousand dollars I borrowed."

Niran stared at her. "When did this happen?"

Noi shrugged. “What does it matter? I will pay back every single cent. I was foolish and let a conman get the better of me. It will never happen again.”

Niran nodded – how could he not agree with her?

So it began. Noi would rise at 6 a.m. and go to work in the doughnut shop from 7 a.m. to 11 a.m. She would then go home, do the housework, and then pick the children up from school. Then when Niran’s mom arrived to babysit them, she would drive to the restaurant to spend the evening cooking.

It was an exhausting schedule and one that would have broken many people. However, she was a determined woman and she would never give up. She knew that when she paid the money back Niran would love her again. But she still yearned to write. As she toiled day after day, an idea came to her for a new story. It was the story of a woman who worked as a cook in a local café, who went on to work in a Michelin starred restaurant and fell in love with the chef. She didn’t have time to write this story down, so she dictated it as she drove to and from the doughnut shop, the school, their home and the restaurant. Listening to it later, she felt it was her best ever story and she couldn’t wait to transcribe it and give a copy to Jinni to read.

Chapter 69

Ellie becomes involved and begins her research

Ellie read the Daily Trends and kept up to date with the gossip, so she knew about the A.I generated version of Danny La Valle who had promised to visit Jenny's BookStop and it turning out to be a fraud. When Jinni told her about the fake Robin Pine and Lulu Bartlett, she was shocked and felt very sad. How cruel to give new authors false hope in this way, and not just that, taking money from them too.

Jinni had put Ellie in touch with Loretta, the private investigator, who had news about the fraudulent company in the Philippines.

"When we followed up with Lorrimar in the Philippines," Loretta explained to Ellie, "it turned out that the company had very few reserves and almost no cash. It has now been taken over by another company, Faro Media. The directors of this company are Harold Nash and Carol Beckett. However, it seems that Faro Media is itself a subsidiary of another media company called Murcia. There is a very long and very complex relationship between these various companies and a firm of CPAs in Los Angeles are trying to get to the bottom of it."

Ellie wondered about the size of the con that had been carried out here.

It was interesting – she found that there were Facebook sites for indie authors that talked about scams and cons similar to this one. Yet both Noi and Glenda seemed to have fallen for it without question.

In addition, there were blogs and websites for authors outlining frauds and warning them to be careful.

Ellie no longer had her YouTube channel but as she searched for information, she became fascinated with this topic. Why would people fall for these scams when there were warnings online? She wanted to encourage people to speak up and so without consulting her husband, Kevin, she decided to make a YouTube video. Glenda agreed to be in the video so long as her face was not shown and she remained anonymous.

Ellie made a short YouTube video where she asked authors who had been approached by scammers or who had been defrauded to come forward.

She posted it online and within a day or two, she was shocked to find a large number of people had made comments:

Barry: I was approached by Robin Pine in 2023 and offered a publishing contract provided I had my book edited first at the cost of $3,000. Robin showed me statistics for authors he said he had helped – these included several best sellers. It was very tempting. I almost went through with it until he asked me to wire the money. I asked a friend who said this was a common ploy when it was a con. I became nervous and did not send the money.

Shelleyauthor: I paid Robin Pine $4,000 in 2023 to publicize my book. He said that the money was for advertising costs. I never saw it advertised anywhere and when I became impatient wanting to know more about where it was advertised, he blocked me."

And so it went on. There were so many horror stories of people who had paid Robin Pine in good faith and received nothing back. Truly shocking.

Ellie responded to the people commenting, asking if a private investigator could contact them to find out more. A few agreed, although the majority did not want to take it any further, as they were too embarrassed.

Claritty: I tried to find out where my money went and just hit brick walls. I could find out nothing. That is the problem of wiring money – it is difficult to trace once you have sent it. I would love to get hold of Robin Pine, believe me, but I am sure whoever it is will be using a different name now. It is a disgrace how someone can do this to indie authors and get away with it.

Glenda had contacted Rosie Banks to ask if she would do a follow-up article, and Rosie agreed to do a Zoom call with Ellie and Loretta.

Rosie Banks was also interested in the YouTube video and Loretta's research. "However," she said, "we need a few more people to come forward who I can interview. Human interest stories are needed here."

Eventually, a person named Teddy Brooks agreed to talk to Rosie about their experience with Robin Pine. Teddy had lost $10,000 and had nothing to show for Robin publicizing their book. The book had never made any best-seller list and Teddy had only sold a few hundred copies.

Rosie agreed to interview Teddy and to put together a follow-up article for the Daily Trends.

Chapter 70

Bill Underwood bares his soul

During these days, Patrice had begun to retreat more and more into herself. She could feel Bill's eyes on her and she resisted any impulse to look back. She kept herself busy with her work at the salon and tried to keep away from him as much as possible.

When she returned on Saturday evening, Bill was waiting for her in the motor court as she parked her car.

"Come out to the pool, darling," he pleaded.

Patrice was wearing stilettos, and found it difficult to walk across the grass. Bill took her arm to help her. They sat down at the table outside the pool house where there was a bottle of rosé cooling in an ice bucket and two glasses. Bill poured the drinks.

"I am going to insist we talk, Patrice." He was watching her very closely. "I will not be put off. I want to talk now and I want to tell you about me. I want to put the record straight."

Patrice sipped her drink. "I don't know what to think, Bill," she said. "I feel you have not told me the truth and I am scared to hear what you have to say. Remember, I moved here away from LA and my family and friends to be with you. I believed in you."

Bill nodded. "I understand how you feel, Patrice. This is why it is important we talk now and stop putting it off."

He was wearing a light T shirt and shorts and they were sitting in the shade, yet there was a fine sheen of sweat on his face and arms.

"You wanted to know about my job, I believe," he said.

Patrice nodded. "I know you have just brought in a new client for Stermer Media, so that should be good news."

"It is," Bill smiled. "Yet you are worrying about my previous job working for Danny La Valle, I believe? My take on that is that you feel I left under a cloud and Danny is investigating me. Am I correct?"

Patrice nodded. "I have heard some rumors about that."

Bill laughed out loud. "Oh Patrice! Believe me, Danny will never investigate or sue me. I know that for sure."

There was silence for a moment and then Bill went on.

"I am going to take us on a little trip tomorrow. I have chartered a small plane to take us to LA and from there I am going to drive you up the coast to meet someone who will put the story straight for you."

"Who is that?" Patrice spluttered.

"Try not to be too impatient – all will be revealed tomorrow."

That was all Bill would say that evening, and after eating a delicious meal that he prepared, Patrice went to bed early and surprisingly, slept well.

She rose early, wondering what to wear for the surprise trip Bill was planning. She decided on a

Breton top and white trousers. She hoped it was not too casual.

As she walked down the stairs, Bill nodded approvingly. “You are stunning, Patrice,” he said. He was wearing chinos and a J Crew T shirt.

They drove to the local airfield where a small private jet was waiting for them. Bill was ever the executive, taking charge as they boarded the plane. Sitting on the plane, Patrice observed him. He was as loving and as gracious as ever. She wanted so badly for there to be a logical explanation for the mystery of the last few weeks.

When they landed at Burbank airport, a car was waiting and they took the 101 freeway towards Ventura. Traffic was heavy and progress was slow. As they drove Bill said, “I am going to introduce you to Lucy. This is why we are driving up the coast. Very few people get to meet Lucy, but I feel you should meet her before I tell you my story.”

“Who is Lucy?” Patrice asked, surprised. This was the first time she had heard of someone by that name.

“You must meet her first, and then we will go for lunch and I will tell you who she is and all about her.”

He would not be drawn any further so Patrice stayed silent. It seemed a long journey.

Finally, Bill took the off ramp towards Oxnard and Port Hueneme. Patrice saw the blue of the ocean and the boats in the marina and felt a deep longing to be living back near to the coast.

They drove alongside the marina where there were townhouses and apartments. Finally, they pulled up in front of a modest townhouse.

Bill stopped the engine and getting out and walking round the car, opened the door for Patrice.

“We are here,” he said. “This is Lucy’s home.”

He rang the doorbell. “I am going to introduce you to Lucy.”

A woman in late middle age opened the door. She was short and stocky and had dark hair streaked with grey. Seeing Bill at the door, she smiled and invited them in.

“Hi Cilla,” Bill said. “This is my wife, Patrice.”

Cilla smiled brightly at Patrice. “Nice to meet you. I am the nurse and carer of Lucy. Come in, she would love to meet you. She gets very few visitors.”

They climbed the stairs to a room with a large glass window and balcony overlooking the boats in the marina. It was a beautiful room, bright, sunny and comfortable.

A woman was sitting in a wheelchair with her back to the main room, looking out over the boats.

Cilla went over to the wheelchair and turned her so she could see Bill and Patrice.

“You have visitors, Lucy,” she said softly, leaning over the chair.

Patrice saw a very young woman sitting in the wheelchair who had once been very pretty. She was supported by straps so she could sit upright and it seemed that her legs had wasted away. Around her neck was a tube that Patrice later found out was a tracheal tube. This was attached to a pacer that stimulated contractions in her diaphragm and forced her body to breathe. This had enabled her to be able to speak. It was hard to put an age on her, but Patrice guessed she was in her early twenties.

Bill walked over and Lucy smiled to see him.

“Hey Bill,” she said.

Bill dropped down so he was on her level and kissed her cheek. He then turned and introduced Patrice as his wife.

Bill and Patrice then sat on the sofa and Cilla brought everyone tea.

They had a chat about life and what Lucy was getting up to. She went to a rehabilitation center now in the mornings, and was starting to interact with other people.

“I haven’t always been like this,” Lucy said, “and I don’t intend to be always like this in the future.”

Sipping her tea and looking at this once beautiful girl, Patrice felt a great sadness. She didn’t know a great deal about quadriplegia but she was not sure if there was a cure.

“I used to dance and do gymnastics,” Lucy went on.

Cilla helped Lucy drink her tea.

They did not stay long, however, the visit was pleasant and friendly. Patrice could see that Lucy was pleased to see Bill and had affection for him.

After leaving, they drove further north to Montecito where Bill had made reservations at Tre Lune restaurant. Bill shushed Patrice in the car saying he would tell her more about Lucy, but all in good time.

He again refused to speak over lunch, saying what he had to tell her was confidential and he did not want to speak in a restaurant. Although the food and wine were delicious, Patrice could not wait for the meal to finish. She had so many questions.

Chapter 71

The truth is revealed

Finally, as they drove back to Burbank airport, Bill began to speak. The traffic was busy and progress was slow but it was now that he started talking – and what a story it was. Patrice had wondered why he had not booked the plane to the small private airfield in Santa Barbara, but she wondered now if he wanted this private time in the car to tell her the story about Lucy.

"Lucy is now twenty years old," he began. "That poor child has lost all quality of life. All because she was star-struck and got mixed up with Danny La Valle."

Bill let that sink in – although Patrice had already guessed this would be something to do with Danny.

"Lucy was brought up by a single mother. She lived in a trailer park in Riverside with her mother and her brother, Glenn. They were poor, I believe, and Lucy had big dreams. As you know Riverside is about a hundred miles from Hollywood, but it might as well be ten thousand.

Lucy never really excelled at anything in school. She liked to dance and act in school plays but was never outstanding. She was very pretty but she was not outstandingly beautiful. She did not have that special something – that star quality. However, she made friends with an older girl at high school called Julie Garcia. They used to take the bus together. Julie was much prettier – in fact, Julie was a very beautiful young woman.

When Julie was eighteen, she signed with an agency that cast background artistes in movies. She moved to Hollywood where she was able to get this type of work in addition to working in a bar on Sunset Boulevard. Julie felt that working in Hollywood she would be discovered and become a famous movie star. She never considered that there would be thousands more like her doing the same thing and waiting for their big break.

Lucy was only seventeen when Julie left, and she wanted to go to Hollywood to be with her really badly. They texted all the time. One weekend, Julie texted her that she had been invited to a party at a mansion in the Hollywood Hills, and did Lucy want to join her?"

Patrice sat staring out of the window. She knew how this would go without Bill having to tell her. It was unbelievably sad.

Bill carried on. "Lucy caught the bus from Riverside and went to Julie's apartment. I believe this was an apartment in a seedy part of Hollywood that she shared with four other people. They spent the afternoon smoking dope and one of the roommates, Kelly, lent Lucy a dress to wear to the party."

Bill stopped here and neither spoke for a few minutes.

"She was underage, I believe, seventeen you said," Patrice commented.

"Yes, that is true," Bill said. "And she wore a tight, low-cut dress that a slut or a prostitute would wear. With her hair and makeup, she could pass for at least twenty-one." He paused then, before saying, with a regrettable tone, "Maybe, she could pass."

"Was the house that the party was at owned by Danny?"

There was another silence and then Bill said, "No, it wasn't. It belonged to an actor called Billy Eto. He is D-list, but he is married to a very rich woman, so owns a beautiful mansion in the Hills."

Patrice had not heard of Billy Eto, but wondered when Danny was going to come into the story.

"Julie was working as a background artiste on a movie where Billy played a serial killer. Billy was known for affairs with young actresses and other people on the set, so it was no surprise he had shown an interest in Julie. I am still not sure how she managed to wangle the invite to the party, but she did, and she managed to get Lucy into the party as well."

Bill concentrated on driving in silence for a few moments before speaking again.

"Danny was completely off his head at this stage in his life. He was in total meltdown. You will remember my role was not simply to do the accounts, it was also to be his minder or fixer. You know the things he did – you were one of the people who we paid money to and who signed a non-disclosure agreement."

Patrice sadly agreed. "Of course, I remember how he groped me and the smell of booze. He was completely off his head."

"The problem with having someone like Danny off his head is that there are vultures in Hollywood," Bill went on. "People who could see that he was in no fit state to manage himself – and they would see this as an opportunity. He's rich, let's have a piece of him.

I employed a doctor to visit him regularly to try to get him off the drugs and booze. Dr. Adam Miesler. I thought he was a reputable Beverly Hills doctor. How wrong was I? One day driving along Mulholland, Danny had an accident where he hit the car in front. We managed to keep this out of the papers, but Danny told Dr. Meisler that he had hurt his back and needed pills. He was only too eager to prescribe Oxycontin, which Danny then became addicted to. After a while it did not do anything to relieve the pain, but he was so addicted he continued to take it.

Other leeches were constantly trying to get access to Danny – and his big wallet."

Patrice believed Bill that this would be the case. "Were you able to protect him?" she asked.

"I tried my best." Bill seemed upset and angry discussing this. "I bloody tried to keep these people away from him. But you have to understand I was dealing with a serial drunk, pill popper and drug addict. Danny would lie, cheat and sell his own mother to get his daily fix."

"Danny knew Billy Eto from a previous film shoot and Billy had invited him to the party. Danny had spent the day, so he told me, at his own home, popping pills for his bad back, smoking a joint and drinking Jack Daniels neat. He did not decide until 10 p.m. to go to the party and by then, he was so off his head he could hardly stand.

I had insisted that José, the handyman, and his wife live in Danny's pool house in case anything bad happened. This is how worried I was about him. However, this weekend, he had given them the weekend off to go to a wedding in San Diego of José's brother. So, on this evening there were no staff at the house. And rather than stay in or call an Uber, he decided to drive himself to the party, which was only about a mile or so away. The man was, sorry is, a complete fool.

He drove over to the party without incident and carried on drinking. This is a man in his fifties, out of shape, drunk and to put it bluntly, a bloody mess. Yet young girls saw a famous director. It will always be beyond me what any young girl would want with a drunken, drug addicted creep like Danny, but perhaps I am jealous. Who knows?"

"You should not be jealous, Bill," Patrice said. "It is a shallow, disgusting world in which young girls chase creeps like Danny to try to get in his movies. Whatever happened to raw talent, huh?"

Bill turned and smiled at her. "I know. What a shitshow huh?"

There was silence for a moment and then he carried on. "But it was my shitshow. I was his minder.

At the party, Danny hooked up with Lucy. Even by his standards she was very young. In his defense, I don't know if he could see straight. I am sure she was already drunk and on drugs when she hooked up with him. Perhaps through an alcoholic haze he looked good. He was totally off his head.

Danny then had this great idea – why not go back to his house and have more fun?

Lucy agreed, but said she had to find Julie to say goodbye. She walked around the house looking for Julie but couldn't find her. Danny grew impatient and basically told her it is now or never.

She went with Danny to his car and Danny drove back down the road to his house. Remember, there was no-one at his house – the staff were away. He got out a cocktail of drink and pills and they tucked in.

He put the sound system on – Motown I believe and when Barry White came on, he was dancing closely with Lucy. He led her up to his bedroom where he managed to have sex with her before passing out."

"Lucy was only seventeen! Oh my God that is disgusting!" Patrice said. "How old was he? In his fifties I believe?"

"Sadly Patrice, that was just the beginning. After sex, Danny passed out on the bed and it seems that Lucy must have got bored. I expect she must have been wide awake and wired. She explored the house and probably drank more and took more pills.

Then, and this is the sad part, Lucy decided she would like to swim. Standing on the balcony outside of the bedroom, she shouted to the sleeping Danny that she wanted to go in the pool.

"Okay go downstairs and jump in?" Danny supposedly mumbled.

Lucy laughed and said, "No need to go downstairs." She clambered naked on the balcony rail and dived into the swimming pool.

The really tragic thing was that she did not know which was the shallow end. She should have jumped further along the balcony if she was going to jump at all.

The fucking stupid child jumped from the balcony into the shallow end!

Danny told me that even in his drunken stupor he heard a loud crack and then Lucy went lifeless.

He ran downstairs and tried to drag Lucy out of the pool. He was screaming loudly and swearing. Eventually he was able to drag her out of the pool, but she was unresponsive. By the way, him dragging her out of the pool may have saved her life, but it was not the right thing to do with regard to the injuries she had suffered.

He immediately rang me. He was now stone cold sober. He spoke to me in between screaming and trying to perform CPR on Lucy.

I rang for Dr. Meisler who went around there immediately. He was able to breathe life into Lucy but she seemed unable to breathe independently.

"We have to get her to hospital now or she will die," he said.

I agreed and we found a small hospital up the coast where discretion was assured. Dr. Miesel and I took her ourselves in my car. Danny was too recognizable so did not go. Dr. Miesel had with him a mechanical ventilator so was able to use this to keep Lucy breathing until we got her to the hospital.

She was admitted just after midnight and went straight to the ER. We did not know the true extent of her injuries at this stage."

It was sickening hearing about this, but it was the first time Patrice had heard about it. "I guess you were able to cover it all up," she said.

Bill nodded. "When you have money like Danny, you can cover anything up. We had to make sure there was no link between his house and the accident. We told the hospital that she had been in a car accident. I don't know if they believed me, but they never queried what I said."

He took a deep breath. "Of course, Danny paid her hospital bill through a company so he could be anonymous. Julie was easy – we told her that Lucy had accepted a lift from someone at the party and been involved in a car accident. We made out that it was someone who was not famous and therefore the accident was not newsworthy. But the real problem, as I saw it, was Lucy's mother."

Patrice groaned. "Oh, her poor mother!"

Bill smiled. "Oh, not so fast Patrice! From my experience anybody can be bought. Yes, the mother cried when I first went to see her, but I told her that the person driving the car would pay all Lucy's bills if we kept this out of the press. I made sure the mother knew this would be ongoing, as Lucy has no chance of recovery."

Patrice sat up, suddenly startled. "You didn't mention Danny's name?"

"No, I certainly didn't. I made out it was a car accident with a wealthy, but non famous person driving."

"How many years ago was this?" asked Patrice.

"Three years. It was just after this horrific incident that Danny knew he had to clean himself up. He checked into the Betty Ford Clinic and, so far as I know, has been sober ever since. After his release from the clinic, he started filming again and the result was Shamrock Isle.

Bill stopped here and smiled. "He is a tortured genius."

Patrice was having difficulty breathing. "Why are you telling me all this?" she asked.

"Because you are worried by gossip and rumors. Patrice, Danny La Valle is no threat to me or to you. He would never, ever, challenge me. Yes, he gave me a reference for my job at Stermer Media. Yes, he would always stand by me. Can you imagine what would happen to Danny if any of this was ever made public?"

"He would go to prison," Patrice said. "This poor, young, naïve, underage girl. Her first time at a Hollywood party and she meets up with him and this happens."

She shook her head sadly. "Why would a man of his age take a girl so young home? Did he never suspect even for a moment that she might be underage? Even if she wasn't underage, she was way too young for him. I feel this is true even by Hollywood standards.

Who are the bastards who hosted this party and let her in? She didn't know them and she was way too young."

Patrice was fighting back tears. She could see that they were approaching Burbank Airport. She knew she had to get on the plane and go back with Bill. She could barely look at him. She was not a mother, but deep inside her something like a motherly instinct surfaced and she longed to hold that young girl and keep her safe. She could picture her sitting in her wheelchair being fed by the carer. If only someone who cared had been there to tell her not to go to the party. She wanted to throw the bastard in prison, or worse. He deserved so much worse.

Bill parked the hire car and they walked out on the tarmac to the waiting plane. He seemed almost relieved that he had told her his secret. There was never any threat from Danny La Valle. In fact, so far as Patrice knew, Danny La Valle might still be financing Bill's lifestyle.

They climbed the steps and sat in their seats on the plane. She sipped the drink that was offered to her, but refused food.

The flight was short, and she turned away looking out of the window. It was only when they had landed and were back in their own car that she plucked up the courage to ask Bill the question that had been playing through her mind.

"Bill, one more question," she said, nervously. "Did you ever, at any time, think about turning Danny in?"

The silence that ensued told her all she would ever want to know.

June 10th, 2024

Danny La Valle's new film is released

The Daily Trends publishes another article

Jinni speaks to Carole Parks again

Bill reflects on sharing his secret

Chapter 72

"The Reluctant Pastor" is released

In the days following the visit to Lucy, Patrice continued to work at the salon and live in the same house as Bill. They were polite and ate meals together and asked about each other's day. Bill said he understood Patrice wanted time to process what he had told her.

"But you must now see," he said, "that the things you felt were threatening our marriage do not exist. I can't stop people spreading rumors, but Danny would never sue me or accuse me of fraud. Danny and I are joined together until the day we both die – by Lucy."

Patrice could see that financially they were not threatened, of course she could. But, she mused, what about morals and caring? What happened there? She could not get the picture of Lucy sitting in her wheelchair in that house out of her mind.

At that time, Danny La Valle began to appear regularly in the Press and on TV to publicize the release of his new movie, *The Reluctant Pastor*. This movie was a resounding success with the critics. The headlines were many:

"A triumph."

"Danny La Valle at his finest."

"Groundbreaking cinema."

She read one review in detail where it talked about Danny La Valle, who was also credited as the writer, being able to show empathy for "human frailties". He was able to create "relatable characters" that mirror our own experiences. He painted vivid scenes of life in the Appalachian Mountains using sensory details, allowing viewers to immerse themselves in the story. Bert, the reluctant pastor of the title, was shown to be a quirky, flawed human being who you felt you could identify with. And on and on it went.

The movie averaged a 5-star rating and 96% on Rotten Tomatoes.

Danny also appeared on various TV shows advertising the movie. On The Late Show a picture was shown of Danny with a young girl who looked about 20 years old. They were on a yacht sailing across a crystal blue sea, and Danny had his arm wrapped around the girl. The host asked Danny about the picture.

"Rona is your eldest daughter and I believe doing very well at USC. She is studying film and media. Is this because Rona is going to follow you into movies?"

Danny laughed and spread his arms. "She loves film. It is all she has ever wanted to do. From a young age she just made movies with her friends. It is almost certain she will follow me into the industry."

This was followed by a video of Rona behind the camera directing some young people in a shoot. Presumably these were her friends.

Looking her up on the internet, Patrice found that Rona lived with her mother – the actress and model, Katrina Firth. She had divorced Danny soon after Rona's birth.

"I wonder how much Rona really knows about her father?" Patrice said out loud to no one in particular.

The Reluctant Pastor was not just a hit with the critics – it took over $100 million in its first weekend at the box office.

After the initial furor died down, Danny was not in the papers and on TV as often, but Patrice still saw his picture and advertisements for the movie on billboards and on the cinema as she drove. Each time she saw his picture, she also saw Lucy in her mind's eye and wondered if he ever thought of her? Or if he did, was it just to worry that he would be exposed? A rich, successful man with a dark, hidden, guilty secret. Then she thought of her husband, Bill Underwood, who had shared the secret with her. Then the tears would come, rolling down her cheeks as she drove, not daring to think of her future.

"It is sad not to love, but it is much sadder not to be able to love."

Miguel de Unamuno

Chapter 73

The Daily Trends publishes a second story

Rosie Banks, the reporter from the Daily Trends, had been able to contact Teddy Brooks who had responded to Ellie's YouTube video. He had agreed to be interviewed and to appear in an article about publishing fraud. She also interviewed Glenda again, and Noi.

Speaking to Loretta, she found out that the trail to find the money that had been wired to the fake agent Robin Pine was very difficult to follow. Rosie was almost certain it would be impossible to get the money back.

Rosie's article included some statistics from the Federal Trade Commission which reported that in 2024 up to $12.5 billion was lost by consumers to fraudulent schemes online.

She also reported second-hand on a Department of Justice report on a multi-million dollar publishing scam which had involved fraudsters convincing elderly authors across the USA that publishers and filmmakers wanted to make their books into blockbusters. However, in order for this to happen, the authors had to pay money up- front first. It seemed the FBI had identified more than 800 victims of this scheme who had collectively lost more than $44 million.

Rosie quoted the following from the Department of Justice article:

"What started as the promise of a Hollywood dream turned into a devastating nightmare for the victims," said U.S. Attorney Tara McGrath. "Authors should stay vigilant, do their research, and think twice before giving money to anyone promising a blockbuster deal. If you or anyone you know has been targeted in a similar scheme, please report it to the FBI immediately."

She then put into the article a few people to contact if you suspect fraud, including the Federal Bureau of Investigations (FBI), the Securities and Exchange Commission (SEC), Internal Revenue Service (IRS) and Federal Trade Commission.

Rosie also mentioned the blog, "Writer Beware" which had good information and case studies on authors affected by fraud. Anyone could write about their own experiences on this blog, and it was an excellent resource, especially for indie authors.

Rosie also said to contact her if you were an author who had been affected by this scam.

There were a number of comments on the article, this time including comments from other authors who had been a victim of the scam with Robin Pine. People who gave their consent were put in touch with Glenda, who started a group of "survivors" who would discuss the way ahead.

This time the article felt more positive and that there may be a way in the future for justice to prevail.

Chapter 74

Jinni

Speaking again with Carole Parks

After taking in the recent events, I knew I had to speak to my CPA again, Ms. Carole Parks. She had told me that Bill Underwood would be a good investor for my business. I was now very worried about who he was and what he was involved with.

I took the elevator up to the 6th floor – it still smelled faintly of urine and perhaps something worse. Everything looked cheap and nasty. The reception area wasn't much better – dismal, dark and slightly smelly. Of course, she kept me waiting for what seemed like an eternity before she ushered me into her own office.

She offered me a cup of coffee, but there were no other pleasantries.

What a plain woman, I thought. She certainly didn't look after herself. The bitten nails, the hair that hung like curtains around her face, the unfashionable, ill-fitting clothes and the glasses slipping down her nose which she constantly kept pushing back up – perhaps I should offer her a day at the salon to have some treatments and a makeover.

She was sitting looking at spreadsheets on her laptop and she turned to me smiling.

"The numbers seem much better now, Jinni," she said. "It seems the beauty salon Patrice Underwood started is really helping your business."

"Yes, that is true. I will give you that," I said.

"Aren't you happy that business is now so much better?"

"Yes, I am happy with the fact that business is better and we have turned a loss into a profit," I said, "of course I am. However, I want to know more about the investment that has been made in my business."

Carole took her glasses off at this point and wiped them on her sleeve. She looked blankly at me.

"Sorry? What do you need to know? Looking at the accounts from your business it seems that since the investment was made, business has been on the up and you now show a profit. There is cash in the bank rather than an overdraft. Reviewing the detailed figures, it seems that the salon Bill's wife started has been very profitable from day one."

"Yes, I know we are now making a profit," I said. "But I wanted to ask about the investment agreement. Can I buy Bill Underwood out?"

Carole appeared bemused. "You certainly do not have enough money in the business to buy him out," she said. "Why would you want to buy him out at this stage? Is there some argument?"

"No, there is no argument," I said.

"Well then, seeing as business is good and actually making a profit, I would leave things as they are for the time being."

At this point she seemed to dismiss me as if the meeting was over.

"I have other questions," I said. "I want to know more about Bill Underwood's background and where he got the money from to invest."

"Jinni." Carole was stern now. "I can assure you that I thoroughly checked Bill out before I put him forward as an investor. He is a qualified CPA and has sufficient funds to invest in your business. Why are you asking these questions now after he has been an investor for the last six months?"

I sat quietly for a few moments wondering what to do. Finally, I could keep quiet no longer.

"I think it is dirty money!" I blurted.

"What on earth are you suggesting?" She was now much more alert and looking angry.

"I think it is dirty money," I repeated. "I know he appears to be a rich man but I am not sure he made the money legally."

Carole now spoke loudly and angrily. "And do you have any evidence for these accusations, Jinni?"

"There is a lot of gossip about him," I said.

"What do you mean by gossip?" Her voice was hard and cold.

"It seems wherever he worked there has been fraud or should I say alleged fraud. This includes his employment in Los Angeles. He worked for the producer Danny La Valle and also for a firm of CPAs – at both places there are allegations of fraud. Then there is the fraud where someone rings authors and pretends to be an agent who can sign them up for a film with Danny La Valle. It is all suspicious."

Carole was now looking at me as if I was raving mad.

"Fraud?" Carole said. "What evidence do you have of any fraud? Now look here, Jinni, I think it is time you faced facts. You came to me almost desperate as you were in debt, your business was, um how can I put this, not exactly thriving." She stopped here and looked me directly in the eyes. "Isn't that true, Jinni? You wanted my help."

"I wanted your help, but I didn't want a fraudster to invest in my business..."

"I would imagine that no-one would want a fraudster to invest! However, what you are saying makes no sense to me. What evidence do you have? By evidence I mean something in writing or the result of an investigation, not gossip or rumors."

I felt like a fool now. Of course I had no evidence. I had just listened to gossip and rumors.

She keyed something into her laptop and showed it to me. It was a search for "Avalon Media fraud" – it had not turned up anything. There were more entries for "Meyer and Co. and fraud". It seemed one of the partners had been sued by a company for negligence when fraud had gone undetected. The partner's name was Jason Rebow. She then keyed in "Bill Underwood and fraud" – nothing of significance came up.

"Bill is an executive at Stermer Media," Carole said. "I find it hard to believe he would have got that position if he had been involved in fraudulent activities in his previous employment."

Her tone now softened. "People get jealous, Jinni. Bill is a very successful CPA. He does hold an executive position with a media company and is highly thought of in the financial community. You are very lucky to have him as an investor in your nail bar. He is also married to a beautiful, successful woman who is running a salon in the upstairs of your premises in the regeneration area."

I felt like a child again, being put in my place by a teacher at school.

"Also, Jinni, remember – people can be nasty and spread rumors when they are jealous."

Carole now pushed her laptop away and looking me direct in the eye, asked if I had further questions.

Shaking my head, I stood up and thanked her for her time. She reached across her desk and shook my hand.

"You can be assured, Jinni, that I am a professional accountant and this meeting will remain confidential between the two of us. I would advise you to go back to your business and be happy that it is thriving."

She saw me out to reception and as I took the elevator back to the street level, I felt I had been dismissed and my concerns glossed over. I walked to the train station with a heavy heart.

Chapter 75

Bill reflects on sharing his secret

When Patrice awoke, Bill was at the foot of the Bed with a tray containing coffee, orange juice, a bowl of muesli and some fruit.

"Good morning, my darling," he said brightly. "Breakfast in bed today. No need to hurry over to the salon."

Patrice sat up and he placed the tray on her lap.

He sat on the side of the bed while she ate and sipped the coffee.

All appeared normal and amicable, but was it really?

Bill knew that since the visit to Lucy, Patrice had allowed him back into her bed and they had made love again regularly. Patrice had made his meal in the evening and they had sat and eaten it together. They had been out to eat on a couple of occasions and to the country club together.

Yet, there was something missing. Bill couldn't put his finger on it. There was a distance between him and Patrice that had not been there before. There was politeness and, on the surface, caring and kindness. However, below the surface, there was something else.

Bill would never understand women, he felt, as long as he lived. He had truly loved Alison. She was, and would always be, his soulmate. He felt it was a match made in Heaven. He could tell her anything – they were best friends. Yet they had the best sex he had ever had. Friends and lovers. Everything he did at Meyer and Co. was for Alison. They both came from ordinary, middle-class families. They had not grown up in poverty, but their families were not wealthy either. Vacations were by the sea at Torquay or Llandudno, in North Wales. Usually in a mobile home with fish and chips for tea. Just a very ordinary upbringing.

When he first met her, Alison had bought dresses and tops from a market stall to wear to the pub on the weekends. Bill couldn't remember where he bought his clothes, but he knew for sure that it wasn't from a designer boutique.

Even in her cheap market clothes, Alison was the most beautiful girl Bill had ever seen. The way she smiled and twirled her hair round her finger when she talked. She had a voluptuous figure, and Bill liked nothing better than undressing her and seeing her naked.

Even now, Bill remembered with longing those days at Aston University in Birmingham. Going to the pub on Friday evening, having a curry and then back to his room for the best sex of his life. Lying in each other's arms, they had planned their future together. A house with a garden big enough for a dog to run around, and two children laughing and playing. It was always sunny in their daydreams.

When Bill got the chance to work for Meyer and Co. in Los Angeles, he felt he had a chance to show Alison the good life. He missed her dreadfully when he went at first, writing or ringing regularly. When he got his permanent US residence papers and he was able to marry Alison and bring her to live with him, he felt he was going to burst with happiness and pride.

The house they had bought in Pasadena was like something out of a fantasy for Bill. It had “beautiful bones” in the words of the realtor, and Alison had transformed it into the most stunning home.

Okay, he reasoned, he had been very busy with his job at Meyer and Co. but he was able to buy Alison things they could only ever have dreamed of when they first met. There were the twin Mercedes cars, the designer clothes and watches.

He remembered a cocktail party at the home of Steve Rogerson, the senior partner, at Meyer and Co. where Alison wore a Zimmerman dress in light blue, accessorized by a Cartier bracelet and watch. He was so proud to have her on his arm. He felt they had made it.

Of course, everything became harder and more complicated when he made it to partner. He was working long hours without a break. He found he didn’t have the time to sit down and just chat with Alison any longer. Of course, they went out to dine and occasionally had meals together at home, but even at these times he felt the intimacy between them seemed to have been lost. If he was to be honest, he felt there was now so much he couldn’t share with anyone, including Alison, and so their conversations became about mundane, everyday things.

Alison worked part-time and renovated the house, while he worked every hour possible. Alison went to the gym and had lunch with girlfriends, while he worked and talked to prospective clients.

They had grown apart, that much was true, the reasons for this he really didn’t know, but one thing was for sure he didn’t feel he could talk about leaving

Meyer and Co. with Alison. On reflection, because the intimacy had been lost, he just told her that he had a new role at Avalon Media earning more money. The money bit was true, but he had glossed over the truth of why he was leaving.

When he worked at Avalon Media, he found the situation at home continued to deteriorate. He had chartered a private jet and flown them to Hawaii for their anniversary. Alison had been polite but not as excited or in love as he would have expected. Even the lovemaking had lost its spark.

There was something about Alison though. She seemed to be glowing, as if she had a secret she was not sharing.

It was not a great surprise when he found out that Alison was "seeing" the pool guy, Barry. It was such a cliché it embarrassed him. Barry was a young, fit man with a suntan and, in Bill's view, room temperature IQ. What did she want with him? He earned next to nothing and drove an old van.

He remembered how cruelly she had talked to him about Barry. "Bill," she had said, "Barry has more love and affection in his little finger than you do in your whole body."

He remembered the fury he had felt inside. Women! He had given that woman everything. The house, the cars, the jewelry, the designer clothes and she felt she had the right to talk to him like that!!

He had been determined Alison would get nothing from him. It was his money and she would not enjoy his money with her stupid pool boy!

The divorce had been acrimonious and Bill had been able to hide money from her. He had almost appeared broke in the court, and Alison had only been able to take the house in Pasadena that was heavily mortgaged.

His view of women changed during the divorce. They wanted your money and even that was not enough for them. How hard he had worked for nothing – no thanks and no caring.

After the divorce, he had dated several women who he saw as “gold diggers”. They were after his money and position, he was sure. He had felt no love for any of these women and had just used them for a while.

Patrice had been different. He had loved Patrice. She cared so much for her work in the beauty salon, and he was able to give her a new salon to work in when they moved. He had given her a beautiful home to live in, designer clothes and jewelry and everything she might want.

Patrice knew better than anyone that he had been Danny’s fixer. After all, that was how they met, when he paid her to keep silent about Danny making unwanted advances on her.

Yet she claimed to be worried about rumors that there had been fraud and that he was going to be exposed, threatening their lifestyle.

He had been sure that when he shared his secret with her, it would put her mind at rest. That fool, Danny La Valle, was never going to sue him, Bill had too much on him for that. Yet Patrice didn’t seem to understand. Surely now he had shared Danny’s guilty secret she would know that they were safe. Nothing in Bill’s past would come back to haunt them.

What the heck was wrong with her? He had noticed the loss of intimacy, the silences and the forced politeness since he had introduced her to Lucy. For goodness' sake. Lucy was well looked after. Probably better looked after by Danny than she would have been by her own mother.

Women!! They were an alien breed and he would never, ever get them.

He smiled at Patrice and took the tray from her lap.

"Shall we take our bikes and ride up to the lakes today?" he asked.

"Yes, okay," Patrice nodded. "That sounds like a good idea, Bill. Let's do it."

June 12th, 2024

Patrice makes a decision

A visitor calls in at Jenny's BookStop

Chapter 76

Patrice makes a decision

Candy, the realtor from Page Elliott, was waiting outside the duplex in her car when Patrice pulled up in her Mercedes. She saw an expensive-looking woman who looked vaguely familiar.

Candy got out of her car and walked over to Patrice.

"Hi, I'm Candy. I am guessing you are Patrice?"

Patrice nodded – she was wearing designer sweats and a Rolex watch. "Yes, I booked an appointment to see the duplex today."

Candy smiled and walked up the path towards the front door. "Will this be for you ma'am? Or are you looking for someone else?"

In Candy's mind, Patrice should have been looking in the Southern Hills, not here in a bland, ordinary northern suburb.

"It is for me, yes," Patrice said. "Provided I like the property."

Candy opened the door and turning left, went into a large open plan area which included a kitchen. The room was flooded with light and overlooked the road at the front, and the yard at the rear. There were doors going out to the yard.

"The yard is included with this apartment," Candy said, "including this porch where you can sit on warm evenings."

There were also two bedrooms and two bathrooms.

By the standards of the homes Patrice had lived in with Bill, the apartment was tiny. But she had lived in apartments like it before, most recently in Burbank when she had met Bill. She would make it beautiful. It was light and airy and that is what she wanted.

“It rents for one thousand four hundred dollars per month, first and last payable upfront, plus security deposit of one thousand four hundred. The landlord will put a new carpet in for you and paint all rooms.”

Patrice agreed to the deal and arranged to go by Candy’s office to sign the paperwork. She would move in on July 1st.

Patrice knew that she could no longer live with Bill. She had to move on and continue her life without him. She loved her salon at the Purple Orchid and there was no way she was going to give it up. Talking to Bill about leaving would involve talking about his investment in the Purple Orchid.

She also knew that she had to talk to Jinni about her decision, as it would almost certainly affect the Purple Orchid.

Since visiting Lucy, Patrice had not been able to get her out of her mind. Seeing her sitting in her wheelchair looking at the boats was heartbreaking. A 20-year-old girl who would never walk again and who was brain damaged, hidden away so that Danny La Valle could continue with his life.

Some days Patrice felt like breaking down in tears, and other days she was gripped by an anger such as she had never known before.

She would keep quiet about what happened. She had given Bill her word. But was she as bad as Bill now that she was involved in the cover-up? Had Bill told her to make sure she could never leave him?

The hardest part was not being able to discuss what she had seen with anyone. When she was working on facials in the salon, customers often commented on Bill working at Stermer Media and the new signing he had made. She always remained upbeat and positive.

But as the days went by, she became more and more sure that she couldn't stay with him. She had to go, and the small apartment would work for now.

She often walked around the house in the Southern Hills touching the furniture and fitments. It was a stunning house and it would, in some ways, be difficult to leave. Yet in other ways it was a constant reminder of what she was sacrificing of herself to live with Bill.

She would make the time to speak to Bill, nearer the end of the month, and tell him of her decision.

In the meantime, she remained calm and polite and as the days passed, she wondered if Bill felt that all was well and there really was a future for them.

Chapter 77

Jenny's BookStop gets a visitor

After the Daily Trends had published the first article on the fraud and A.I Danny La Valle, Jenny's BookStop had been busy. People were obviously fascinated by the fake Danny La Valle and the promise of a visit to the shop. The second article had not generated as much trade, but Jenny was pleased her shop remained busy.

Today she was serving a customer when Rosie Banks, the reporter, walked in accompanied by a tall, flamboyant looking man with floppy hair.

After she had finished serving the customer, Rosie came over and introduced the person with her as Ben Carter.

She explained that Ben was going to be making a documentary about fraud in the literary world. He was really interested in self-published authors who had been offered blockbuster deals to produce their book into a movie.

Ben was very interested to feature in his documentary the scheme that had been reported in the Daily Trends.

"Would you be willing to be involved?" Ben asked Jenny.

Jenny indicated that she would, and she was sure that Glenda and Noi would be interested too.

"I can assure you that I am a legitimate filmmaker," said Ben, showing her his card.

Jenny promised to get in touch with Noi and Glenda.

When she did get in touch though, she was more than a bit taken aback by their reactions.

"How do you know that this isn't just another fraud?" said Glenda. "I thought we were being wary of people now?"

"He came into the shop with Rosie Banks, the reporter, so I felt that gave him some legitimacy," said Jenny.

"Have we ever heard of him?" Glenda was persistent. "Has he made any films in the past?"

She was frantically googling as she spoke.

"It seems he is small time – an amateur," Glenda said. "He does have a distribution deal and his last documentary was on human trafficking. But this only had a few thousand views."

"If he is small time, then this is not fraud," Jenny said. "Plus, he has not asked for any money upfront."

"Yay – not yet!" Glenda said cynically. "I have my job to think about. It is embarrassing for the school if I am seen to be involved in fraudulent schemes! I really have to give this some thought."

Jenny said she understood and then spoke to Noi.

Noi seemed genuinely scared to go ahead with speaking to the filmmaker. Jenny got the impression there had been a lot of trouble between Noi and her husband as a result of the fraud. She knew, through the grapevine, that Noi was working an extra job to pay off the money she had lost.

Jenny had already told Ben that she would cooperate in the making of the documentary, and he assured her he would be in touch soon to come over to interview her.

She sent messages to both Noi and Glenda saying:

"Please reconsider your decision about the upcoming documentary. What happened to all of us was appalling and will continue to go on unless we share with the public that there are fraudulent people out there willing to prey on unsuspecting authors and bookstore owners. We would be doing a public service by appearing in this documentary."

She pressed send and waited to see what the response would be. She was determined to bring the fraudsters to justice no matter what the consequences for her and her shop.

Chapter 78

Jinni

Speaking with Patrice, June 25th

I was not reassured by Carole Parks' comments about Bill Underwood. I knew the business was making a profit now and this had been made possible by the investment he made. Without him I would not have been able to open the premises in the regeneration area. These new premises had been very successful. Also, I knew Patrice and her salon had helped the business to thrive.

I was still mulling over the meeting and the best way to go forward when Patrice asked to see me after the salon closed for the day. We agreed to meet in the coffee bar area.

I arrived first and poured myself a cup of iced water. I sat at a table wondering what she wanted to talk about. She arrived after I had been sitting there for about 5 minutes.

Patrice poured herself a cup of iced water and sat opposite me. Although on the surface she looked her normal self, when I looked closely at her I could see that her eyes looked tired and there was strain showing on her face.

She spread her hands out in front of her on the table. There was a sadness about her as she looked at me and started to speak.

“I wish to speak to you, at this stage in confidence, Jinni,” she said.

I nodded. “Of course.”

“I think setting up my beauty salon in your nail bar has been a success so far. Would you not agree? Even the bad publicity we got about Keesha just resulted in more business. I am so busy I have had to take on an assistant. Profits are higher than we could have imagined.”

I was getting a sinking feeling and I looked at her, worried what she would say.

“I have been happy in the salon…” she continued.

Oh no, I thought, what is coming next?

“But sadly, not happy in my personal life.” She looked at me. “There was so much I didn’t know about Bill when I married him. It was all so quick. I thought I was in love with him and he seemed perfect.”

I wanted to say no-one is perfect, but I kept quiet and let her go on.

“I knew from day one that he worked for Danny La Valle. His main job was looking after Danny’s finances, but I also knew he helped, shall we say, smooth things over for Danny. We lived in a beautiful home in Calabasas, and I was running my small salon in Burbank.”

She stopped there, taking a deep breath. Again, I kept silent, allowing her to go on.

“When Bill agreed to come here with Stermer Media, he promised to find me a salon to replace the one I had to sell in Burbank. We were lucky that you wanted someone to invest in the Purple Orchid at that time."

I was now feeling very nervous. Had that bitch Carole Parks told Bill what I said? Was he now going to pull out from his investment?

What the heck was I supposed to say other than, "Yes, I agree I was lucky Bill invested and you started the salon."

Patrice then went on. "But then there have been these strange rumors going around about fraud. It seems that wherever Bill goes, he is followed by rumors of fraud."

"But these are rumors." I spread my hands open. "There is no evidence."

Patrice got up and walked around the coffee bar. I did not take this as a good sign. She seemed agitated and nervous.

"Jinni," she announced as she returned to sit at the table. "I can't go on living with Bill. I feel that he is not an honest and straight-living man."

This was a big shock to me. I guess I had guilty feelings about my conversation with Carole Parks and thought this was going to be about that. I had not expected Patrice to feel so strongly about her husband.

I stared at her, at first not sure what to say. "You are planning on leaving him?" I stuttered.

"Yes." Patrice was fighting back tears. "I can no longer go on living a lie."

It sounded like a cliché but I expect she knew much more than I did about Bill and his dealings.

"I'm so sorry Patrice." I knew it sounded hollow, but the end of a marriage is painful for all involved. I knew this from personal experience, when my own marriage broke down and I moved here to be near my brother, Somchai.

"You have, of course, discussed this with Bill," I said.

"Yes, that is where the problem is – I have asked Bill a lot of questions and he has told me very confidential things about his previous life. Things that mean I can no longer live with him. However, I did not want to discuss my moving out until I have talked to you about our business here at the Purple Orchid."

I am well aware I may sound self-absorbed but the Purple Orchid was first in my mind now. If Patrice left Bill, would he want to take his investment out of the business? Was that even possible?

"I believe," said Patrice, leaning over the table, "that Bill will allow me to keep my business here in the Purple Orchid as part of any separation agreement. However, his name is on the agreement as an investor with mine. This is why I wanted to talk to you about it. Would you be happy to go ahead with Bill being an investor when he and I were separated?"

I must have looked confused and bewildered as she then said, "Look, I know I have dropped this on you. Please take a couple of days to think about it and let me know. I would want to know by the end of the month as I have signed up for a rental apartment and that is when I am leaving him."

I was at a loss for words. Thoughts swirled round my head. "Wouldn't it be better if Bill transferred his investment to you, as part of the separation agreement? We could then continue to work as partners and he would have no interest in the Purple Orchid."

Patrice looked bewildered. I got the impression she was very skilled as a beauty therapist, but not so skilled when it came to money and business agreements.

I tried again. "Would Bill consider transferring his investment to you? That way we would not have to include him in any business decisions or profit sharing."

"I can try," Patrice said. "But so long as you are happy to go ahead in any event I will now talk to Bill."

I felt like she wasn't the brightest person I had ever met, but I also knew she wouldn't give up her life in the big house with her rich husband easily. Maybe there was truth in the fraud rumors and she wanted to get away from him. I wondered why she didn't turn him in, or why she hadn't thought about asking him to give up his investment in the Purple Orchid.

I left the Purple Orchid that evening and caught the train home with a very heavy heart. I knew one thing though, the Purple Orchid was my baby, and I would fight with all I had to make sure that it was a success. If Bill Underwood took the money away, I would find a way – and it seemed that whatever, Patrice would be my ally now.

Success is not final; failure is not fatal: it is the courage to continue that counts."

Winston Churchill, the former Prime Minister of the United Kingdom

Chapter 79

Bill and Patrice sit down and talk

There had been the polite interactions, there had been the attempts to act as if all was normal again and then there had been the times when Bill knew deep down that this marriage was over.

Today was one of those days. When he reached for her to kiss her and hold her, he could sense the reluctance in Patrice to respond. He held on to her and began to talk.

"Patrice, we must talk," he said, the desperation coming through in his voice. "I want you to know that I love you with all my heart and I want more than anything to spend the rest of my life with you."

There was silence for a moment and then, gently removing herself from his embrace, Patrice said, "Okay let's talk."

They sat down on a sofa in the primary bedroom – side by side but not touching. The sofa faced the south facing window and the view of the golf course and hills in the distance was stunning.

"I love you, but I feel that you have fallen out of love with me," he pleaded. "What have I done that is wrong? I have given you everything you ever wanted. You have your salon – I know you love your salon and it is doing well. I know you love this house and we have been happy living here. There is your car, the jewelry, the holidays."

Patrice felt tears welling up. "But these are all material things, Bill. Yes, I have loved the material things. But it is real love that I crave. A man who loves people before possessions."

"But I do love you Patrice," Bill persisted. "I have always treated you with respect and caring. When can you say I have not treated you with love?"

"You have shown me love by giving me gifts and possessions and this is not what I want," said Patrice. "So long as I stay with you, I can never look at these possessions without thinking about where the money came from to buy them."

Bill withdrew then and looked at her. "What?" he said. "What did you just say?" He shook his head. "Patrice, I met you when I asked you to sign an NDA and I arranged for you to be paid for your silence. That money bought you your first salon in Burbank. You knew I was Danny's fixer and that is what I did. I looked after him and I made sure his indiscretions remained private. I will always remain in Danny's confidence and everything will remain private. This is why I told you about Lucy. She is my ace in the hole. Danny will never do anything to me. On the contrary, as you should have worked out, a lot of the lifestyle you have been enjoying is courtesy of Danny."

The tears were rolling down Patrice's cheeks now.

"I know that is true, Bill," she sobbed. "Of course I know that is true and it is what I can't handle. A young girl, Lucy, whose life has been ruined is hidden away and sacrificed so Danny can pursue his career as a big Hollywood producer. All the time aided and abetted by you. And now by me."

She saw the look of alarm on Bill's face.

"What are you talking about, Patrice? You were worried about Danny and there is no need to be worried. Our life is secure."

Patrice was openly sobbing now. She had to get away from him, she knew. He seemed to be devoid of human emotion.

"Oh, I see," he said. "You are now intending to hold this incident over me, are you? When I shared this secret with you, it was in good faith. But now I can see that you see a chance to hold me to ransom. I should have seen what you really were from day one."

"Please stop," Patrice said. "You have it so wrong, Bill. I don't think you even begin to realize how wrong you are."

There was silence then for what seemed like an eternity. Then Patrice spoke again. "I am leaving you, Bill. I don't want much from you. I don't want your money. You keep the house, the cars, the jewelry. What I do want though is to continue at the Purple Orchid. I will take your investment in the Purple Orchid as my share of separation."

Bill sneered. "You don't want money, yet you want me to continue to invest in your beauty business. I see. I really don't have much choice, do I."

He stood up and began to pace the room. "What a fool I have been. I thought you loved me as much as I loved you, Patrice. It turns out you were just waiting for something to hold over me so you could leave." He was pacing back and forth, back and forth. "Well, if that is what you want, fuck off, just go. Go now and don't come back. You can have your little business and good luck with it. But get out of my house." He paused for effect and then added. "Now."

Patrice could see that there were tears in his eyes and part of her wanted to go and hold him.

"I just can't go on," she wept.

"Fuck off now, Patrice," he said. "I am going out for a drive and when I get back, I expect you to be gone."

He turned and walked out of the room and slamming the front door, she heard the car start and he sped away.

Sobbing, Patrice packed a few clothes and within half an hour she too drove away from the beautiful home in the Southern Hills. She checked into a cheap motel as she did not get the keys to her new apartment until the following day. Laying on the bed she knew she had to stop her tears and start planning for the future. She had just walked away from one of the most beautiful homes in the Southern Hills to live in a small, rented apartment in the Northern suburbs which she needed to furnish and make her own. She was 29 years old and here she was beginning all over again. Her mother had taught her to be strong and resilient and she knew that despite the pain she felt today, this was the best way forward. She would make the Purple Orchid the best salon in the Southern States. Of that, she was sure.

Sitting up, she took her cell phone from her purse and dialed Jinni's number. Jinni picked up immediately.

"Hi Jinni," Patrice said. "I'm at the Keyshore Motel on the 135 highway. I've left Bill and am going to move into my own place tomorrow. I wanted you to be the first to know."

Chapter 80

Jinni

Patrice leaves Bill

I was in shock. So Patrice went ahead with it. She had decided to leave Bill and start her own life. When my cell phone rang that night and it was Patrice telling me she was staying in the motel, I have to admit it, floored me.

“Shall I come over to you now?” I asked.

At first Patrice said not to come over, and then she broke down in tears.

“I’m on my way over,” I said.

I quickly got dressed and drove over to the motel. Patrice answered the door and I went into the room. It was obvious that she had been crying. I sat next to her on the bed and hugged her.

“I’m so sorry, Patrice.” I realized this sounded inadequate but was feeling in shock and not sure what to say.

Patrice was sobbing. “I couldn’t go on, Jinni,” she said. “I was living a lie.”

This sounded like a cliché, but I wanted to know more. I let her go on.

“When I met Bill, I thought he was the most wonderful, kind man I had ever met. He treated me with respect and like a lady. He was a gentleman. I moved in with him very quickly after I met him as I felt cared for and loved.”

"It is lovely that he cared for you and you felt loved." I was hugging her.

"But I moved in with a man I didn't know," she wailed. "I moved in with him and then I married him. But I knew nothing about him."

I knew how she felt. I had let Bill invest in my business when I also knew nothing about him.

"I hadn't met his family because they were in England. He told me his ex-wife had gone back to England, but that was a lie because she was living in LA all the time. However, I met no-one from his past and therefore I knew nothing about him."

I was quiet as I knew I had to let her rant.

"There always seemed to be a lot of money. But I didn't ask too many questions – I just enjoyed being with him and the lifestyle we enjoyed. Plus, I had my salon in Burbank and was busy with that. Then when we moved here, I had my salon with you at the Purple Orchid."

I was stroking her back now.

"But...but then the rumors started. And there were some small things that were strange. The whole protective behavior around his cell phone – at first I wondered if he was having an affair. But then I decided that it was something..." here she hesitated for a long time. "Worse."

I continued stroking her back.

"I hired a private investigator to find out about him and what I found out shocked me. It was then that I realized he was not the man I thought he was."

I still had not spoken.

"He has secrets. There is so much I can't tell you."

The sobbing continued. There had been no mention that Bill was the investor in our joint business and she had now left him.

"So where is your new place?" I asked, trying to sound optimistic. "Did you say it's ready tomorrow?"

Patrice blew her nose and wiped her eyes. She sniffed and blew her nose again. "It's on Bradley Street."

"I know Bradley Street. It's near me," I said, smiling.

"Yes, it's ready, I can move in tomorrow." Patrice wiped her tears and continued. "I walked out with nothing – but the house was leased anyway so the furniture was not ours. I have to buy furniture – I have to buy everything."

"Will you need any help doing that?" I asked.

"I can find furniture and put a home together. Believe me, I have done it before." She sniffed and wiped her eyes. "I will be fine, Jinni. I am a survivor."

I hugged her again. "Are you sure you don't want to come and stay with me in the meantime?" I asked.

"No, I will be perfectly alright." She was composed again now. "But thank you."

Standing she said, "Also, Jinni don't worry about the investment, that is secure. I may not walk away from this marriage with much, but my salon is very important to me and I want to be sure that nothing happens to threaten the Purple Orchid. Bill will continue to invest."

I knew then that Patrice would make sure her investment was secure and that we would remain business partners for the foreseeable future.

It was only when I got home that I started to wonder where the money came from and if it related to Bill Underwood's secrets in any way.

July, 2024

A business meeting is held

The Open Day – and Keesha attends

Chapter 81

Jinni

A business meeting takes place

On July 10th I found myself again in Carole Parks' office with Patrice and Bill Underwood. He seemed to be his usual self, with his expressionless face and condescending British accent.

Patrice had taken a few days off from the salon to set up her new apartment. She seemed as poised and elegant as ever, and there was no outward hint of the inner turmoil she must have been feeling.

I nodded to Bill and Patrice as I took my seat for the meeting. Carole was behind her extremely untidy desk, looking ungroomed and untidy herself. She smiled and looked around at us all. Then she launched forth:

"Bill and Patrice have called this meeting regarding the investment in the Purple Orchid. As we are all aware, this investment is in the names of Bill Underwood, who has thirty percent, and Patrice Underwood, who has twenty percent. Due to personal issues, Bill will now transfer his ownership of this investment to Patrice."

She paused briefly. "This makes Patrice Underwood a fifty percent investor and owner of the Purple Orchid."

Bill spoke then. "I have agreed to sign over my interest to Patrice and going forward, I now have no further interest in the Purple Orchid."

Carole nodded. "There are forms to complete to transfer the ownership to Patrice that all three of you need to complete."

We then completed the necessary paperwork.

The atmosphere was professional, but I couldn't help feeling that it must have been extremely difficult for Patrice.

I looked at Bill. He was a man of mystery, that much I knew. I wondered again what Patrice knew and I did not know. Perhaps it was best that I did not know. But the business was now owned by myself and Patrice, and Bill no longer had any part to play.

We ended the meeting amicably, shaking hands and walking to the elevator together. We rode down in the elevator without speaking. When we reached the entrance of the building, Patrice asked me if I wanted to join her for a drink to celebrate our new partnership.

Bill said his goodbyes, and we went to a local cocktail bar where we both ordered martinis and sat at a corner table.

"To the Purple Orchid, may it continue to grow and prosper." Patrice raised her glass.

"The Purple Orchid." I raised my glass and we chinked glasses.

"I have so many ideas going forward," Patrice said. "I feel we can do so much to make the business grow even more."

She seemed to want to look to the future and not to discuss the past, which I thought was a good thing.

"I feel we should bring Keesha back if she would agree," Patrice went on. "This time we should show her with a "make up free" look. Much more natural and show her nails with summer colors."

"Yes, I agree, she was good for publicity last time she posed for us. I can get in touch with her again."

"Let's set a time for an open day. We could demonstrate some of the products we use and sell. I could do a facial demonstration using the products. We could then offer a limited number of free consultations. We could also do some free manicures and pedicures using the latest products." Patrice had obviously been thinking about this.

"The coffee bar has never really taken off – we could use an open day to encourage people to come in and enjoy it," I said, starting to imagine what the day would look like. "And perhaps Keesha would come in and talk about her beauty routine."

"That is a really great idea," agreed Patrice. "We should go ahead and fix a date and then plan the day. It will be the best event we have done so far!"

And so with that, Bill Underwood was dismissed from our lives, and Patrice and I took over the Purple Orchid salons.

Chapter 82

Jinni

The Open Day

Patrice and I worked hard planning the open day. We invited Keesha, who agreed to come and model for us and give a short talk about her beauty routine. She felt it would be good PR and she agreed with us that we would photograph the event and she could have copies of the photos for her own use.

The local radio station KAVC98 sent a reporter who interviewed Keesha, and this time myself and Patrice. We talked about the way we saw the salon developing in the next few months. It would be a full-service salon, with nails downstairs and beauty treatments upstairs.

We were very busy all day, with new and existing customers visiting us. Robbie demonstrated the well-being products as well as nail art downstairs. Patrice and Clarrie demonstrated facials and makeup in the upstairs salon.

By the end of the day, Patrice and I were exhausted. When everyone had left, we sat in the coffee bar with our feet up discussing the day. We were both so happy with how it had gone.

“The future seems bright.” Patrice smiled at me. “I feel we make a great partnership and we can go forward and do great things together.”

I raised my coffee cup in a toast. “To the future of the Purple Orchid and to our future as business partners.”

It was a lovely end to a successful day.

Yet inside I had so many questions that I knew at this stage would never be answered.

Who was Bill Underwood? Why had Patrice decided to leave him after such a short period of time? What secrets did he hold?

Was the Purple Orchid now tainted by the money he had invested? I knew he no longer had any influence and any money he had invested was now passed to Patrice.

I wondered about the book frauds that had taken place since Bill had been associated with the Purple Orchid. Authors had been told that Danny La Valle would make their books into films. I knew Bill had been Danny's accountant and fixer. Was there any link there?

Deep down I knew I would never have answers to these questions and I had to put them out of my mind. I felt blessed to have Patrice as a business partner and I decided to think about the future in a positive way.

Leaving that evening I took an Uber downtown and met Robbie for drinks and a meal at an upscale restaurant. I ordered champagne and we toasted the day and the Purple Orchid. Looking at Robbie, I felt that I was the luckiest woman in the world.

Epilogue

October, 2024

Steve Cannon makes a shocking discovery

The Underwood Residence in Fishponds, Bristol

Epilogue

Steve Cannon makes a shocking discovery

Steve Cannon was sitting in his corner office at the Stermer Media head office in LA. He was feeling content and sure that his bonus would be coming his way this year. Business in the boutique publishing house owned by Stermer had been good this year.

There had been times when he had been worried during the year. There was the issue of the royalties last spring, but he had been able to sort this out fairly quickly. The account to “Stout & Bing” had been set up by a temporary worker when Glenys was on vacation. It had been signed off by Bill Underwood. Steve had insisted on a face-to-face meeting about that and put Bill on a performance review. In addition, he had stopped all payments to “Stout & Bing” and introduced very rigorous procedures for setting up new accounts. Problem solved. Bill Underwood was an idiot in his view. If he had been behind this fraud, and Steve had no proof he was, then it was pretty pathetic and easily discovered. Otherwise, he was very incompetent and they should consider getting rid of him soon. Either way, Steve had solved the issue.

There was a knock on his door as Kim, the audit manager, arrived to discuss “something important” found during the audit.

He indicated that Kim should come in and sit down.

“What can I do for you?” He smiled ear to ear.

"I wanted to share some discrepancies we have found in the accounts." Kim had brought a laptop and logging in, turned it to face Steve.

"There have been large payments made out of the Publishing Advance account that I feel may be fraudulent."

"Surely not." Steve beamed at her. "We have good systems and controls here."

"Did you use a PR agency this year called Lorimar?"

Steve thought for a moment. "We were thinking about using them, but we never actually did a campaign with them."

"How would you spell their name?" asked Kim.

Steve looked at her as if she was crazy, although he had started to have a sick feeling. "L. O. R. I. M. A. R," he parroted.

Kim nodded. "So what are all these payments to *Lorrimar*, with two r's?"

Steve was aware his mouth was gaping open and his face was going red.

"How much?" he demanded.

"There is about a million dollars going to Lorrimar, all approved by Bill Underwood. This includes regular, smaller payments last year and obtaining a copy of the management accounts, I can see that the payments are much bigger in recent months. In May, five hundred thousand dollars was sent.

Lorrimar has a registered office in the Philippines and the directors are Lulu Bartlett and Robin Pine.

However, it seems they are in financial difficulties and are currently being taken over."

Steve felt for a moment that he was going to spontaneously combust. After dismissing Kim with the promise of a bigger meeting with the audit team, he composed himself for a moment and then picking up the phone, he rang a number on speed dial.

Shocked, he got an answer phone. "I am out of the office at the moment and will get back to you as soon as possible. Please leave a message."

Underwood! Out of the office! He would find out where the bastard was. Ringing reception at Bill's office, he was told that Bill was not available and had not been in the office for a few days.

It seemed he had disappeared into thin air!

Epilogue

The Underwood Residence – Fishponds, Bristol

The figure pushing the trolley around the Morrisons supermarket in Fishponds was slightly stooped and wearing an anorak and polyester pants. No-one paid him the slightest attention as he picked up bread, milk, tea bags, cheese, ham and mayonnaise. He decided to buy, at the last minute, a bottle of Merlot to drink after lunch. He would have a cup of tea with lunch. Down the next aisle he found chocolate éclairs with cream – his favorites. There was a beautiful blonde lady in the chocolate éclair aisle, but she did not give him a second glance as he stood next to her and picked up a package of éclairs. “Excuse me,” he said politely as he reached across her. She ignored him.

Paying for his purchases he walked along the high street past the Old Mail House pub, at first, fighting the temptation to go in and sample a pint of bitter beer and then giving in and sitting at a table in the bar area. Again, no-one paid him the slightest bit of attention. Sometimes he wondered if he was invisible.

Finishing the beer, he left the pub and began walking. Turning into a street of Victorian terrace houses, he juggled the shopping bags as he searched for his keys in his anorak pocket.

The house was a large bay-winded terrace that had seen better days. The front door needed replacing, and the small front garden was full of litter dropped by people waiting at the nearby bus stop.

He opened the front door and walking into the hallway, took off his anorak and hung it up. He then went into the kitchen and made two sandwiches and two beakers of tea. Putting these onto a tray he climbed the stairs – one flight and then another flight to the converted loft.

Maddi was sitting at a computer under the Plexi glass loft window which had been opened to allow some air into her workspace.

“Oh, you are back,” she observed. “I signed up three this morning while you were out gallivanting around the shops.”

He smiled. She was always dour, but such an asset.

“My wife won’t be Zooming again,” he said. “She has now left me on the moral high ground.”

Maddi nodded. “And I am sure it is well deserved!”

At this they both smiled.

“She believed all you said. Why did you not tell her mum and dad are now in a care home in Weston-Super-Mare?”

“I thought it added to the pathos. She seemed almost upset at what I had to put up with.”

Here they both had a chuckle.

“I’m a very good liar, I do it for my living.” Maddi was smiling and enjoying herself now. “Also, it is funny she had not been given that information at home by her husband.”

They ate their sandwiches in companionable silence.

“I can only stay until later this afternoon,” he said. “I have business to do in the Philippines. Oh, by the way, I'm no longer at Stermer Media, so we can't use their systems."

Here Maddi sharply interrupted him. "For goodness' sake, Bill. How many times do I have to tell you about using companies you work for. You don't shit where you eat. Try to remember that, why don't you!"

Suitably chastised, Bill went on. "Also, there has been some publicity about Danny and the supposed visit to the bookstore."

Maddi nodded. "People are so stupid though, they will still think it is him even if they have been warned. Actually, I shouldn't say stupid – it is greed, pure and simple. The allure of money makes fools out of them."

He nodded. "Perhaps use someone else though for the time being. Danny is still helping to keep me in the style to which I have become accustomed remember," Bill laughed, "we can't keep using him for everything!"

They moved on to chat about the issue in the Philippines, where it seemed they had to change the name of the operation to avoid being prosecuted. They also needed to talk about the workers in the Philippines who worked remotely for Maddi, and them making calls using voice-disguising software.

Then there was the money that was in the account in the Bahamas in the name of an offshore company, plus the accounts in Panama.

So much business to discuss. 3 p.m. rolled round quickly and the limousine arrived to take him to Heathrow airport.

They embraced briefly and he left in the limousine with only a small cabin bag with him.

By 6 p.m. he was in the VIP lounge dressed in Hugo Boss and sipping a glass of champagne. By 8 p.m. he was in business class flying to Manila, in the Philippines. He wondered if he would ever be able to go back to the States – maybe he would be on a poster, “Wanted by the FBI”. He laughed to himself about that.

Sitting sipping champagne, his thoughts turned to the bank accounts he had seen this afternoon. All offshore and hidden from creditors or a woman seeking a divorce. Maddi was a genius – so much cleverer than he. Musing about the future, he was sure they could give up their activities soon as they had enough for a wonderful retirement in an offshore tax haven.

He smiled at the flight attendant who came by to check if he needed anything. She’s a stunner, he thought to himself. She was very solicitous to the wealthy men in business class. Watching her, he knew with his money and connections he would have no problems finding a replacement wife. For a second, a cloud passed briefly over his horizon – would he ever find true love, though? It was easy to find women who would enjoy the good life with him. But for them to love him? He thought he had love with Alison but that had soured. And then there was Patrice. He was a genuine guy who just wanted a woman to love. Would he ever find that one woman who would love him for himself and see past the trappings of wealth? A humble, genuine person – just like himself, who would love him unconditionally?

Raising his glass, he said out loud, “To love,” to nobody in particular. A man sitting opposite smiled and joined him in the toast.

All in all, he was in a good place and he knew that for a rich man like him the future would be rosy. With that he fell asleep and did not awaken until the plane began its descent into Manila.

Leaving the plane, he smiled as he slipped Anna, the flight attendant, his card. He knew, of course, that she would call him. And of course, he would be ready for her.

About the Author – S. Cunliffe

I am a passionate writer about American fiction. I am British, and I lived in the USA for a number of years and attended university in Los Angeles at USC. I now live in Bristol, England and am a university lecturer.

This is the third book I have written about Jinni and the ladies of the Purple Orchid:

The first book is *The Purple Orchid*, which tells the story of the Purple Orchid – an upscale nail salon in the Southern States owned by Jinni, a Thai immigrant. The salon is a beautiful place full of exotic flowers and gossip and chatter.

The women of the Purple Orchid have so many tales to tell. Whether it be:

Jinni's illicit love affair with Song – a beautiful Chinese woman who is in the USA illegally – the resulting fallout threatening to destroy both her well-being and her business;

Jinni's betrayal of family ties, interfering in a close relative's marriage breakup;

Amara, dropping out of college and struggling to find her own way in life;

Ellie, the English content creator, releasing provocative YouTube videos and gossiping online about Meghan Markle and Prince Harry with dire consequences;

Janine, helping an elderly granny and her friend to get fit and healthy.

And at the heart of it all, the Purple Orchid becomes a place where opinions are valued, people can engage in stimulating conversations, but most importantly, it becomes a sanctuary from the outside world.

The second book is *Purple Orchid Blues*. It is 2023 and the ladies of the Purple Orchid want to obtain justice for a crime committed in Atlanta, Georgia against an illegal immigrant who previously worked at the Purple Orchid. In a small suburb of this southern city, injustice is rife. A Black man sits in a prison cell accused of a violent crime he says he did not commit. A cafe owner is in hospital seriously injured, keeping secret his abusive treatment of the illegal immigrants he employed.

This story looks at how obtaining justice can be difficult when it seems no one hears your voice…

I love to hear from my readers, and I rely heavily upon your feedback to develop my writing and the stories I tell.

Please let me know what you think!

Please leave a review on Amazon or Goodreads.

You can also contact me through my website:

Home | Scunliffe Author

ACKNOWLEDGEMENTS

The Writer Beware website (http://writerbeware.blog) for the wonderful work they do advising authors how to avoid scams and frauds such as those written about in this book which is a work of fiction.

Printed in Dunstable, United Kingdom

68002859R00228